GIANT DAYS

VOLUME NINE

BOOM! BOX

BOOM! BOX

GIANT DAYS Volume Nine, February 2019. Published by BOOM! Box, a division of Boom Entertainment, Inc. Giant Days is ™ & © 2019 John Allison. Originally published in single magazine form as GIANT DAYS No. 33-36. ™ & © 2017-2018 John Allison. All rights reserved. BOOM! Box™ and the BOOM! Box logo are trademarks of Boom Entertainment, Inc., registered in various countries and categories. All characters, events, and institutions depicted herein are fictional. Any similarity between any of the names, characters, persons, events, and/or institutions in this publication to actual names, characters, and persons, whether living or dead, events, and/or institutions is unintended and purely coincidental. BOOM! Box does not read or accept unsolicited submissions of ideas, stories, or artwork.

For information regarding the CPSIA on this printed material, call: (203) 595-3636 and provide reference #RICH – 825777.

BOOM! Studios, 5670 Wilshire Boulevard, Suite 400, Los Angeles, CA 90036-5679. Printed in the USA. First Printing.

ISBN: 978-1-68415-310-7, eISBN: 978-1-64144-163-6

GIANT DAYS™

CREATED & WRITTEN BY
JOHN ALLISON

PENCILS BY
MAX SARIN

INKS BY
LIZ FLEMING
(CHAPTERS 33-35)

WITH
JENNA AYOUB
(CHAPTER 35)

AND
MAX SARIN
(CHAPTER 36)

COLORS BY
WHITNEY COGAR

LETTERS BY
JIM CAMPBELL

COVER BY
LISSA TREIMAN

SERIES DESIGNER
MICHELLE ANKLEY

COLLECTION DESIGNER
KARA LEOPARD

ASSISTANT EDITOR
SOPHIE PHILIPS-ROBERTS

EDITOR
SHANNON WATTERS

CHAPTER
THIRTY-THREE

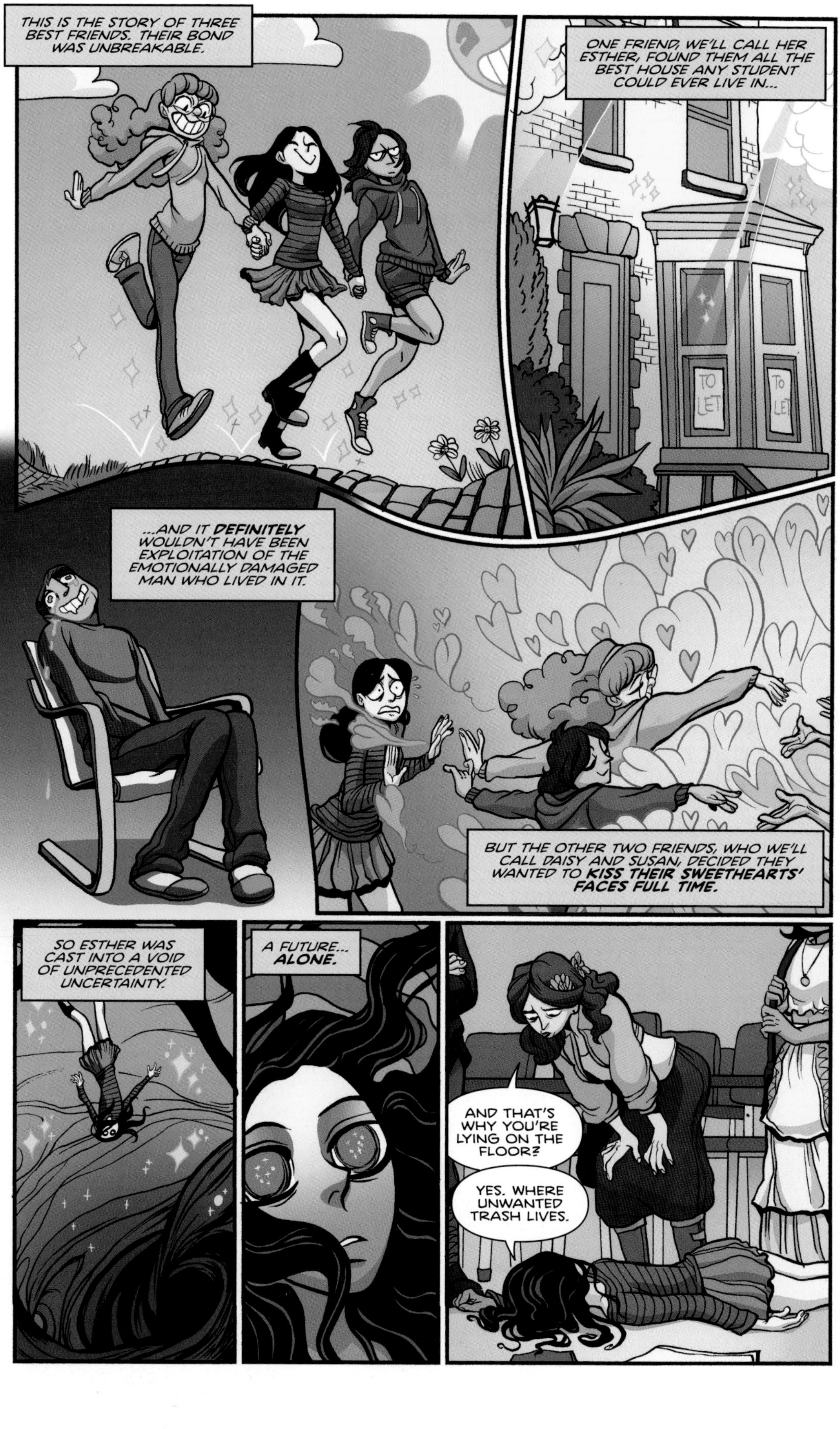
THIS IS THE STORY OF THREE BEST FRIENDS. THEIR BOND WAS UNBREAKABLE.
ONE FRIEND, WE'LL CALL HER ESTHER, FOUND THEM ALL THE BEST HOUSE ANY STUDENT COULD EVER LIVE IN...
TO LET
TO LET
...AND IT DEFINITELY WOULDN'T HAVE BEEN EXPLOITATION OF THE EMOTIONALLY DAMAGED MAN WHO LIVED IN IT.
BUT THE OTHER TWO FRIENDS, WHO WE'LL CALL DAISY AND SUSAN, DECIDED THEY WANTED TO KISS THEIR SWEETHEARTS' FACES FULL TIME.
SO ESTHER WAS CAST INTO A VOID OF UNPRECEDENTED UNCERTAINTY.
A FUTURE... ALONE.
AND THAT'S WHY YOU'RE LYING ON THE FLOOR?
YES. WHERE UNWANTED TRASH LIVES.

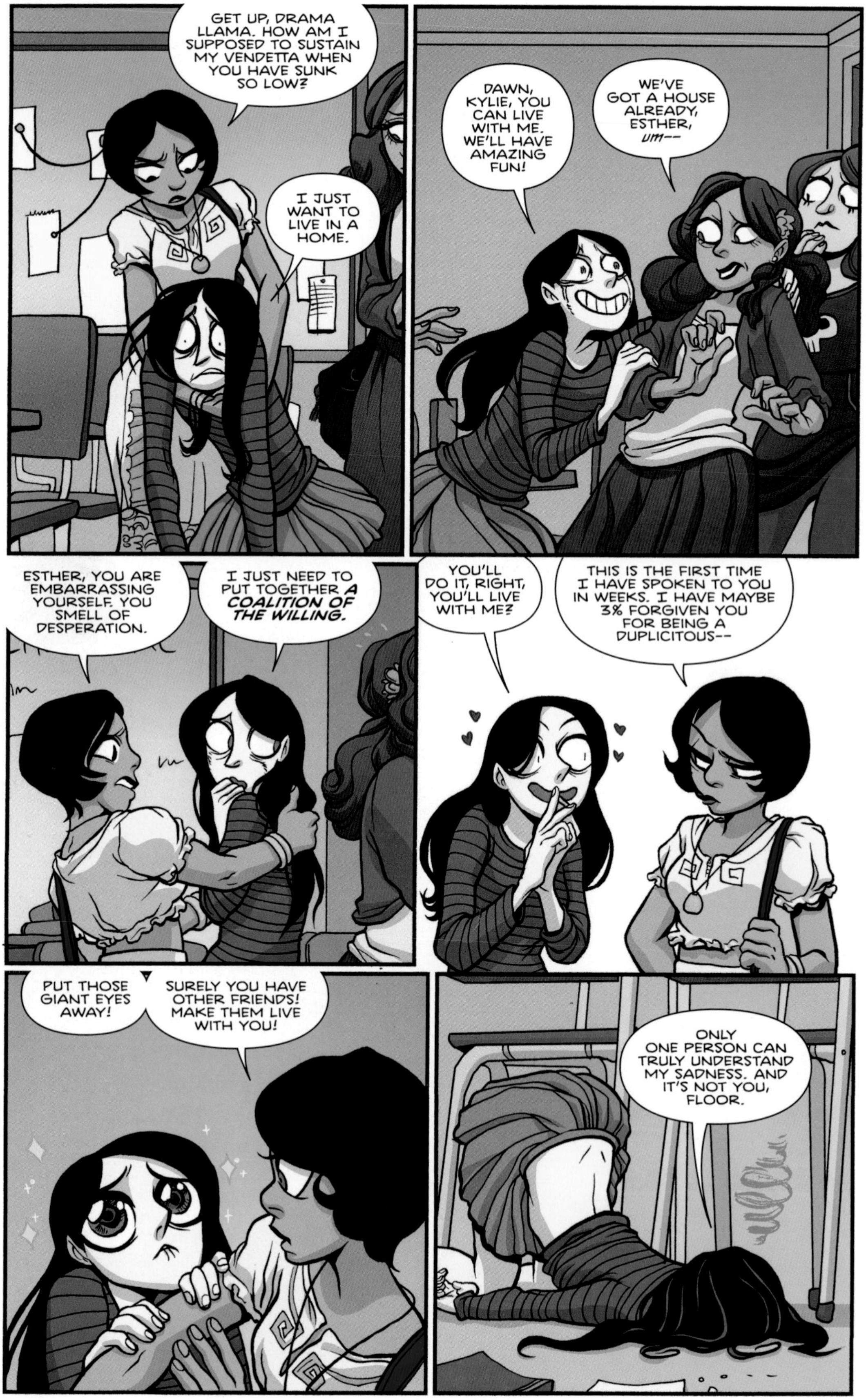
GET UP, DRAMA LLAMA. HOW AM I SUPPOSED TO SUSTAIN MY VENDETTA WHEN YOU HAVE SUNK SO LOW?
I JUST WANT TO LIVE IN A HOME.
DAWN, KYLIE, YOU CAN LIVE WITH ME. WE'LL HAVE AMAZING FUN!
WE'VE GOT A HOUSE ALREADY, ESTHER, UM--
ESTHER, YOU ARE EMBARRASSING YOURSELF. YOU SMELL OF DESPERATION.
I JUST NEED TO PUT TOGETHER A COALITION OF THE WILLING.
YOU'LL DO IT, RIGHT, YOU'LL LIVE WITH ME?
THIS IS THE FIRST TIME I HAVE SPOKEN TO YOU IN WEEKS. I HAVE MAYBE 3% FORGIVEN YOU FOR BEING A DUPLICITOUS--
PUT THOSE GIANT EYES AWAY!
SURELY YOU HAVE OTHER FRIENDS! MAKE THEM LIVE WITH YOU!
ONLY ONE PERSON CAN TRULY UNDERSTAND MY SADNESS. AND IT'S NOT YOU, FLOOR.

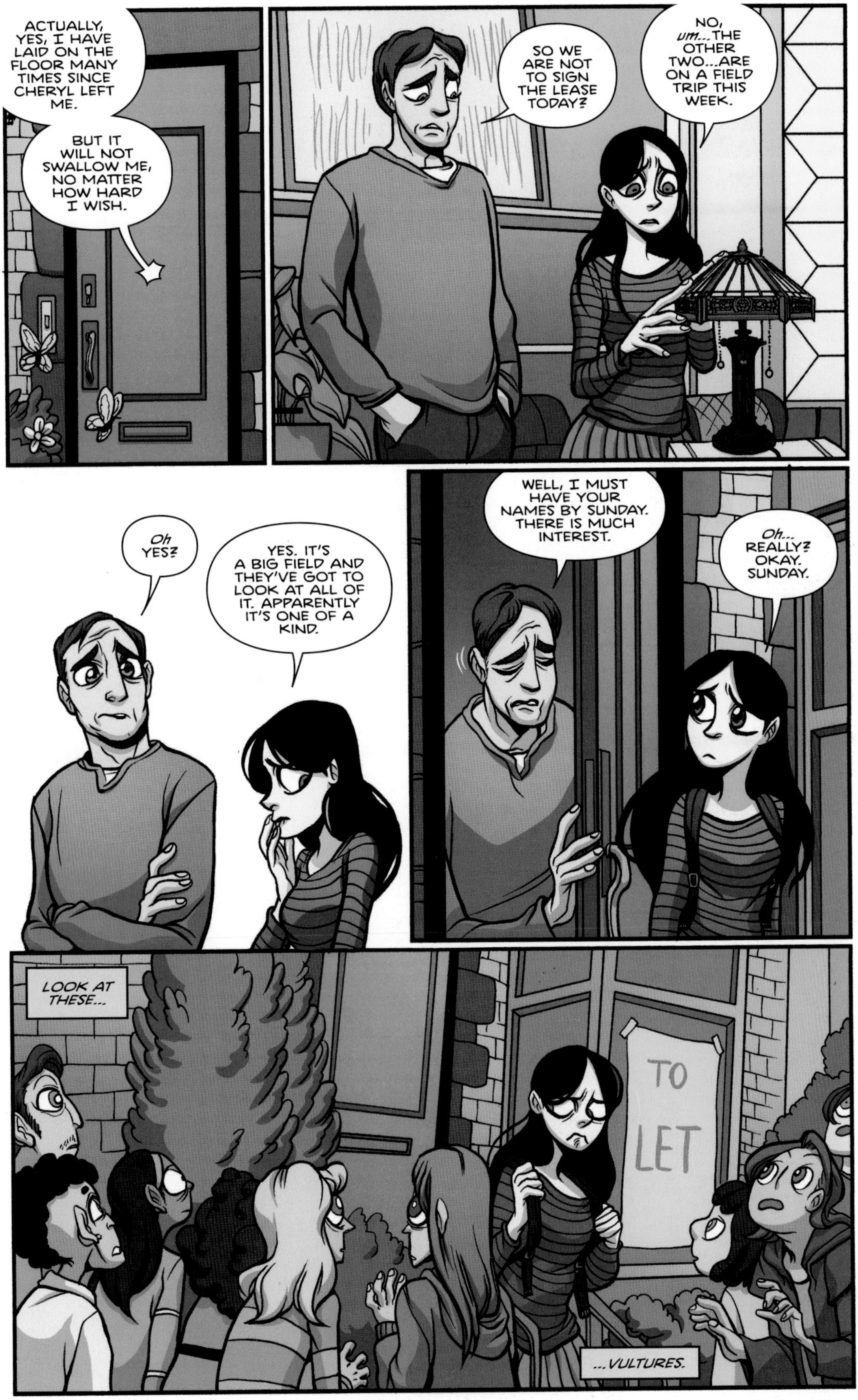
ACTUALLY, YES, I HAVE LAID ON THE FLOOR MANY TIMES SINCE CHERYL LEFT ME.
BUT IT WILL NOT SWALLOW ME, NO MATTER HOW HARD I WISH.
SO WE ARE NOT TO SIGN THE LEASE TODAY?
NO, *UM...* THE OTHER TWO... ARE ON A FIELD TRIP THIS WEEK.
Oh YES?
YES. IT'S A BIG FIELD AND THEY'VE GOT TO LOOK AT ALL OF IT. APPARENTLY IT'S ONE OF A KIND.
WELL, I MUST HAVE YOUR NAMES BY SUNDAY. THERE IS MUCH INTEREST.
Oh... REALLY? OKAY. SUNDAY.
LOOK AT THESE...
TO LET
...VULTURES.

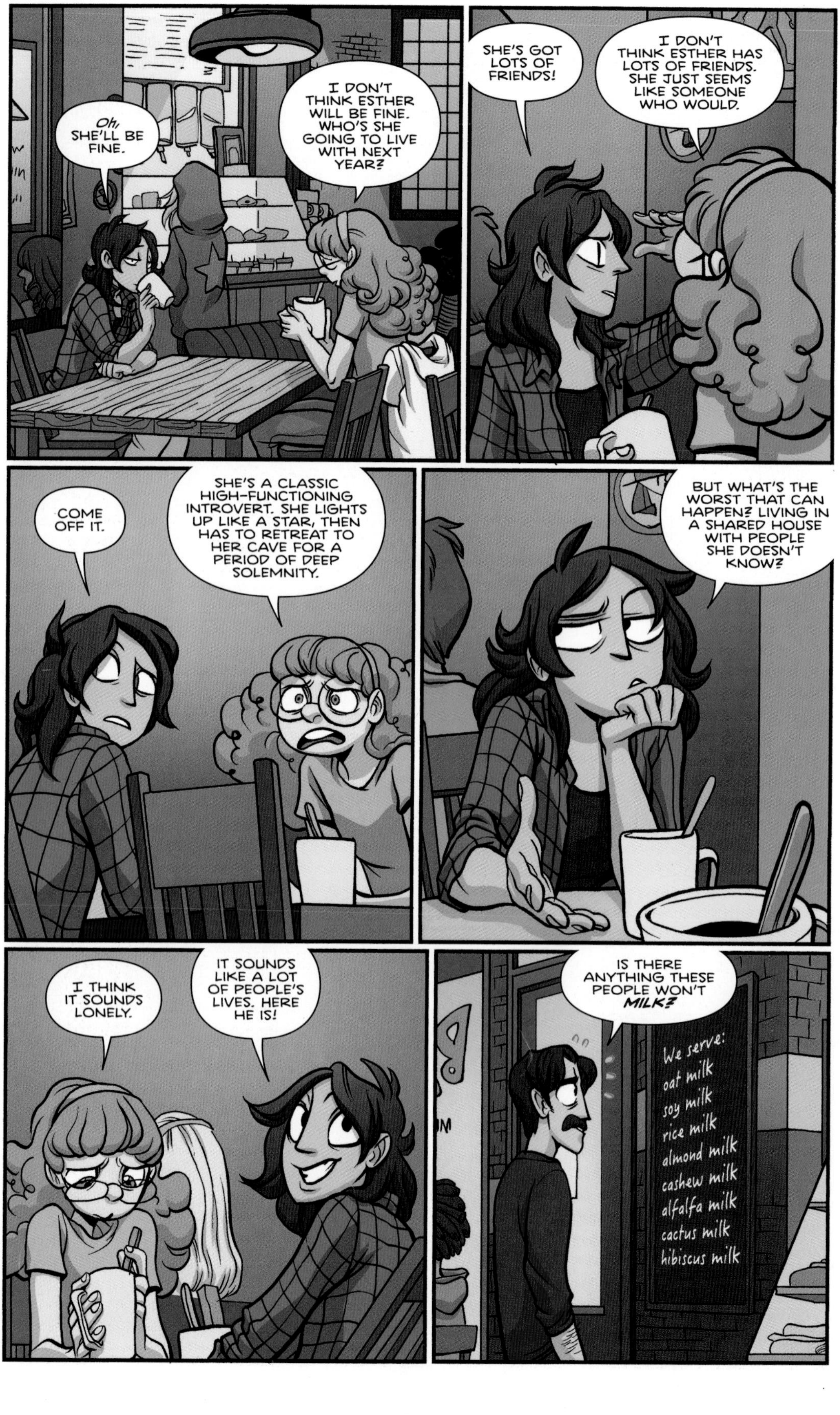

Oh, SHE'LL BE FINE.
I DON'T THINK ESTHER WILL BE FINE. WHO'S SHE GOING TO LIVE WITH NEXT YEAR?
SHE'S GOT LOTS OF FRIENDS!
I DON'T THINK ESTHER HAS LOTS OF FRIENDS. SHE JUST SEEMS LIKE SOMEONE WHO WOULD.
COME OFF IT.
SHE'S A CLASSIC HIGH-FUNCTIONING INTROVERT. SHE LIGHTS UP LIKE A STAR, THEN HAS TO RETREAT TO HER CAVE FOR A PERIOD OF DEEP SOLEMNITY.
BUT WHAT'S THE WORST THAT CAN HAPPEN? LIVING IN A SHARED HOUSE WITH PEOPLE SHE DOESN'T KNOW?
I THINK IT SOUNDS LONELY.
IT SOUNDS LIKE A LOT OF PEOPLE'S LIVES. HERE HE IS!
IS THERE ANYTHING THESE PEOPLE WON'T MILK?
We serve:
oat milk
soy milk
rice milk
almond milk
cashew milk
alfalfa milk
cactus milk
hibiscus milk

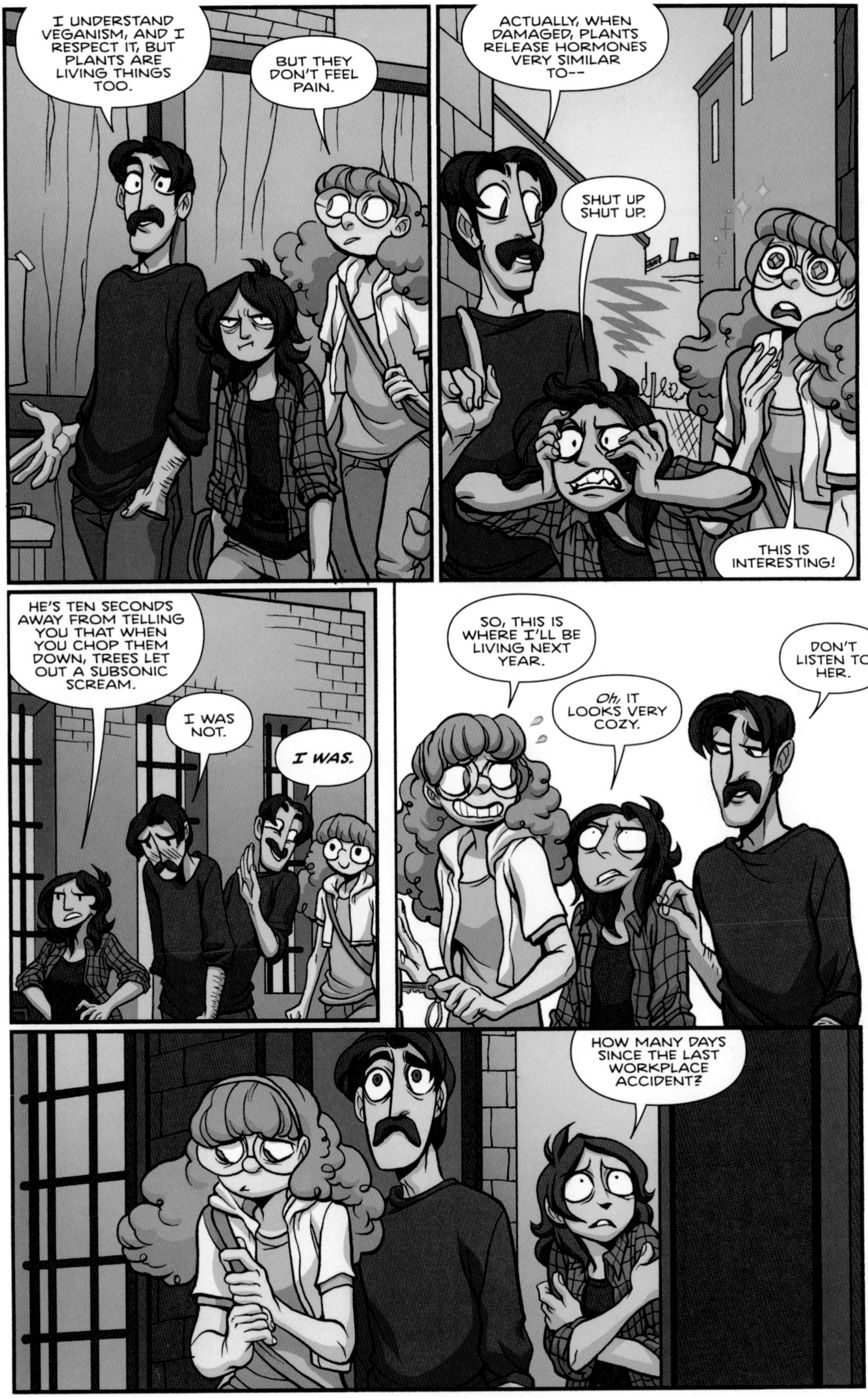
I UNDERSTAND VEGANISM, AND I RESPECT IT, BUT PLANTS ARE LIVING THINGS TOO.
BUT THEY DON'T FEEL PAIN.
ACTUALLY, WHEN DAMAGED, PLANTS RELEASE HORMONES VERY SIMILAR TO--
SHUT UP SHUT UP.
THIS IS INTERESTING!
HE'S TEN SECONDS AWAY FROM TELLING YOU THAT WHEN YOU CHOP THEM DOWN, TREES LET OUT A SUBSONIC SCREAM.
I WAS NOT.
I WAS.
SO, THIS IS WHERE I'LL BE LIVING NEXT YEAR.
Oh, IT LOOKS VERY COZY.
DON'T LISTEN TO HER.
HOW MANY DAYS SINCE THE LAST WORKPLACE ACCIDENT?

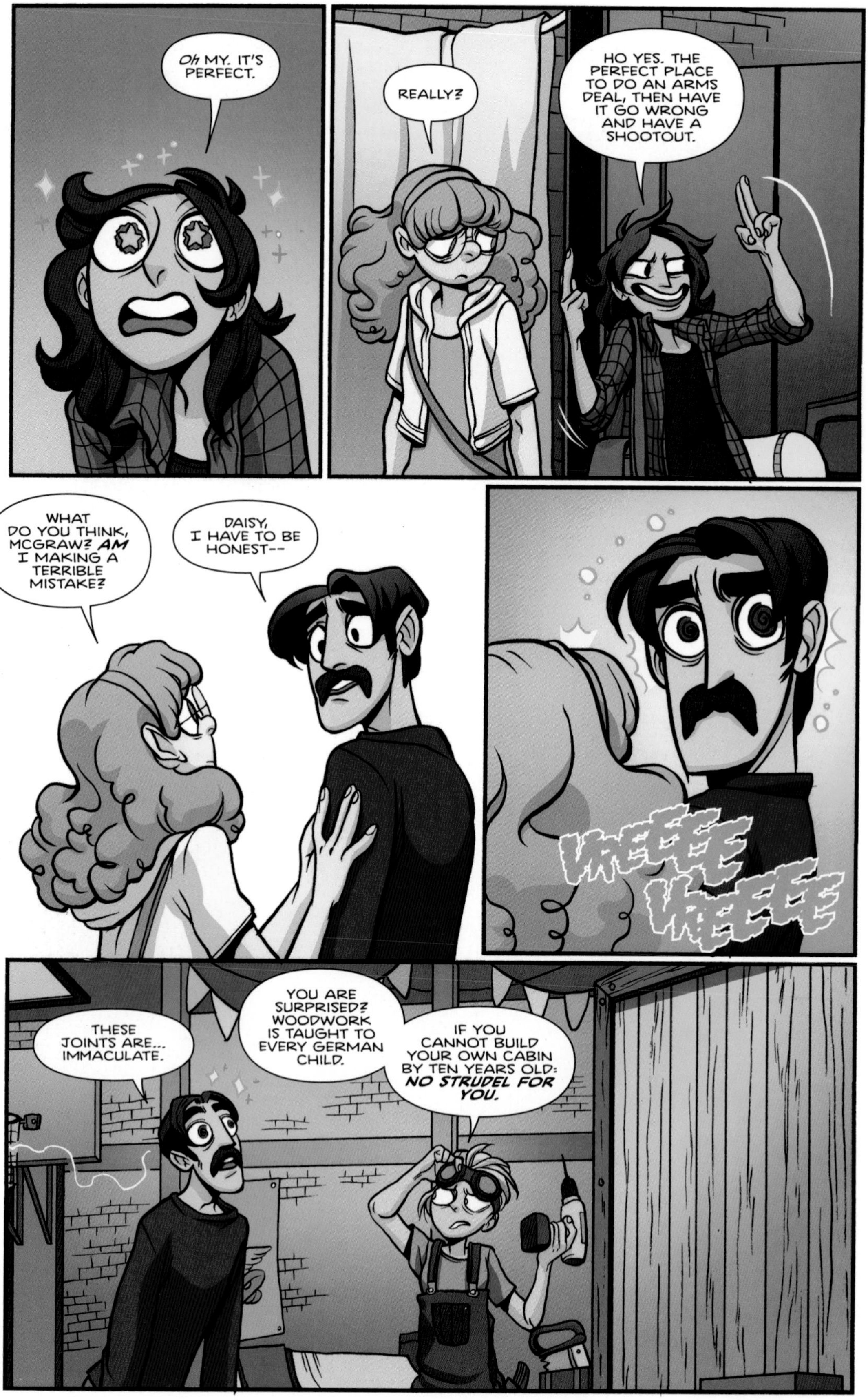
Oh MY. IT'S PERFECT.
REALLY?
HO YES. THE PERFECT PLACE TO DO AN ARMS DEAL, THEN HAVE IT GO WRONG AND HAVE A SHOOTOUT.
WHAT DO YOU THINK, MCGRAW? AM I MAKING A TERRIBLE MISTAKE?
DAISY, I HAVE TO BE HONEST--
VREEEE VREEEE
THESE JOINTS ARE... IMMACULATE.
YOU ARE SURPRISED? WOODWORK IS TAUGHT TO EVERY GERMAN CHILD.
IF YOU CANNOT BUILD YOUR OWN CABIN BY TEN YEARS OLD: NO STRUDEL FOR YOU.

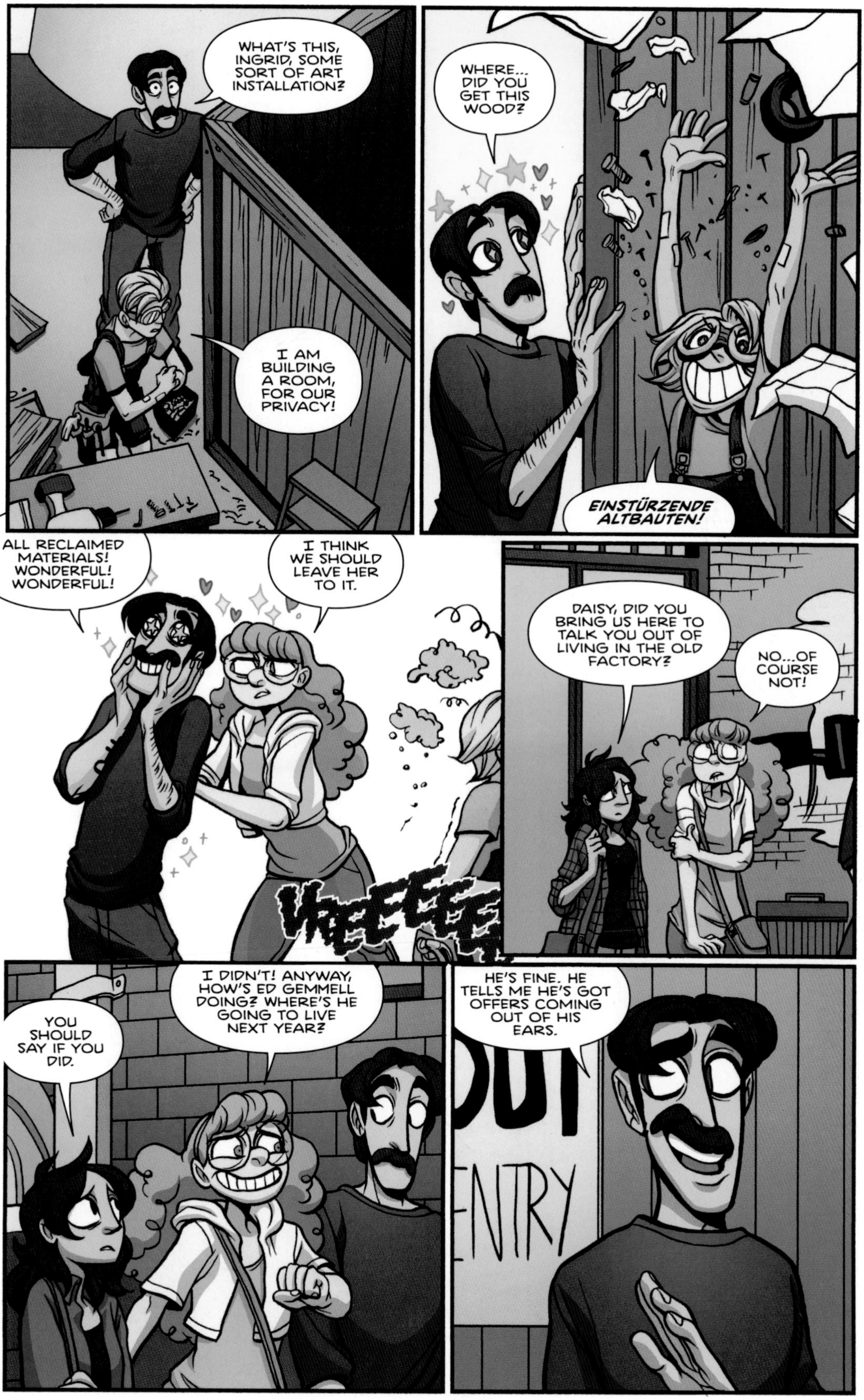
WHAT'S THIS, INGRID, SOME SORT OF ART INSTALLATION?
I AM BUILDING A ROOM, FOR OUR PRIVACY!
WHERE... DID YOU GET THIS WOOD?
EINSTÜRZENDE ALTBAUTEN!
ALL RECLAIMED MATERIALS! WONDERFUL! WONDERFUL!
I THINK WE SHOULD LEAVE HER TO IT.
VREEEEE
DAISY, DID YOU BRING US HERE TO TALK YOU OUT OF LIVING IN THE OLD FACTORY?
NO...OF COURSE NOT!
YOU SHOULD SAY IF YOU DID.
I DIDN'T! ANYWAY, HOW'S ED GEMMELL DOING? WHERE'S HE GOING TO LIVE NEXT YEAR?
HE'S FINE. HE TELLS ME HE'S GOT OFFERS COMING OUT OF HIS EARS.
ENTRY

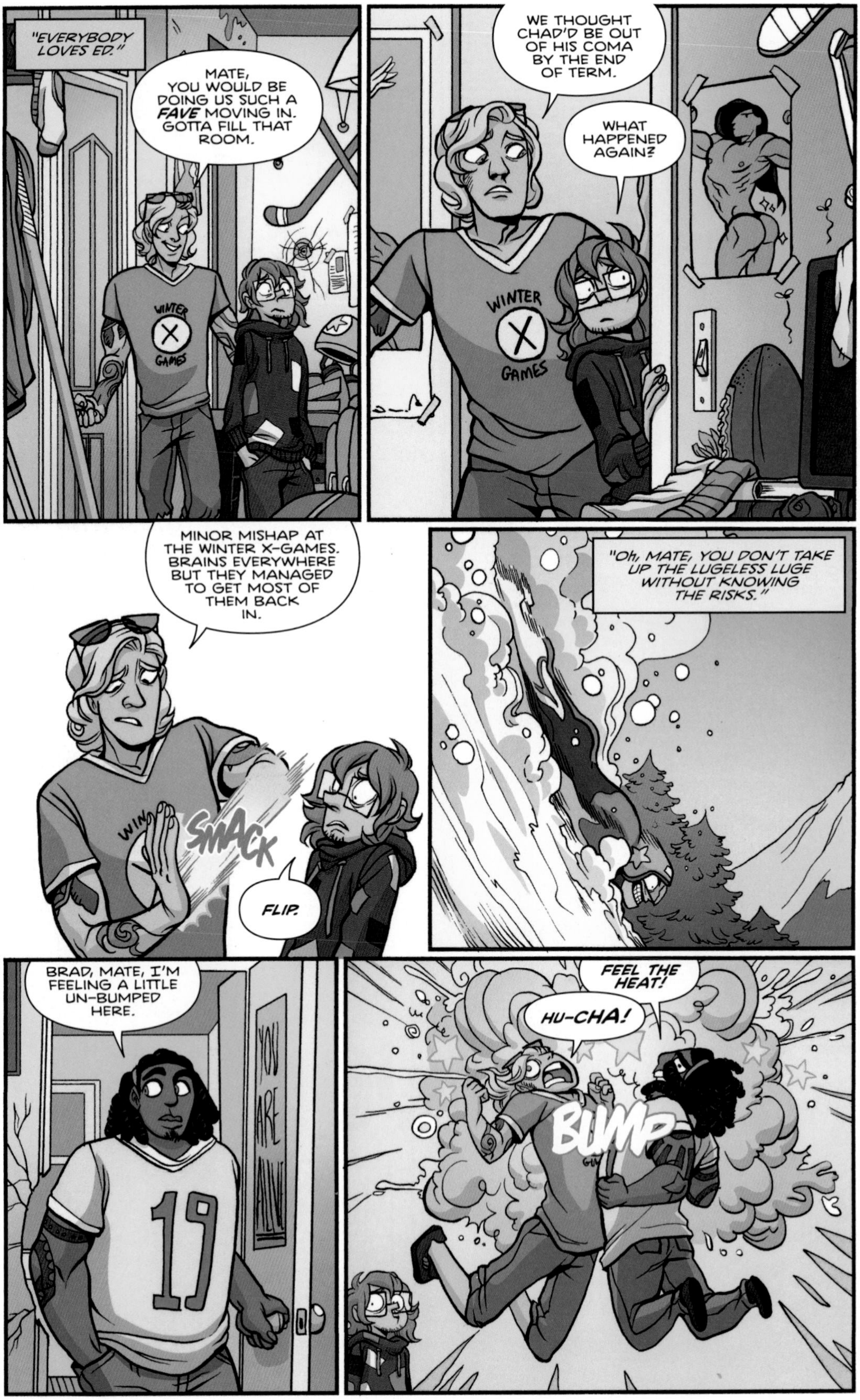
"EVERYBODY LOVES ED."
MATE, YOU WOULD BE DOING US SUCH A FAVE MOVING IN. GOTTA FILL THAT ROOM.
WINTER X GAMES
WE THOUGHT CHAD'D BE OUT OF HIS COMA BY THE END OF TERM.
WHAT HAPPENED AGAIN?
MINOR MISHAP AT THE WINTER X-GAMES. BRAINS EVERYWHERE BUT THEY MANAGED TO GET MOST OF THEM BACK IN.
SMACK
FLIP.
"Oh, MATE, YOU DON'T TAKE UP THE LUGELESS LUGE WITHOUT KNOWING THE RISKS."
BRAD, MATE, I'M FEELING A LITTLE UN-BUMPED HERE.
YOU ARE ALIVE
19
FEEL THE HEAT!
HU-CHA!
BUMP

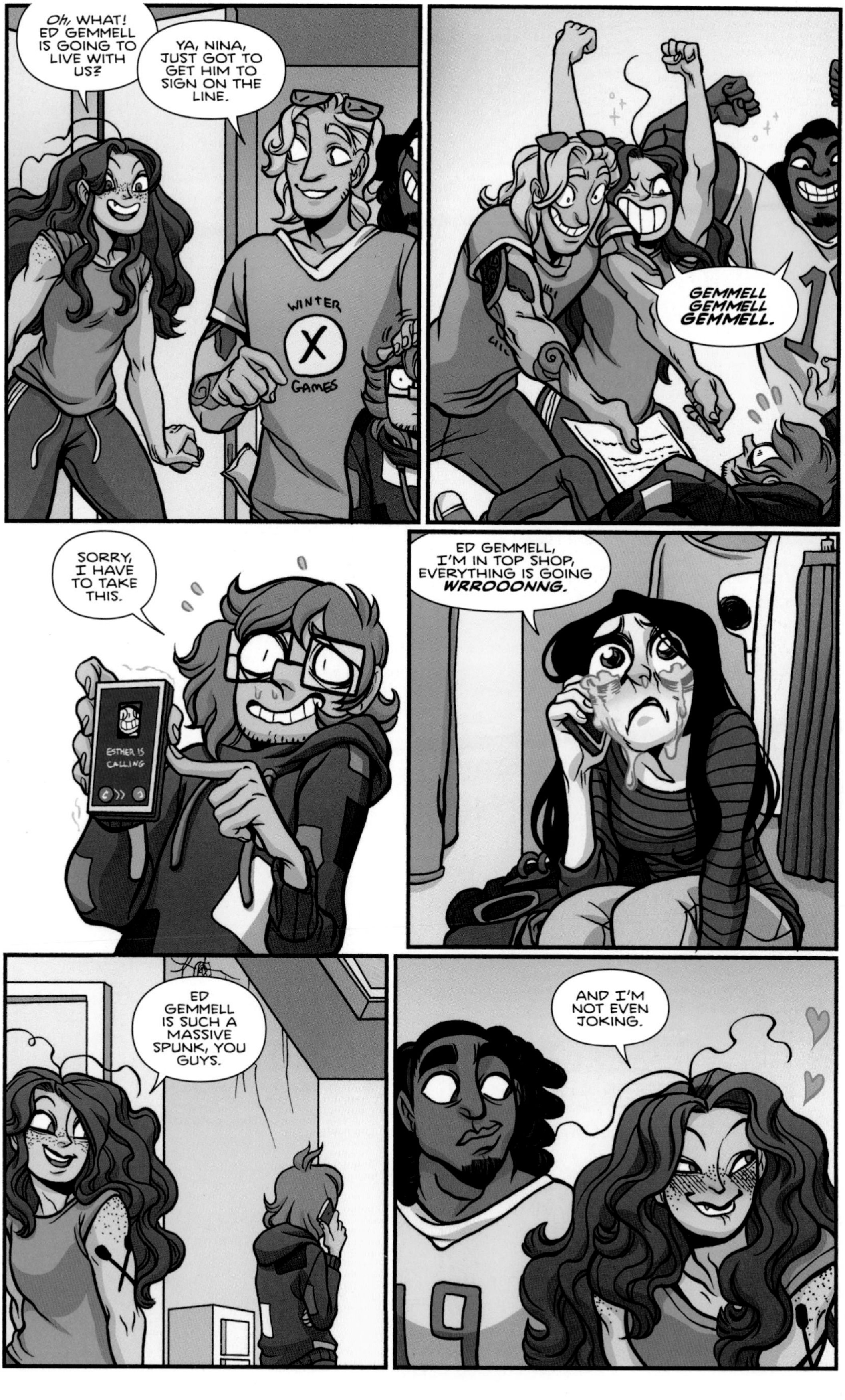
Oh, WHAT! ED GEMMELL IS GOING TO LIVE WITH US?
YA, NINA, JUST GOT TO GET HIM TO SIGN ON THE LINE.
WINTER X GAMES
GEMMELL GEMMELL GEMMELL.
SORRY, I HAVE TO TAKE THIS.
ESTHER IS CALLING
ED GEMMELL, I'M IN TOP SHOP, EVERYTHING IS GOING WRROOONNG.
ED GEMMELL IS SUCH A MASSIVE SPUNK, YOU GUYS.
AND I'M NOT EVEN JOKING.

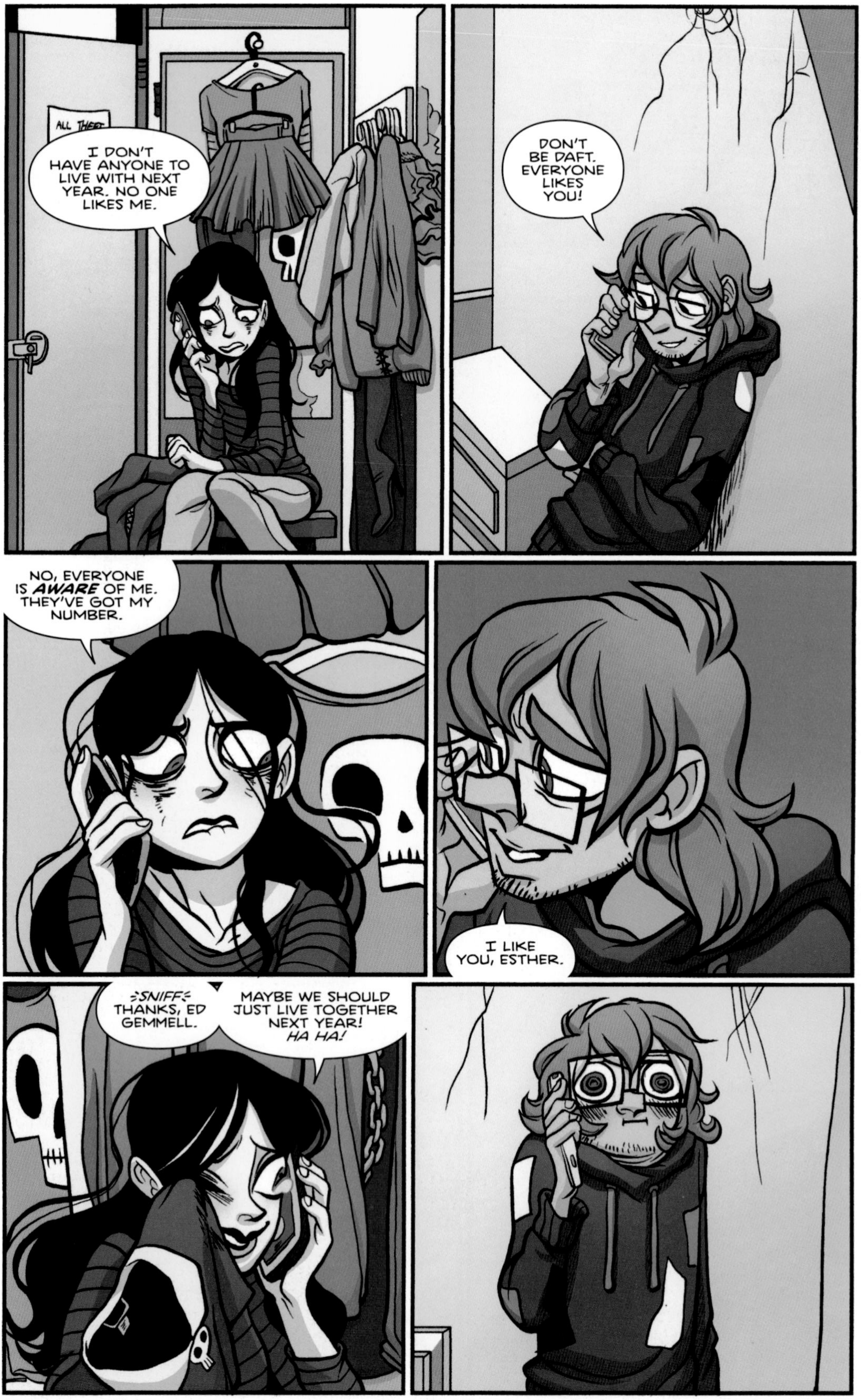
I DON'T HAVE ANYONE TO LIVE WITH NEXT YEAR. NO ONE LIKES ME.
DON'T BE DAFT. EVERYONE LIKES YOU!
NO, EVERYONE IS ***AWARE*** OF ME. THEY'VE GOT MY NUMBER.
I LIKE YOU, ESTHER.
SNIFF THANKS, ED GEMMELL.
MAYBE WE SHOULD JUST LIVE TOGETHER NEXT YEAR! *HA HA!*

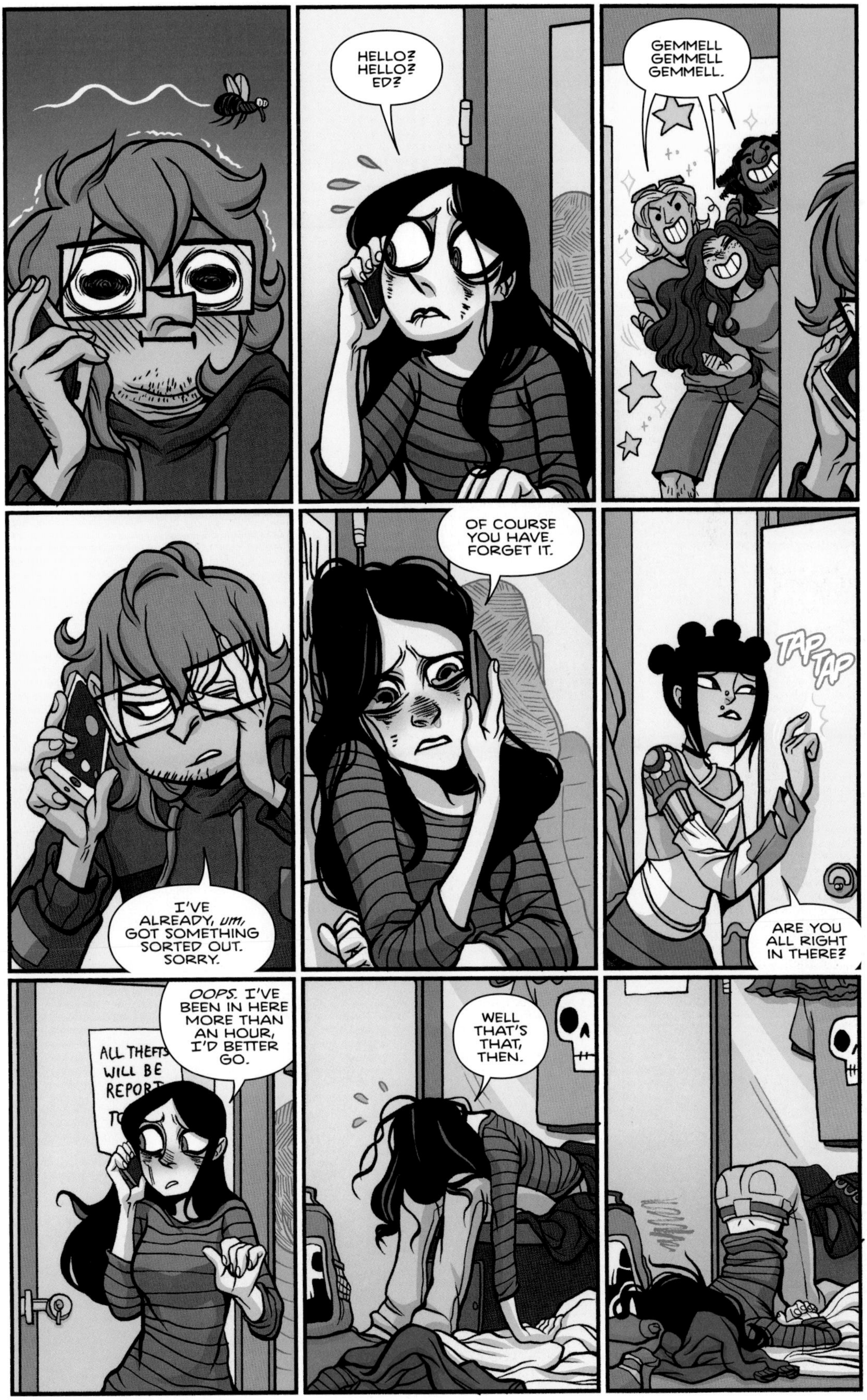

HELLO?
HELLO?
ED?
GEMMELL
GEMMELL
GEMMELL.
I'VE ALREADY, UM, GOT SOMETHING SORTED OUT. SORRY.
OF COURSE YOU HAVE. FORGET IT.
TAP TAP
ARE YOU ALL RIGHT IN THERE?
ALL THEFTS WILL BE REPORT
OOPS. I'VE BEEN IN HERE MORE THAN AN HOUR, I'D BETTER GO.
WELL THAT'S THAT, THEN.

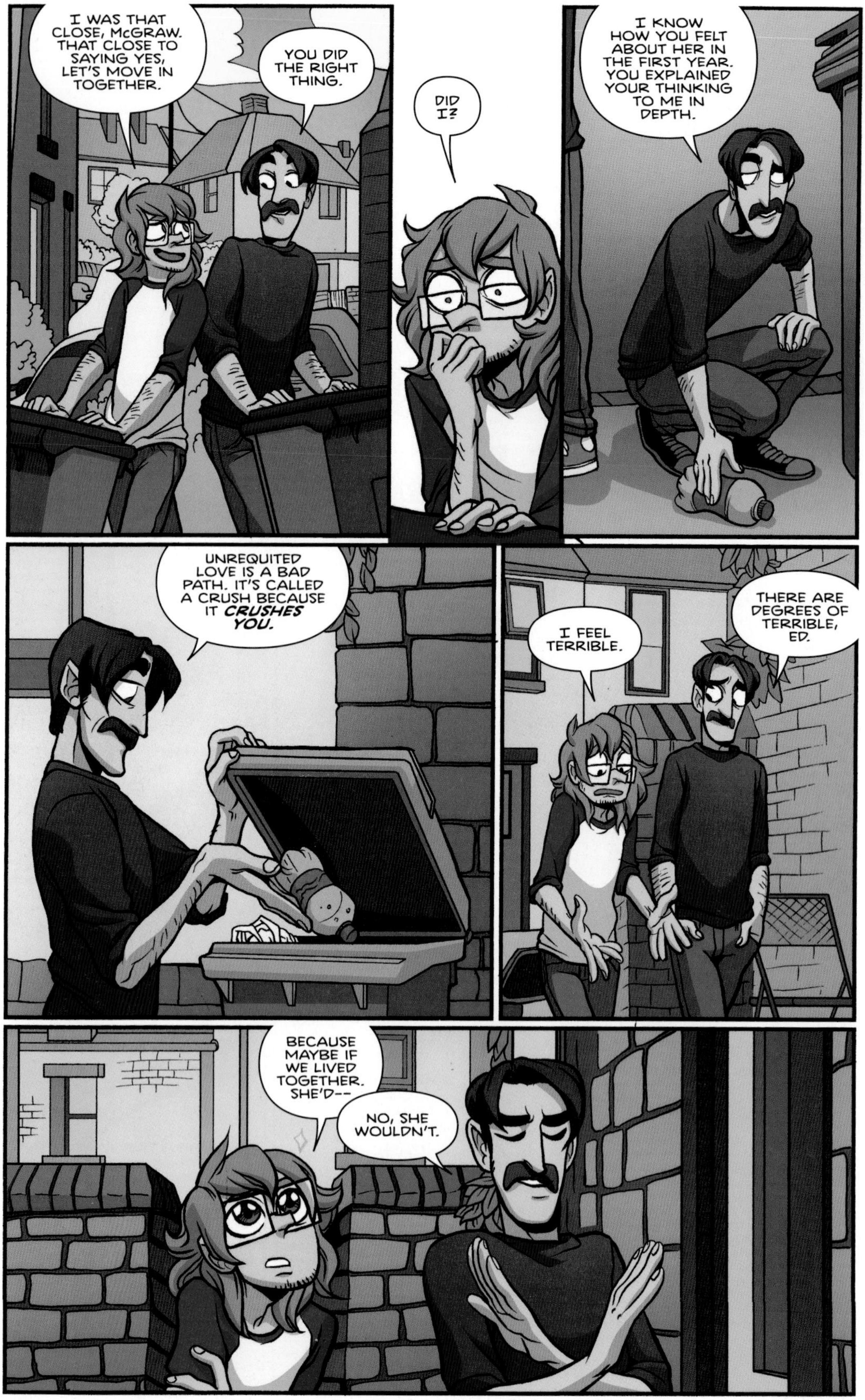
I WAS THAT CLOSE, McGRAW. THAT CLOSE TO SAYING YES, LET'S MOVE IN TOGETHER.
YOU DID THE RIGHT THING.
DID I?
I KNOW HOW YOU FELT ABOUT HER IN THE FIRST YEAR. YOU EXPLAINED YOUR THINKING TO ME IN DEPTH.
UNREQUITED LOVE IS A BAD PATH. IT'S CALLED A CRUSH BECAUSE IT *CRUSHES YOU.*
I FEEL TERRIBLE.
THERE ARE DEGREES OF TERRIBLE, ED.
BECAUSE MAYBE IF WE LIVED TOGETHER. SHE'D--
NO, SHE WOULDN'T.

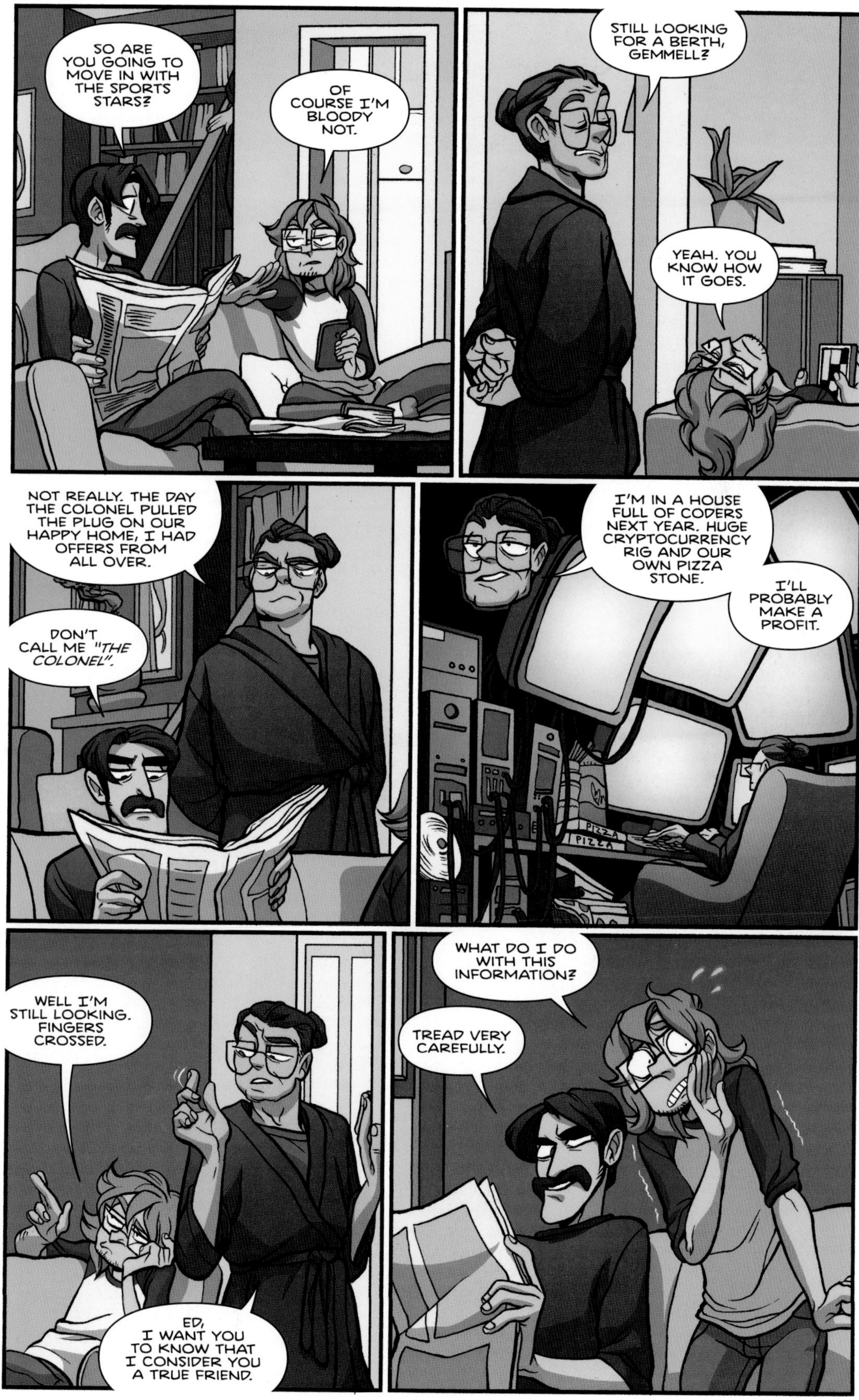
SO ARE YOU GOING TO MOVE IN WITH THE SPORTS STARS?
OF COURSE I'M BLOODY NOT.
STILL LOOKING FOR A BERTH, GEMMELL?
YEAH. YOU KNOW HOW IT GOES.
NOT REALLY. THE DAY THE COLONEL PULLED THE PLUG ON OUR HAPPY HOME, I HAD OFFERS FROM ALL OVER.
DON'T CALL ME *"THE COLONEL"*.
I'M IN A HOUSE FULL OF CODERS NEXT YEAR. HUGE CRYPTOCURRENCY RIG AND OUR OWN PIZZA STONE.
I'LL PROBABLY MAKE A PROFIT.
PIZZA
PIZZA
WELL I'M STILL LOOKING. FINGERS CROSSED.
ED, I WANT YOU TO KNOW THAT I CONSIDER YOU A TRUE FRIEND.
WHAT DO I DO WITH THIS INFORMATION?
TREAD VERY CAREFULLY.

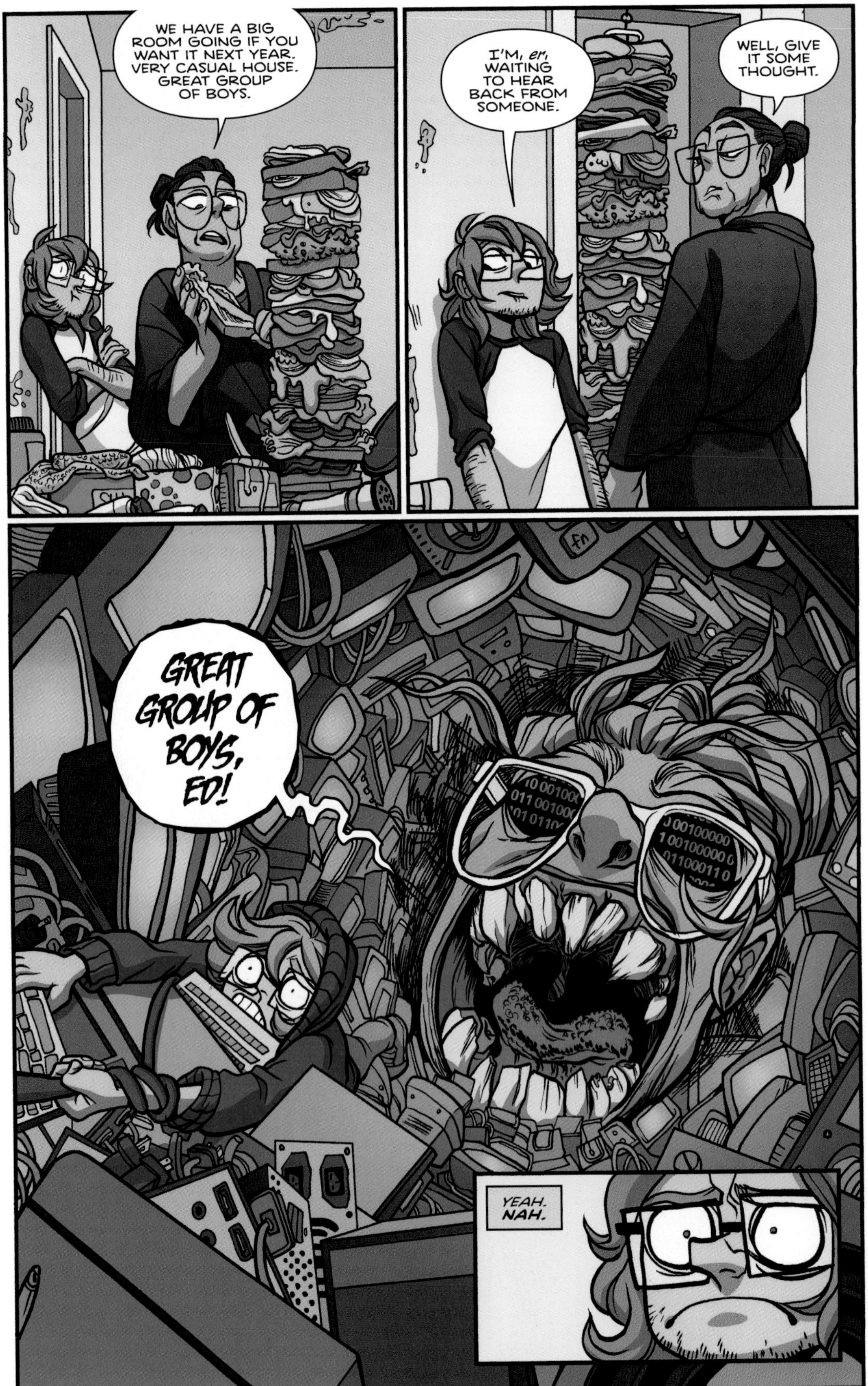
WE HAVE A BIG ROOM GOING IF YOU WANT IT NEXT YEAR. VERY CASUAL HOUSE. GREAT GROUP OF BOYS.
I'M, *er*, WAITING TO HEAR BACK FROM SOMEONE.
WELL, GIVE IT SOME THOUGHT.
GREAT GROUP OF BOYS, ED!
YEAH. NAH.

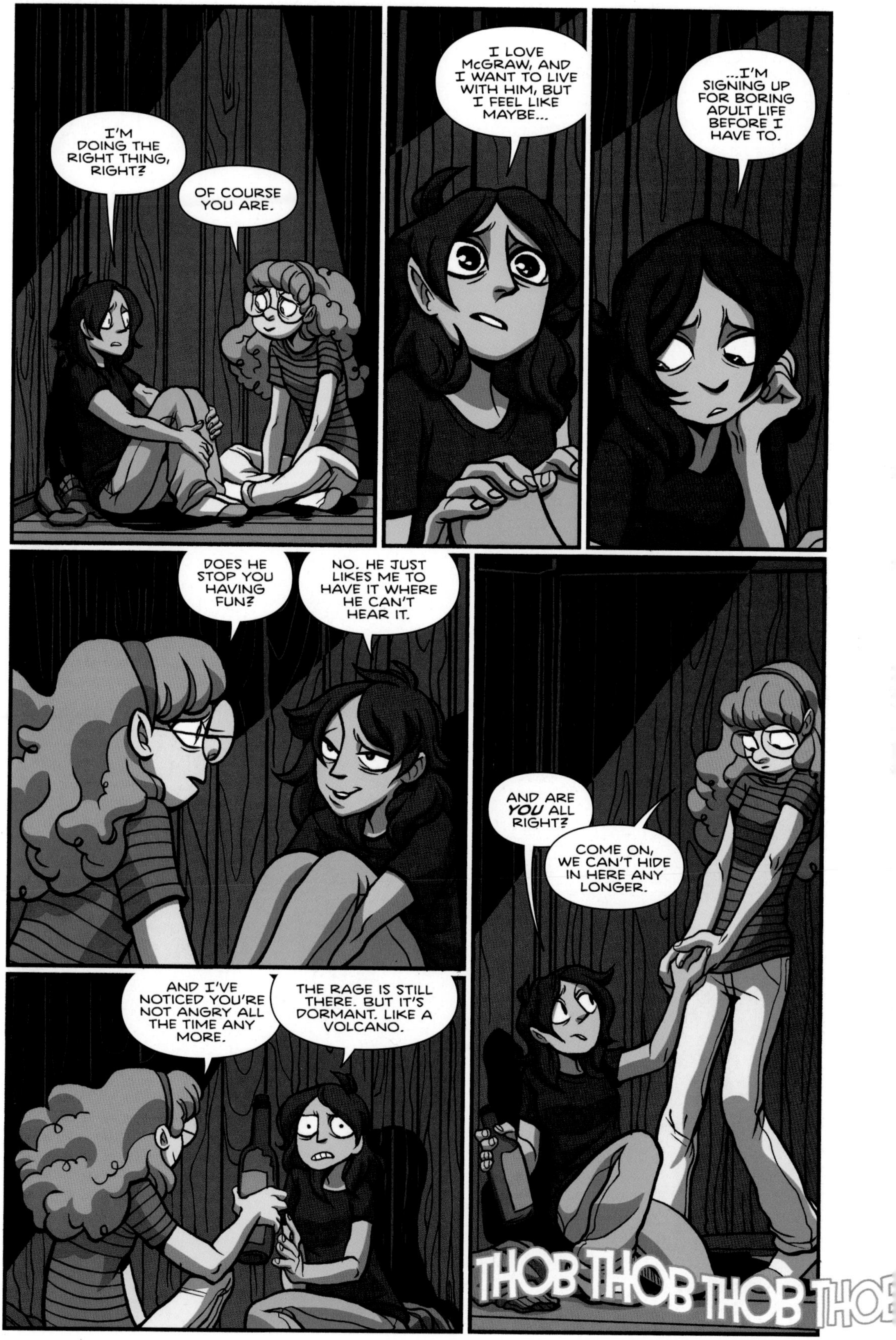
I'M DOING THE RIGHT THING, RIGHT?
OF COURSE YOU ARE.
I LOVE McGRAW, AND I WANT TO LIVE WITH HIM, BUT I FEEL LIKE MAYBE...
...I'M SIGNING UP FOR BORING ADULT LIFE BEFORE I HAVE TO.
DOES HE STOP YOU HAVING FUN?
NO. HE JUST LIKES ME TO HAVE IT WHERE HE CAN'T HEAR IT.
AND I'VE NOTICED YOU'RE NOT ANGRY ALL THE TIME ANY MORE.
THE RAGE IS STILL THERE. BUT IT'S DORMANT. LIKE A VOLCANO.
AND ARE *YOU* ALL RIGHT?
COME ON, WE CAN'T HIDE IN HERE ANY LONGER.
THOB THOB THOB THOB

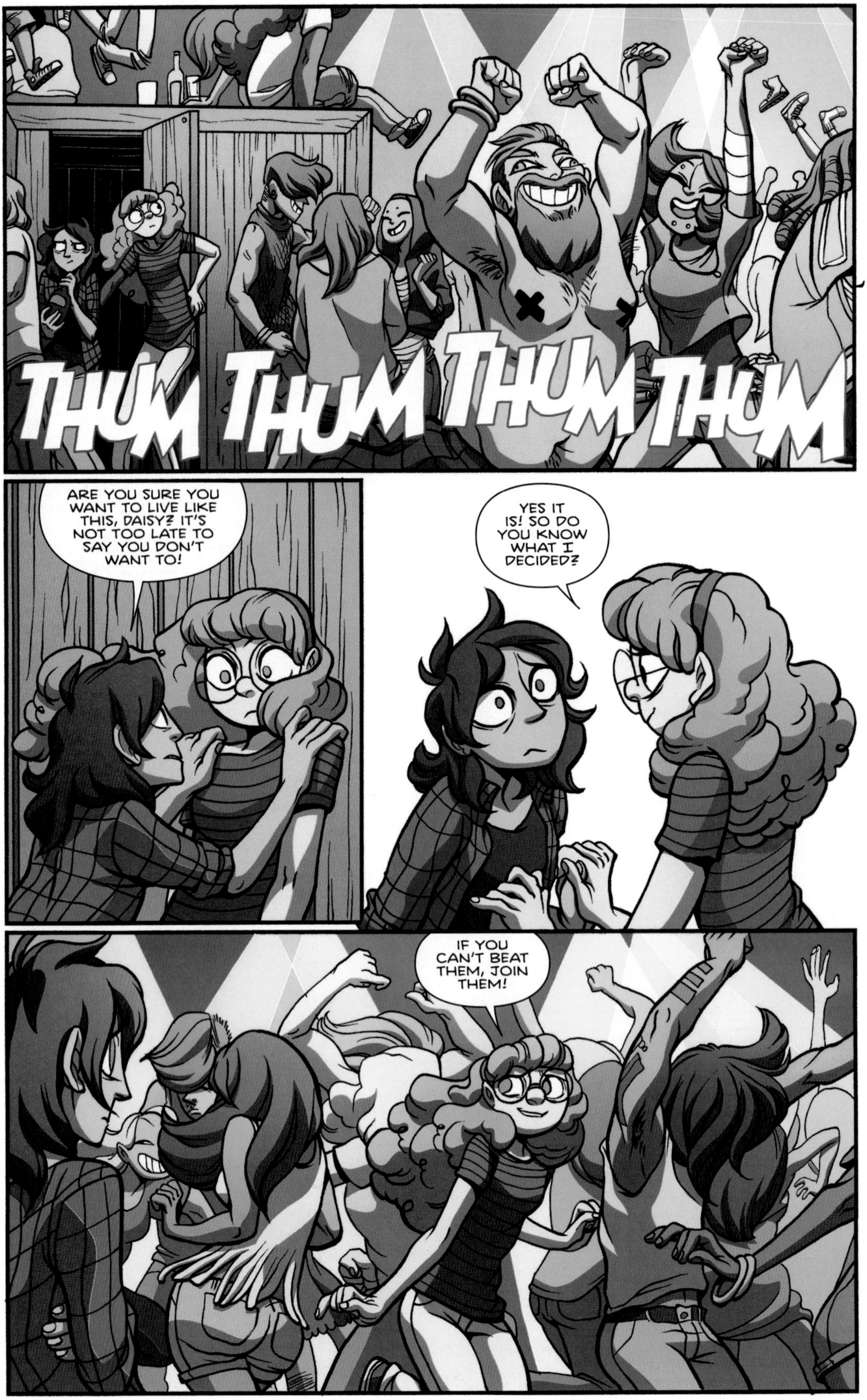
THUM THUM THUM THUM
ARE YOU SURE YOU WANT TO LIVE LIKE THIS, DAISY? IT'S NOT TOO LATE TO SAY YOU DON'T WANT TO!
YES IT IS! SO DO YOU KNOW WHAT I DECIDED?
IF YOU CAN'T BEAT THEM, JOIN THEM!

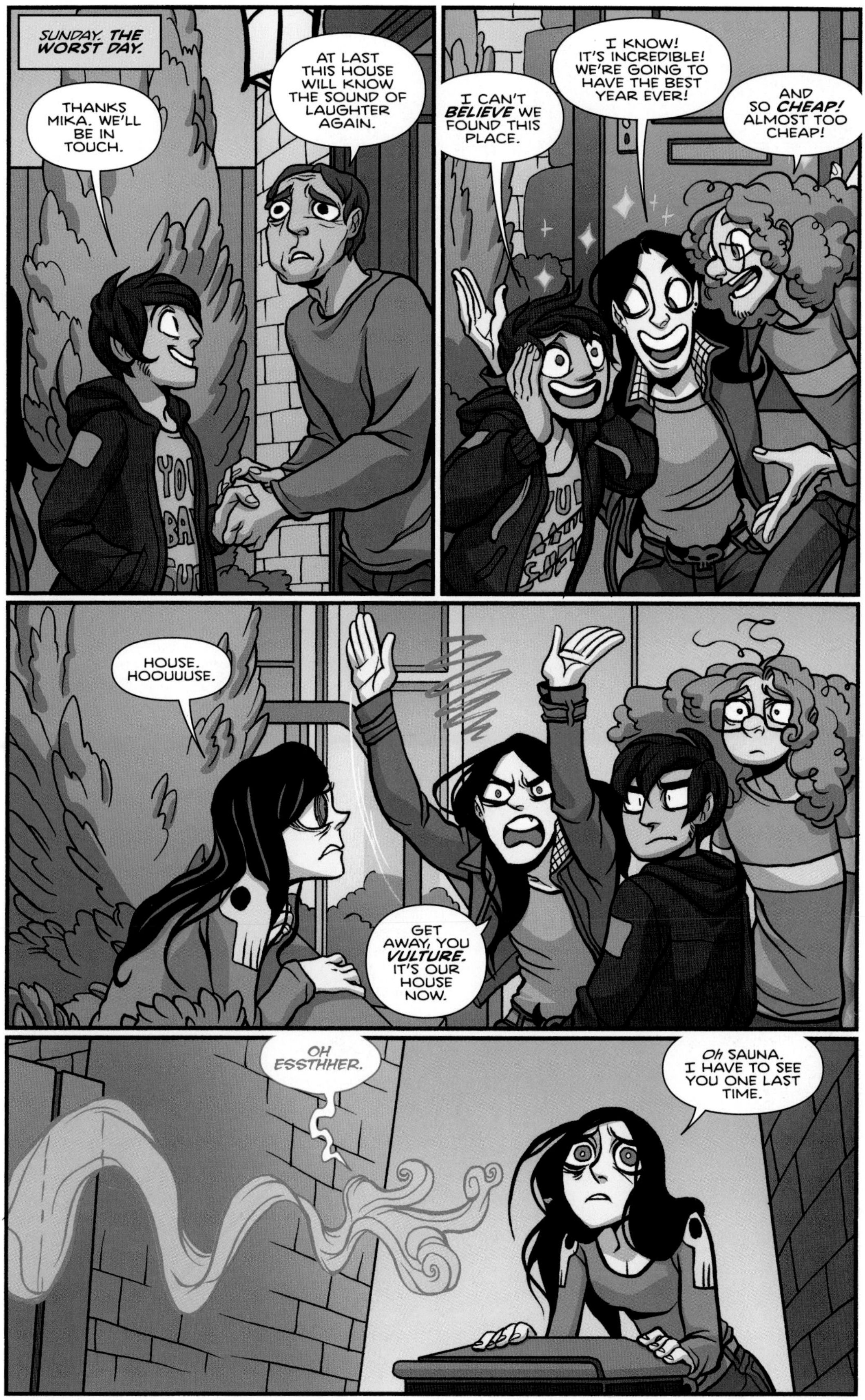
SUNDAY. THE WORST DAY.
THANKS MIKA. WE'LL BE IN TOUCH.
AT LAST THIS HOUSE WILL KNOW THE SOUND OF LAUGHTER AGAIN.
I CAN'T BELIEVE WE FOUND THIS PLACE.
I KNOW! IT'S INCREDIBLE! WE'RE GOING TO HAVE THE BEST YEAR EVER!
AND SO CHEAP! ALMOST TOO CHEAP!
HOUSE. HOOUUUSE.
GET AWAY, YOU VULTURE. IT'S OUR HOUSE NOW.
OH ESSTHHER.
Oh SAUNA. I HAVE TO SEE YOU ONE LAST TIME.

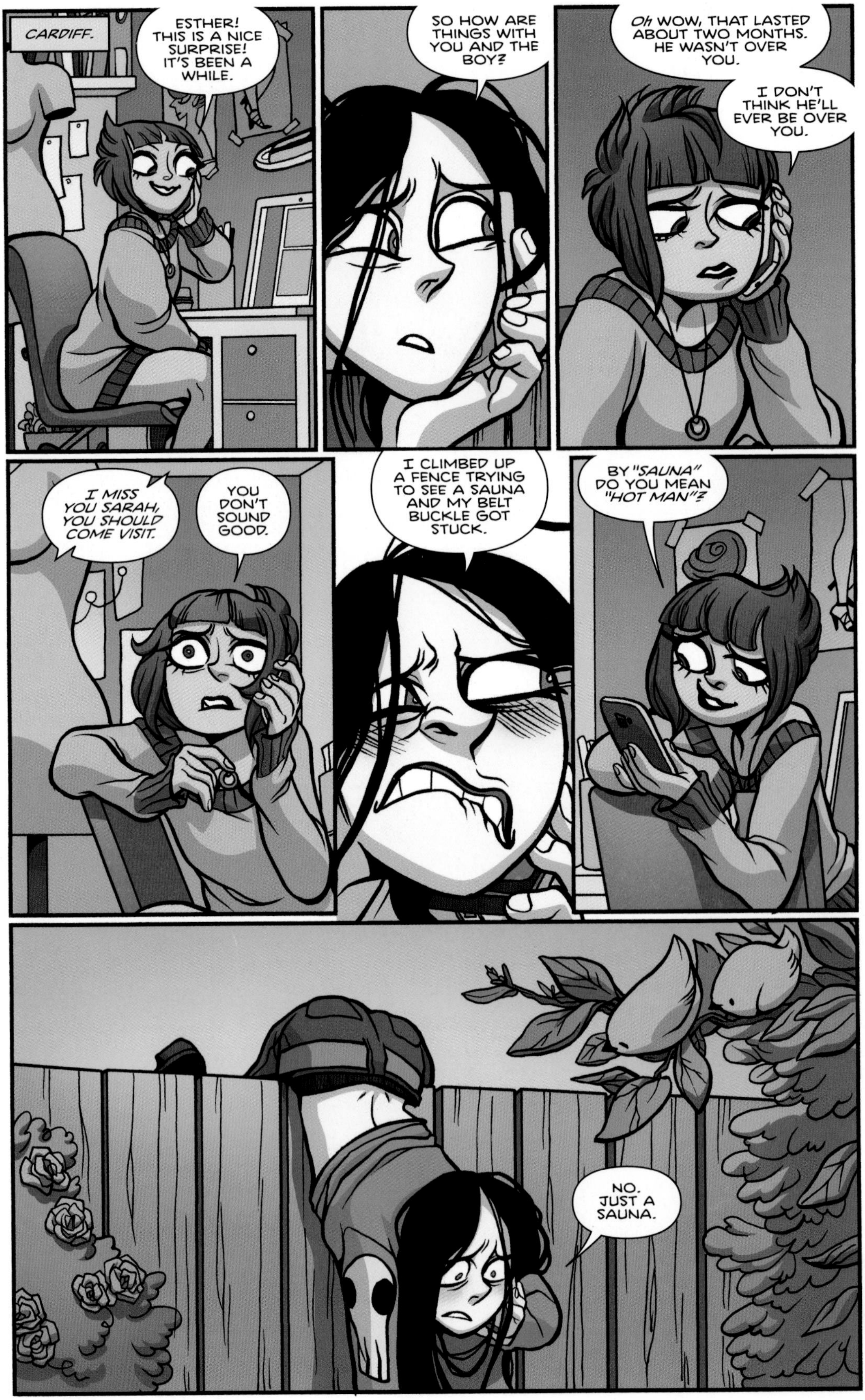
CARDIFF.
ESTHER! THIS IS A NICE SURPRISE! IT'S BEEN A WHILE.
SO HOW ARE THINGS WITH YOU AND THE BOY?
Oh WOW, THAT LASTED ABOUT TWO MONTHS. HE WASN'T OVER YOU.
I DON'T THINK HE'LL EVER BE OVER YOU.
I MISS YOU SARAH, YOU SHOULD COME VISIT.
YOU DON'T SOUND GOOD.
I CLIMBED UP A FENCE TRYING TO SEE A SAUNA AND MY BELT BUCKLE GOT STUCK.
BY "SAUNA" DO YOU MEAN "HOT MAN"?
NO. JUST A SAUNA.

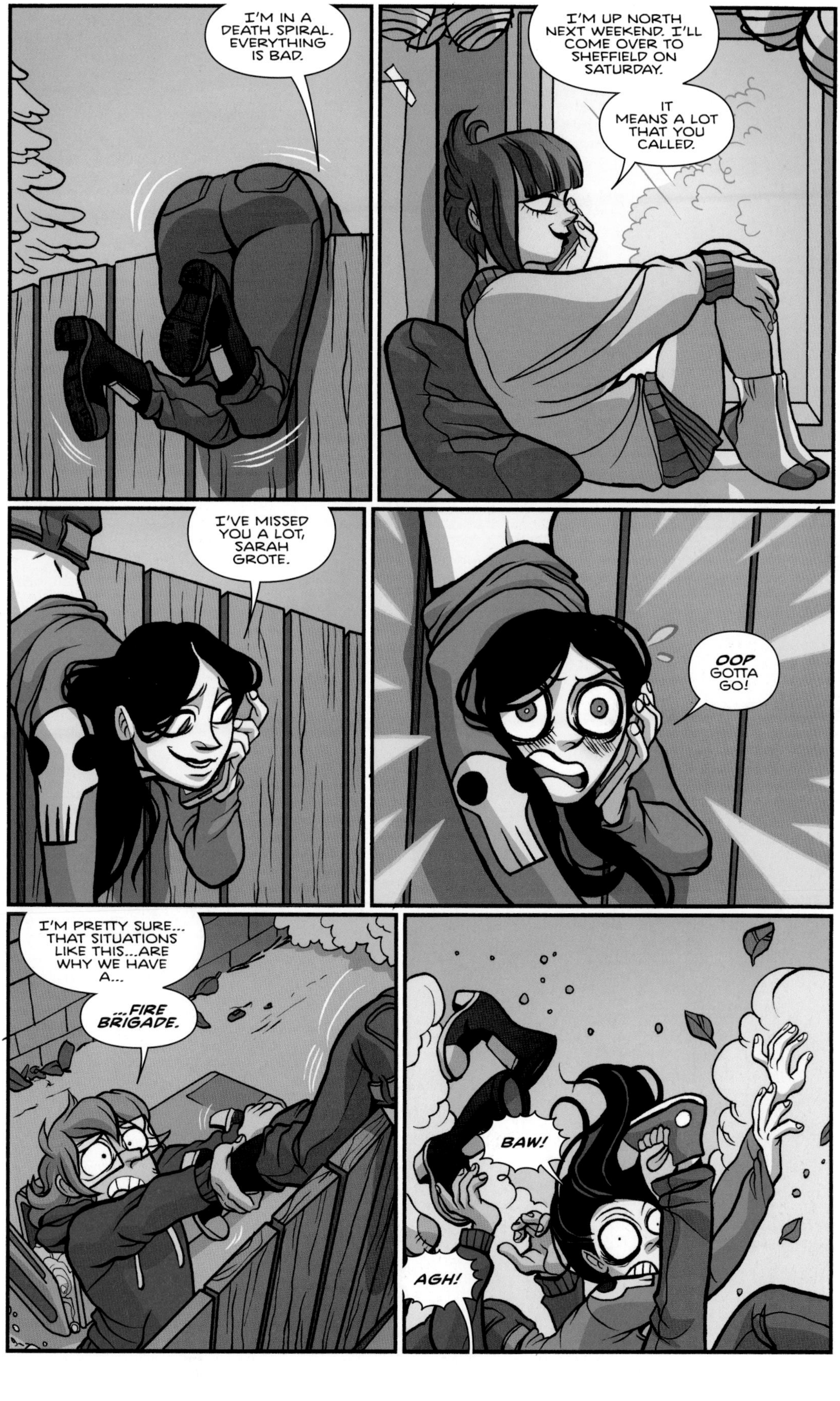
I'M IN A DEATH SPIRAL. EVERYTHING IS BAD.
I'M UP NORTH NEXT WEEKEND. I'LL COME OVER TO SHEFFIELD ON SATURDAY.
IT MEANS A LOT THAT YOU CALLED.
I'VE MISSED YOU A LOT, SARAH GROTE.
OOP GOTTA GO!
I'M PRETTY SURE... THAT SITUATIONS LIKE THIS...ARE WHY WE HAVE A...
...FIRE BRIGADE.
BAW!
AGH!

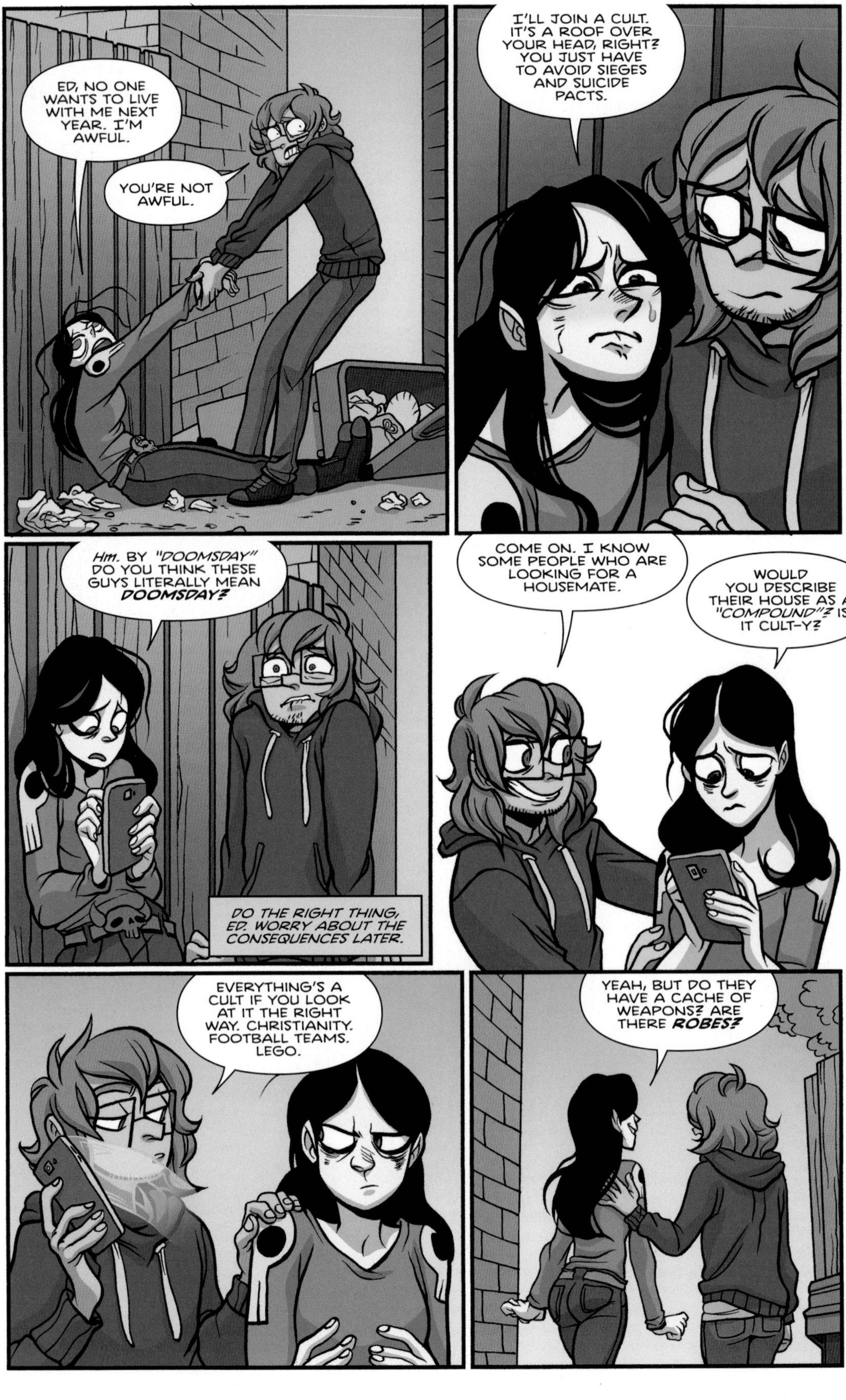
ED, NO ONE WANTS TO LIVE WITH ME NEXT YEAR. I'M AWFUL.
YOU'RE NOT AWFUL.
I'LL JOIN A CULT. IT'S A ROOF OVER YOUR HEAD, RIGHT? YOU JUST HAVE TO AVOID SIEGES AND SUICIDE PACTS.
Hm. BY "DOOMSDAY" DO YOU THINK THESE GUYS LITERALLY MEAN DOOMSDAY?
DO THE RIGHT THING, ED. WORRY ABOUT THE CONSEQUENCES LATER.
COME ON. I KNOW SOME PEOPLE WHO ARE LOOKING FOR A HOUSEMATE.
WOULD YOU DESCRIBE THEIR HOUSE AS A "COMPOUND"? IS IT CULT-Y?
EVERYTHING'S A CULT IF YOU LOOK AT IT THE RIGHT WAY. CHRISTIANITY. FOOTBALL TEAMS. LEGO.
YEAH, BUT DO THEY HAVE A CACHE OF WEAPONS? ARE THERE ROBES?

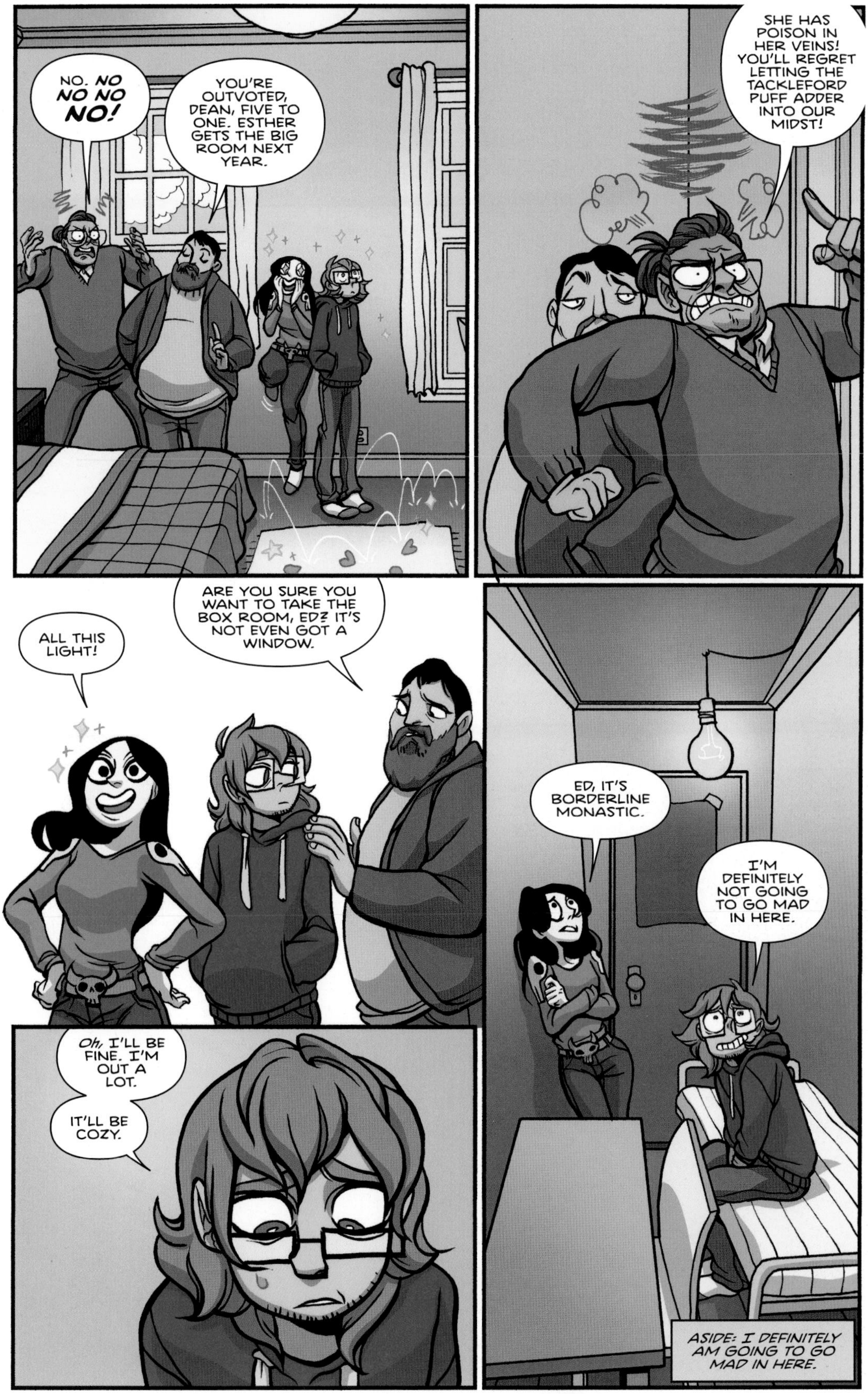
NO. *NO NO NO* ***NO!***
YOU'RE OUTVOTED, DEAN, FIVE TO ONE. ESTHER GETS THE BIG ROOM NEXT YEAR.
SHE HAS POISON IN HER VEINS! YOU'LL REGRET LETTING THE TACKLEFORD PUFF ADDER INTO OUR MIDST!
ALL THIS LIGHT!
ARE YOU SURE YOU WANT TO TAKE THE BOX ROOM, ED? IT'S NOT EVEN GOT A WINDOW.
Oh, I'LL BE FINE. I'M OUT A LOT.
IT'LL BE COZY.
ED, IT'S BORDERLINE MONASTIC.
I'M DEFINITELY NOT GOING TO GO MAD IN HERE.
ASIDE: I DEFINITELY AM GOING TO GO MAD IN HERE.

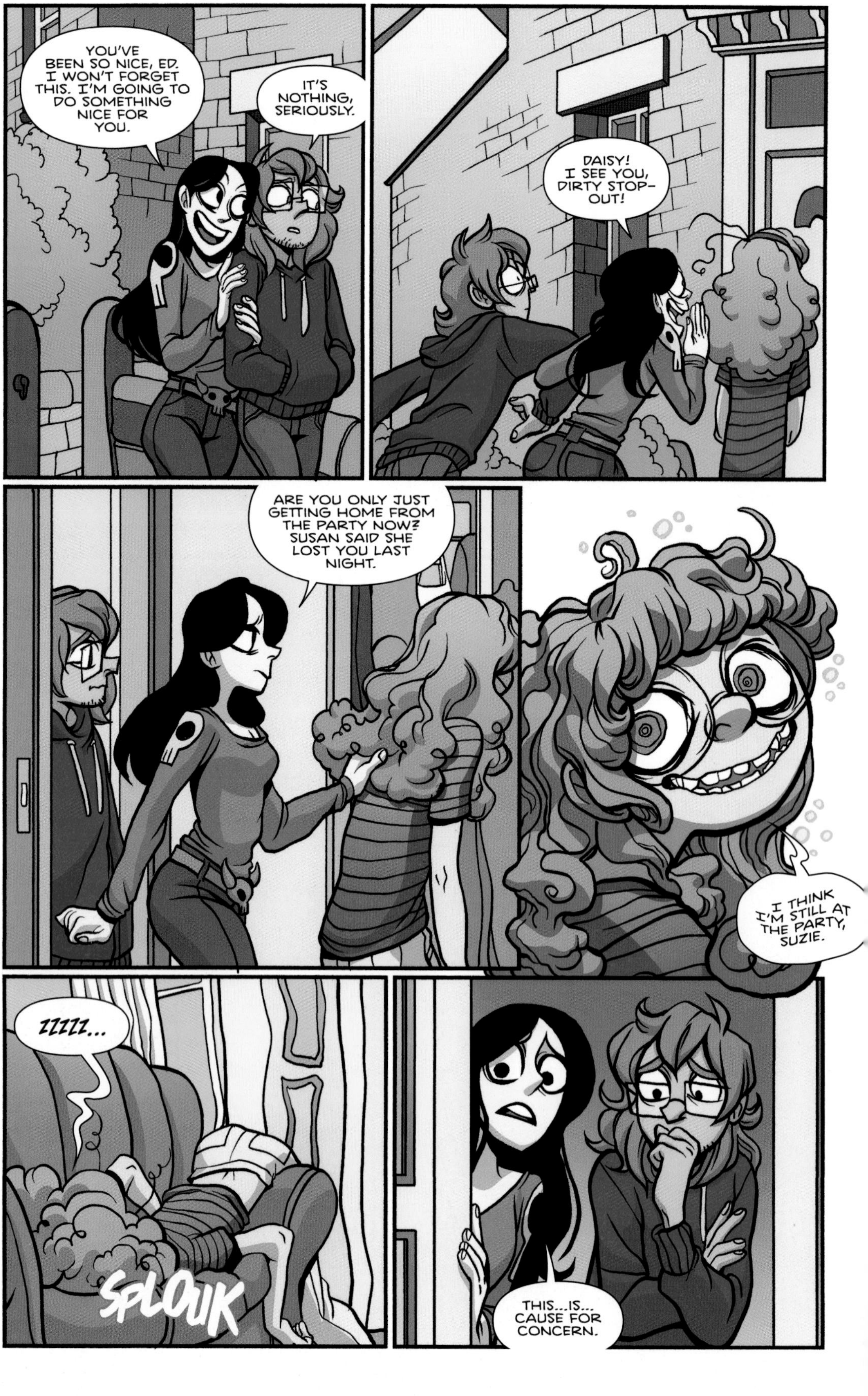
YOU'VE BEEN SO NICE, ED. I WON'T FORGET THIS. I'M GOING TO DO SOMETHING NICE FOR YOU.
IT'S NOTHING, SERIOUSLY.
DAISY! I SEE YOU, DIRTY STOP-OUT!
ARE YOU ONLY JUST GETTING HOME FROM THE PARTY NOW? SUSAN SAID SHE LOST YOU LAST NIGHT.
I THINK I'M STILL AT THE PARTY, SUZIE.
ZZZZZ...
SPLOUK
THIS...IS... CAUSE FOR CONCERN.

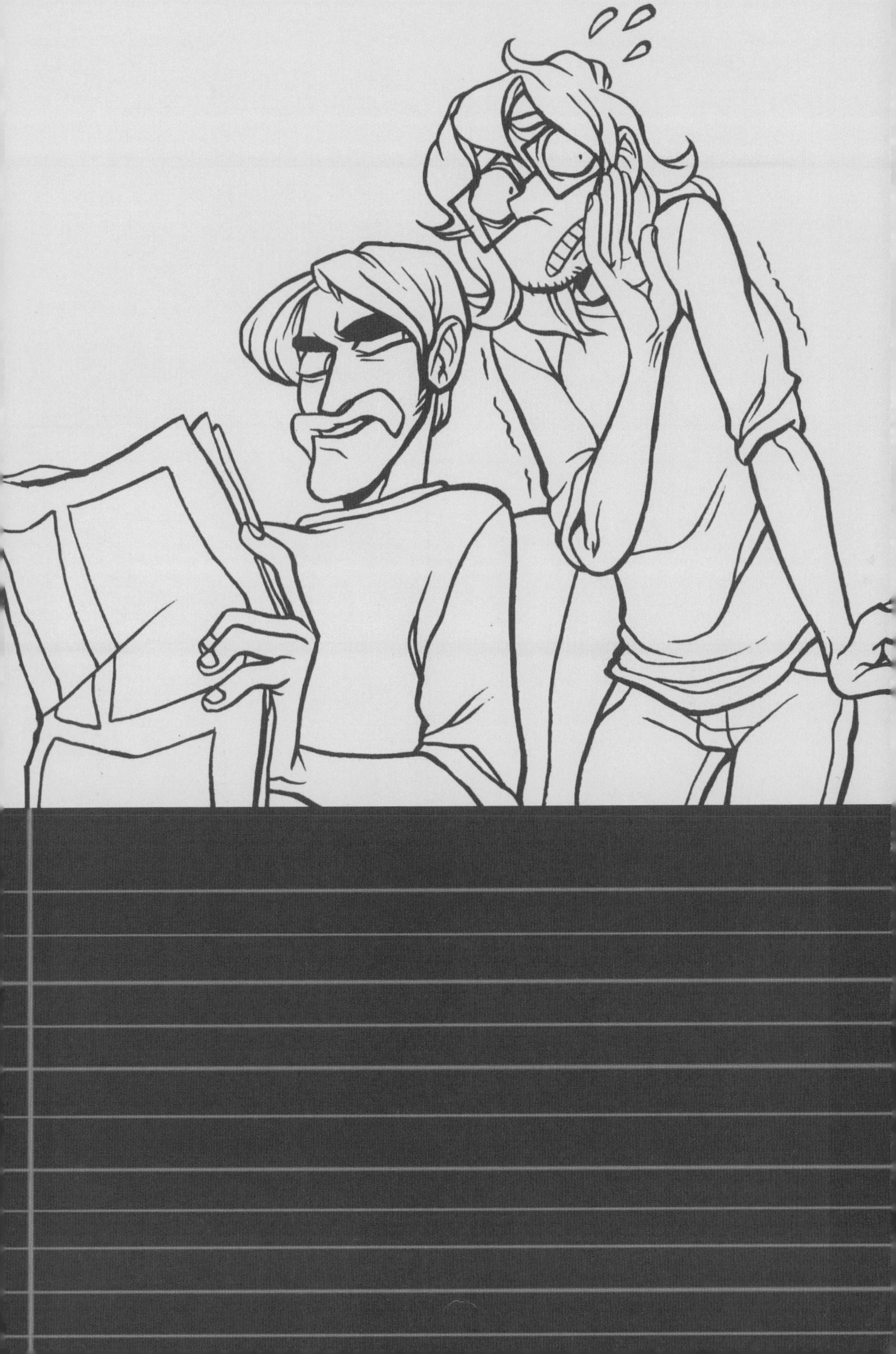

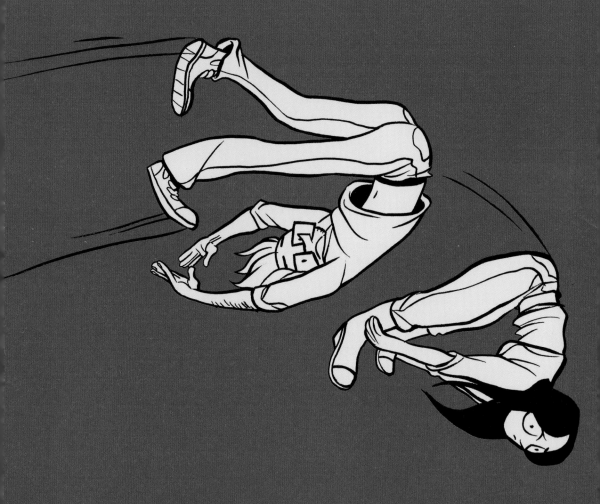

CHAPTER
THIRTY-FOUR

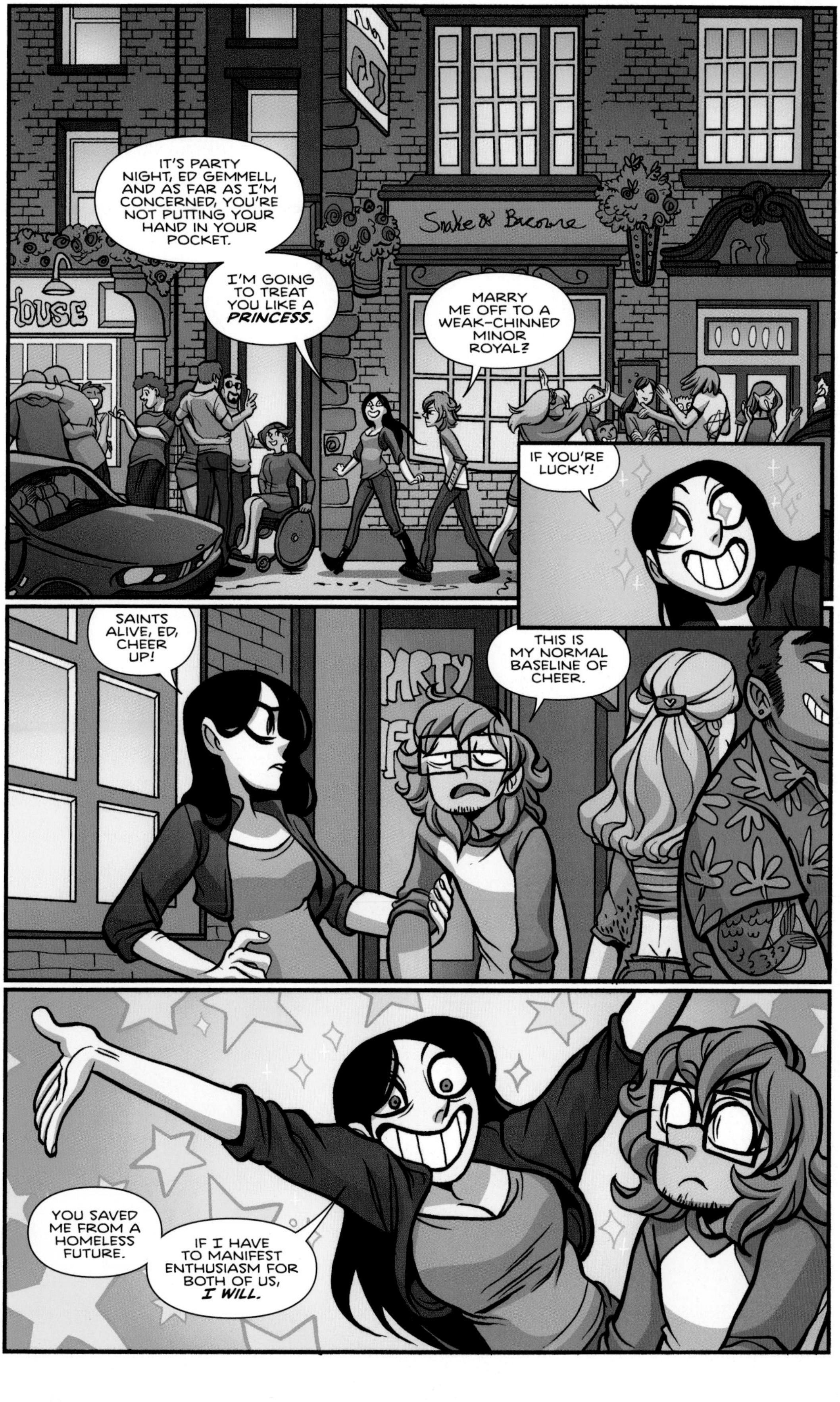
Snake & Barome
IT'S PARTY NIGHT, ED GEMMELL, AND AS FAR AS I'M CONCERNED, YOU'RE NOT PUTTING YOUR HAND IN YOUR POCKET.
I'M GOING TO TREAT YOU LIKE A PRINCESS.
MARRY ME OFF TO A WEAK-CHINNED MINOR ROYAL?
IF YOU'RE LUCKY!
SAINTS ALIVE, ED, CHEER UP!
THIS IS MY NORMAL BASELINE OF CHEER.
YOU SAVED ME FROM A HOMELESS FUTURE.
IF I HAVE TO MANIFEST ENTHUSIASM FOR BOTH OF US, I WILL.

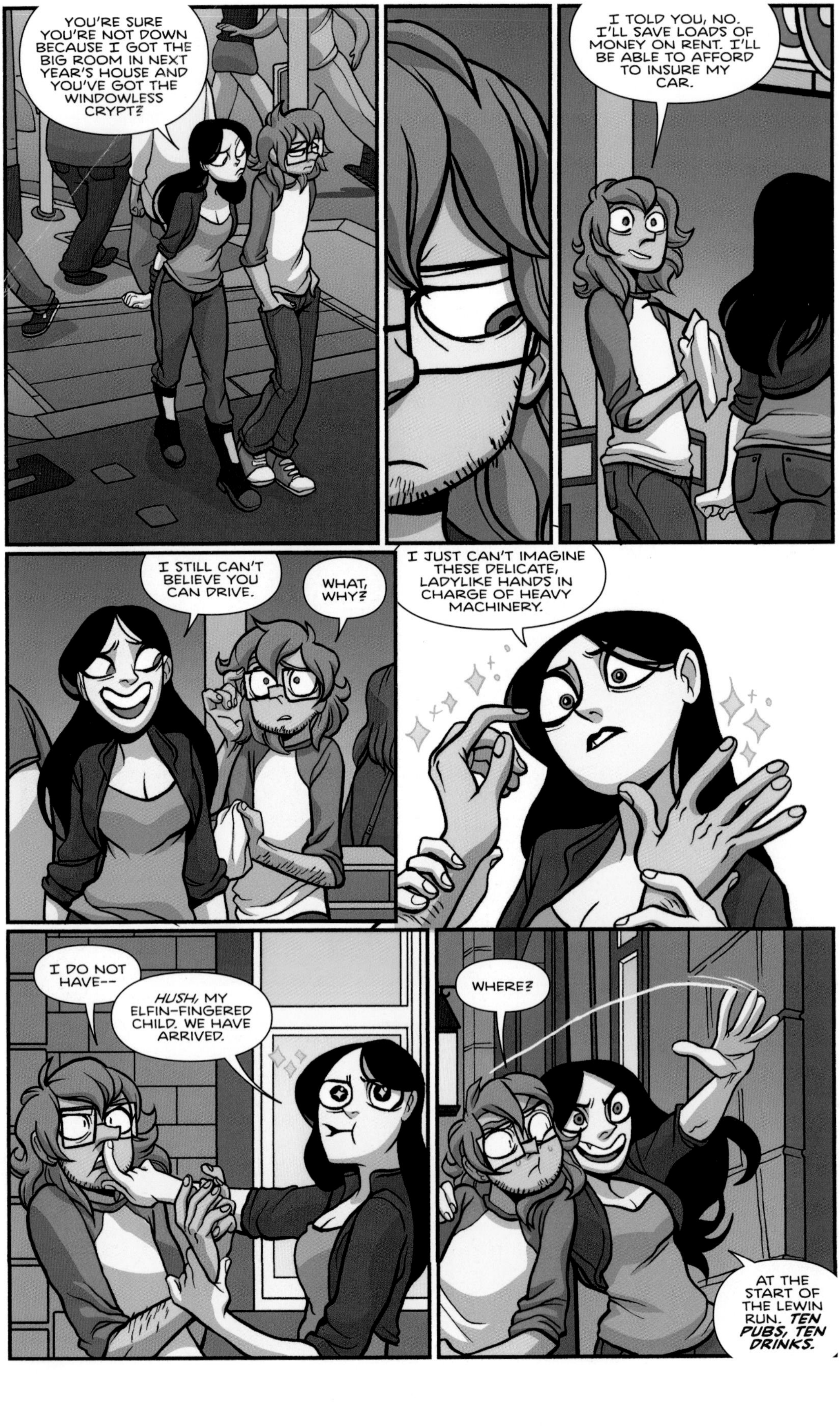
YOU'RE SURE YOU'RE NOT DOWN BECAUSE I GOT THE BIG ROOM IN NEXT YEAR'S HOUSE AND YOU'VE GOT THE WINDOWLESS CRYPT?
I TOLD YOU, NO. I'LL SAVE LOADS OF MONEY ON RENT. I'LL BE ABLE TO AFFORD TO INSURE MY CAR.
I STILL CAN'T BELIEVE YOU CAN DRIVE.
WHAT, WHY?
I JUST CAN'T IMAGINE THESE DELICATE, LADYLIKE HANDS IN CHARGE OF HEAVY MACHINERY.
I DO NOT HAVE--
HUSH, MY ELFIN-FINGERED CHILD. WE HAVE ARRIVED.
WHERE?
AT THE START OF THE LEWIN RUN. ***TEN PUBS, TEN DRINKS.***

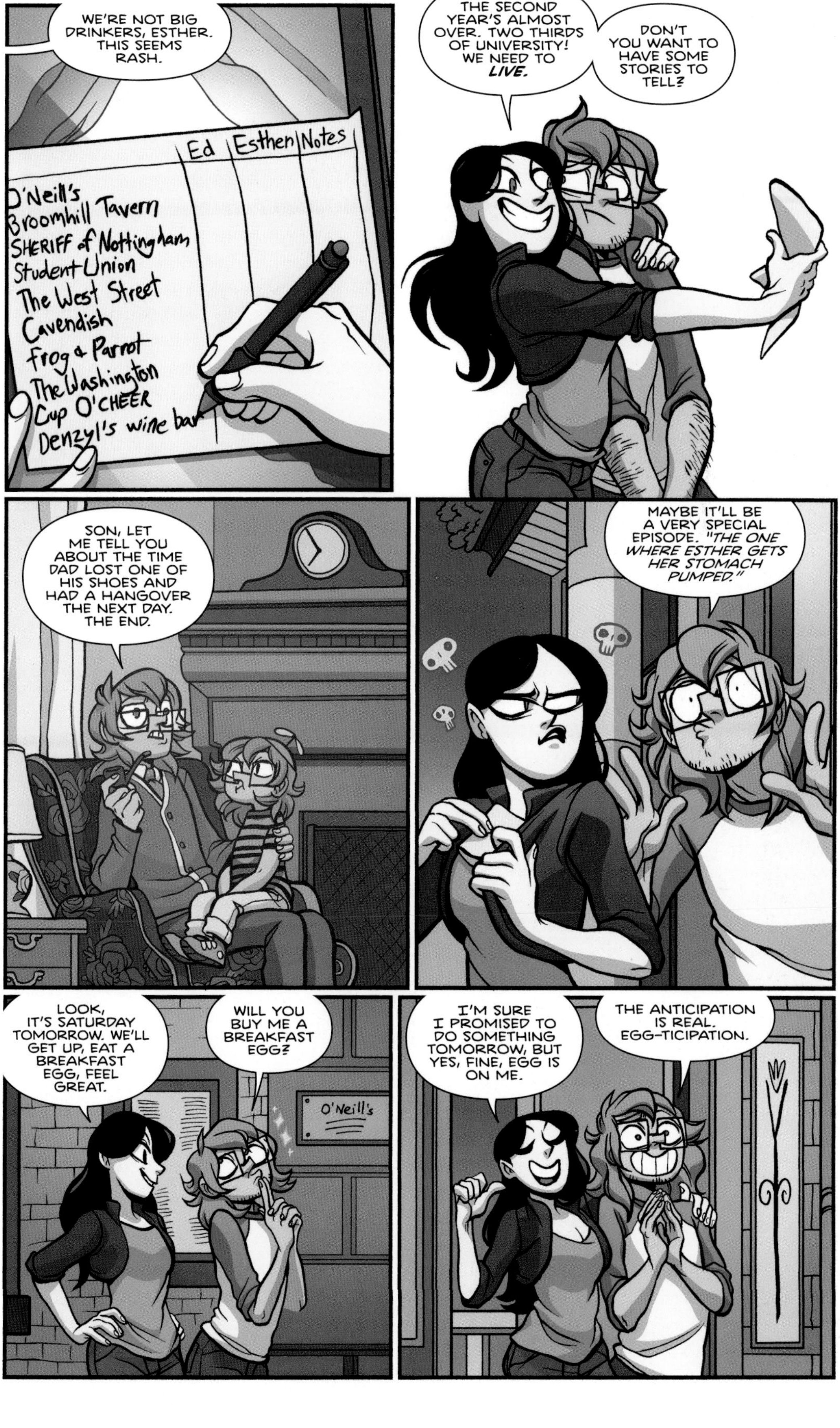
WE'RE NOT BIG DRINKERS, ESTHER. THIS SEEMS RASH.
Ed
Esther
Notes
O'Neill's
Broomhill Tavern
SHERIFF of Nottingham
Student Union
The West Street
Cavendish
Frog & Parrot
The Washington
Cup O'CHEER
Denzyl's wine bar
THE SECOND YEAR'S ALMOST OVER. TWO THIRDS OF UNIVERSITY! WE NEED TO LIVE.
DON'T YOU WANT TO HAVE SOME STORIES TO TELL?
SON, LET ME TELL YOU ABOUT THE TIME DAD LOST ONE OF HIS SHOES AND HAD A HANGOVER THE NEXT DAY. THE END.
MAYBE IT'LL BE A VERY SPECIAL EPISODE. "THE ONE WHERE ESTHER GETS HER STOMACH PUMPED."
LOOK, IT'S SATURDAY TOMORROW. WE'LL GET UP, EAT A BREAKFAST EGG, FEEL GREAT.
WILL YOU BUY ME A BREAKFAST EGG?
O'Neill's
I'M SURE I PROMISED TO DO SOMETHING TOMORROW, BUT YES, FINE, EGG IS ON ME.
THE ANTICIPATION IS REAL. EGG-TICIPATION.

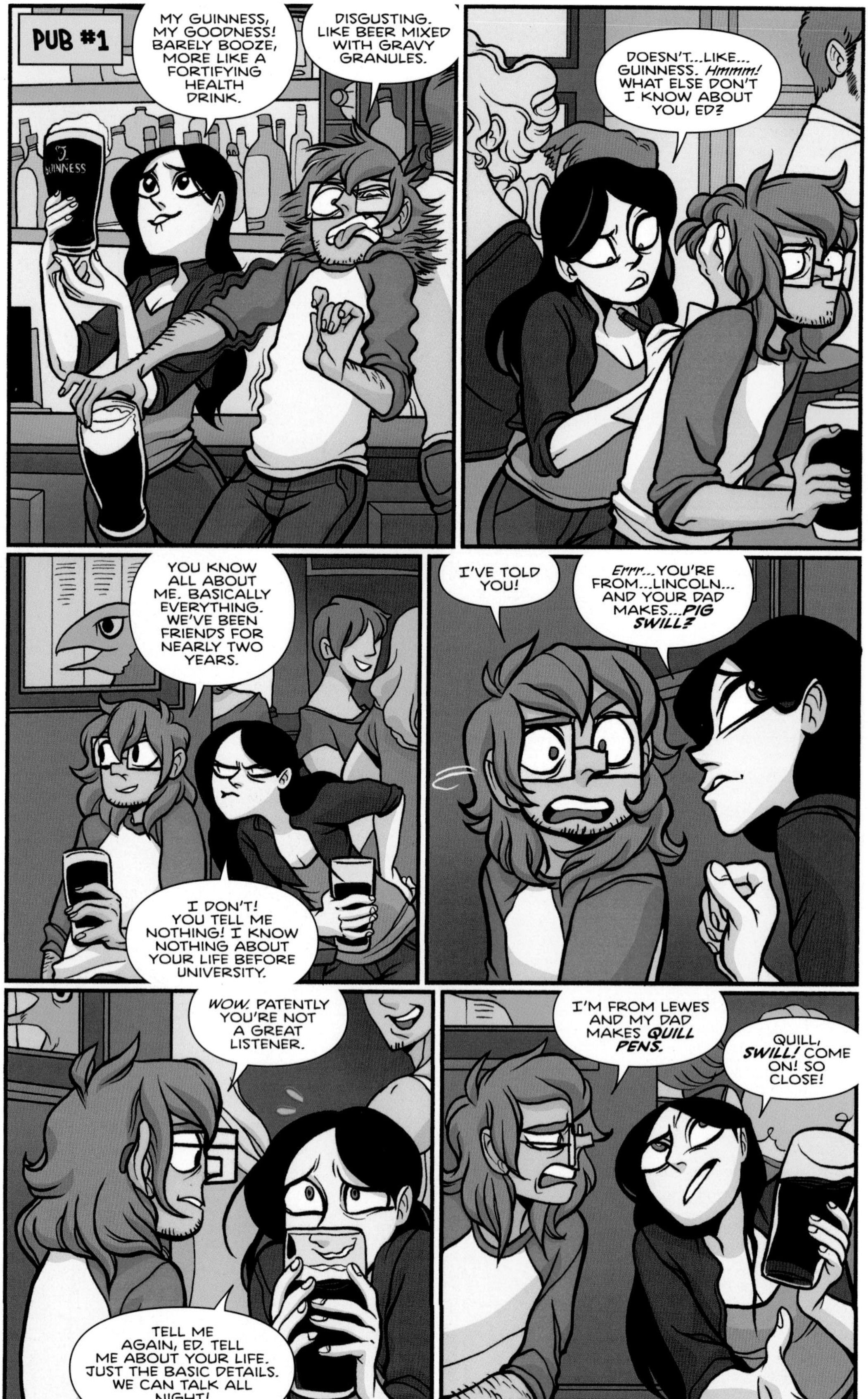
PUB #1
MY GUINNESS, MY GOODNESS! BARELY BOOZE, MORE LIKE A FORTIFYING HEALTH DRINK.
DISGUSTING. LIKE BEER MIXED WITH GRAVY GRANULES.
GUINNESS
DOESN'T...LIKE... GUINNESS. *Hmmm!* WHAT ELSE DON'T I KNOW ABOUT YOU, ED?
YOU KNOW ALL ABOUT ME. BASICALLY EVERYTHING. WE'VE BEEN FRIENDS FOR NEARLY TWO YEARS.
I DON'T! YOU TELL ME NOTHING! I KNOW NOTHING ABOUT YOUR LIFE BEFORE UNIVERSITY.
I'VE TOLD YOU!
Errr... YOU'RE FROM...LINCOLN... AND YOUR DAD MAKES...***PIG SWILL?***
WOW. PATENTLY YOU'RE NOT A GREAT LISTENER.
TELL ME AGAIN, ED. TELL ME ABOUT YOUR LIFE. JUST THE BASIC DETAILS. WE CAN TALK ALL NIGHT!
I'M FROM LEWES AND MY DAD MAKES ***QUILL PENS.***
QUILL, ***SWILL!*** COME ON! SO CLOSE!

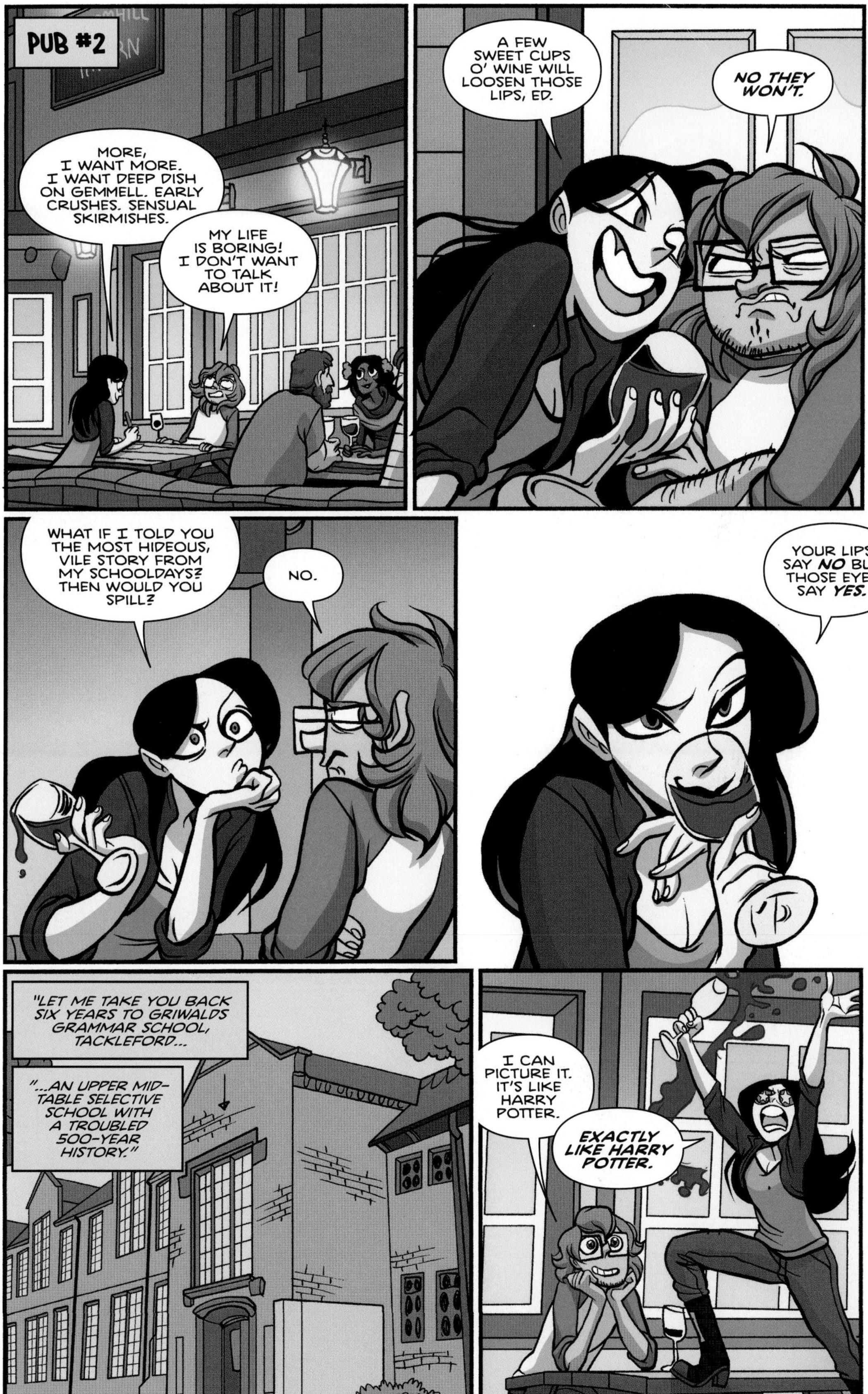
PUB #2
MORE, I WANT MORE. I WANT DEEP DISH ON GEMMELL. EARLY CRUSHES. SENSUAL SKIRMISHES.
MY LIFE IS BORING! I DON'T WANT TO TALK ABOUT IT!
A FEW SWEET CUPS O' WINE WILL LOOSEN THOSE LIPS, ED.
NO THEY WON'T.
WHAT IF I TOLD YOU THE MOST HIDEOUS, VILE STORY FROM MY SCHOOLDAYS? THEN WOULD YOU SPILL?
NO.
YOUR LIPS SAY NO BUT THOSE EYES SAY YES.
"LET ME TAKE YOU BACK SIX YEARS TO GRIWALDS GRAMMAR SCHOOL, TACKLEFORD...
"...AN UPPER MID-TABLE SELECTIVE SCHOOL WITH A TROUBLED 500-YEAR HISTORY."
I CAN PICTURE IT. IT'S LIKE HARRY POTTER.
EXACTLY LIKE HARRY POTTER.

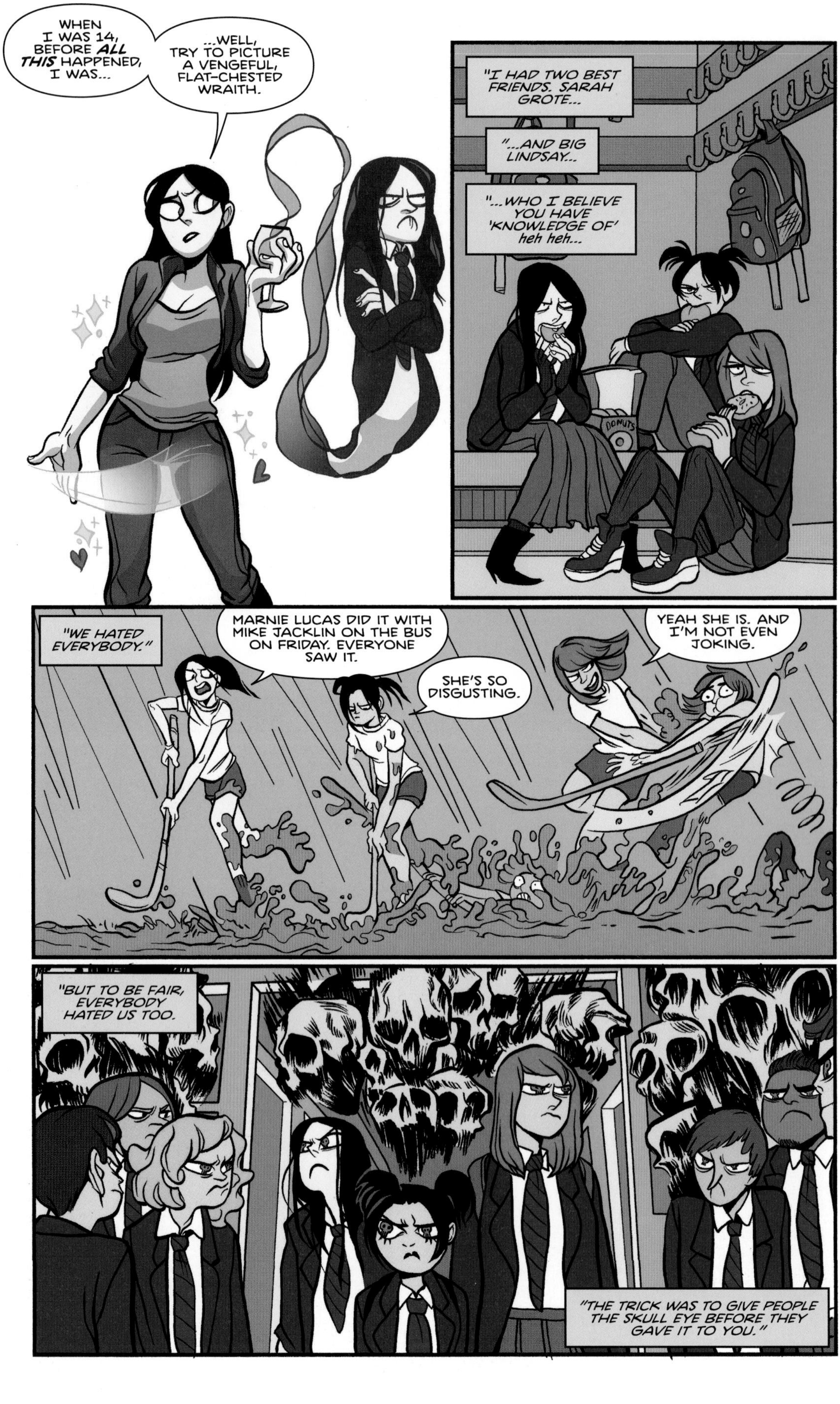

WHEN I WAS 14, BEFORE ALL THIS HAPPENED, I WAS...
...WELL, TRY TO PICTURE A VENGEFUL, FLAT-CHESTED WRAITH.
"I HAD TWO BEST FRIENDS. SARAH GROTE...
"...AND BIG LINDSAY...
"...WHO I BELIEVE YOU HAVE 'KNOWLEDGE OF' heh heh...
DONUTS
"WE HATED EVERYBODY."
MARNIE LUCAS DID IT WITH MIKE JACKLIN ON THE BUS ON FRIDAY. EVERYONE SAW IT.
SHE'S SO DISGUSTING.
YEAH SHE IS. AND I'M NOT EVEN JOKING.
"BUT TO BE FAIR, EVERYBODY HATED US TOO.
"THE TRICK WAS TO GIVE PEOPLE THE SKULL EYE BEFORE THEY GAVE IT TO YOU."

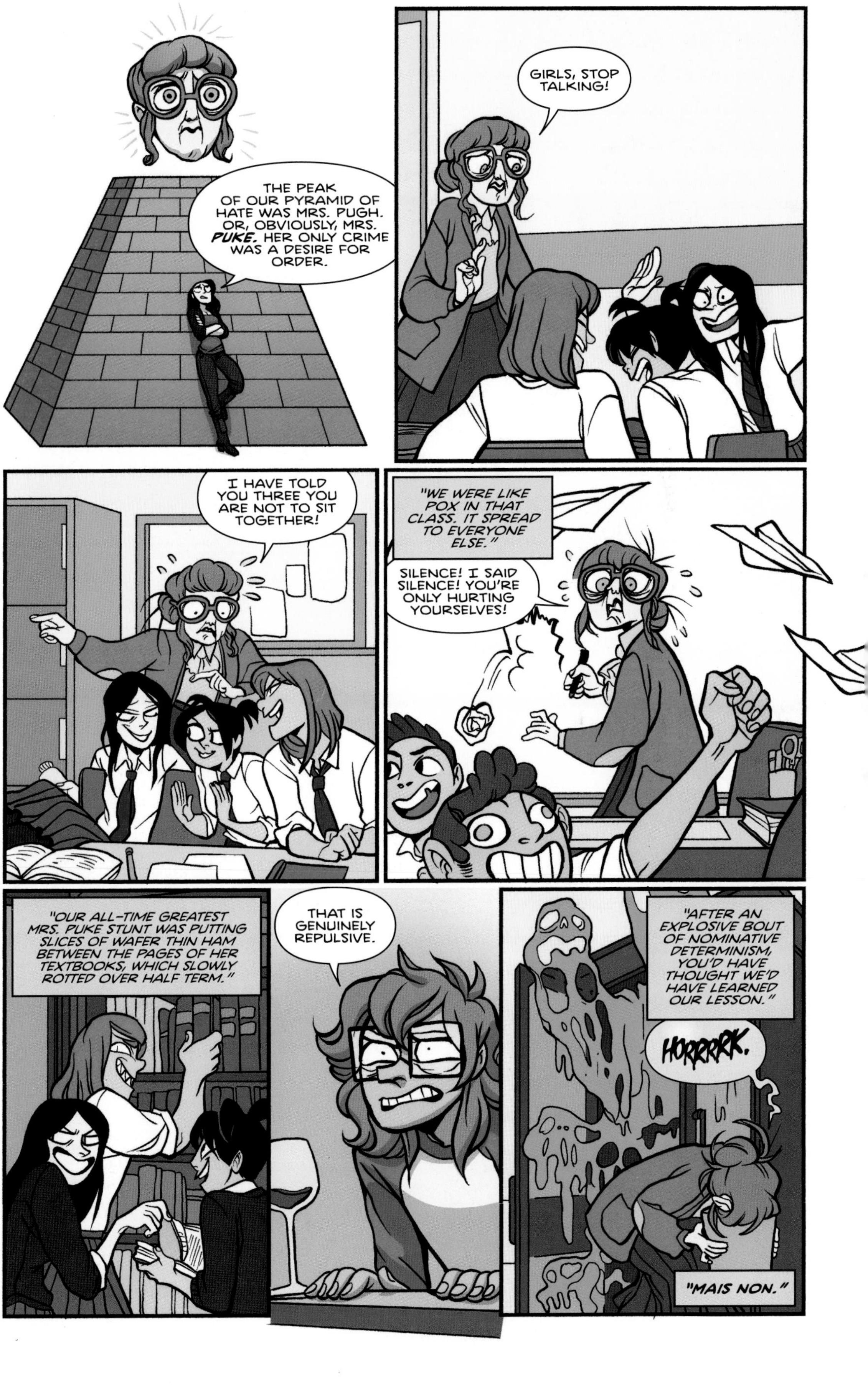
THE PEAK OF OUR PYRAMID OF HATE WAS MRS. PUGH. OR, OBVIOUSLY, MRS. PUKE. HER ONLY CRIME WAS A DESIRE FOR ORDER.
GIRLS, STOP TALKING!
I HAVE TOLD YOU THREE YOU ARE NOT TO SIT TOGETHER!
"WE WERE LIKE POX IN THAT CLASS. IT SPREAD TO EVERYONE ELSE."
SILENCE! I SAID SILENCE! YOU'RE ONLY HURTING YOURSELVES!
"OUR ALL-TIME GREATEST MRS. PUKE STUNT WAS PUTTING SLICES OF WAFER THIN HAM BETWEEN THE PAGES OF HER TEXTBOOKS, WHICH SLOWLY ROTTED OVER HALF TERM."
THAT IS GENUINELY REPULSIVE.
"AFTER AN EXPLOSIVE BOUT OF NOMINATIVE DETERMINISM, YOU'D HAVE THOUGHT WE'D HAVE LEARNED OUR LESSON."
HORRRRK.
"MAIS NON."

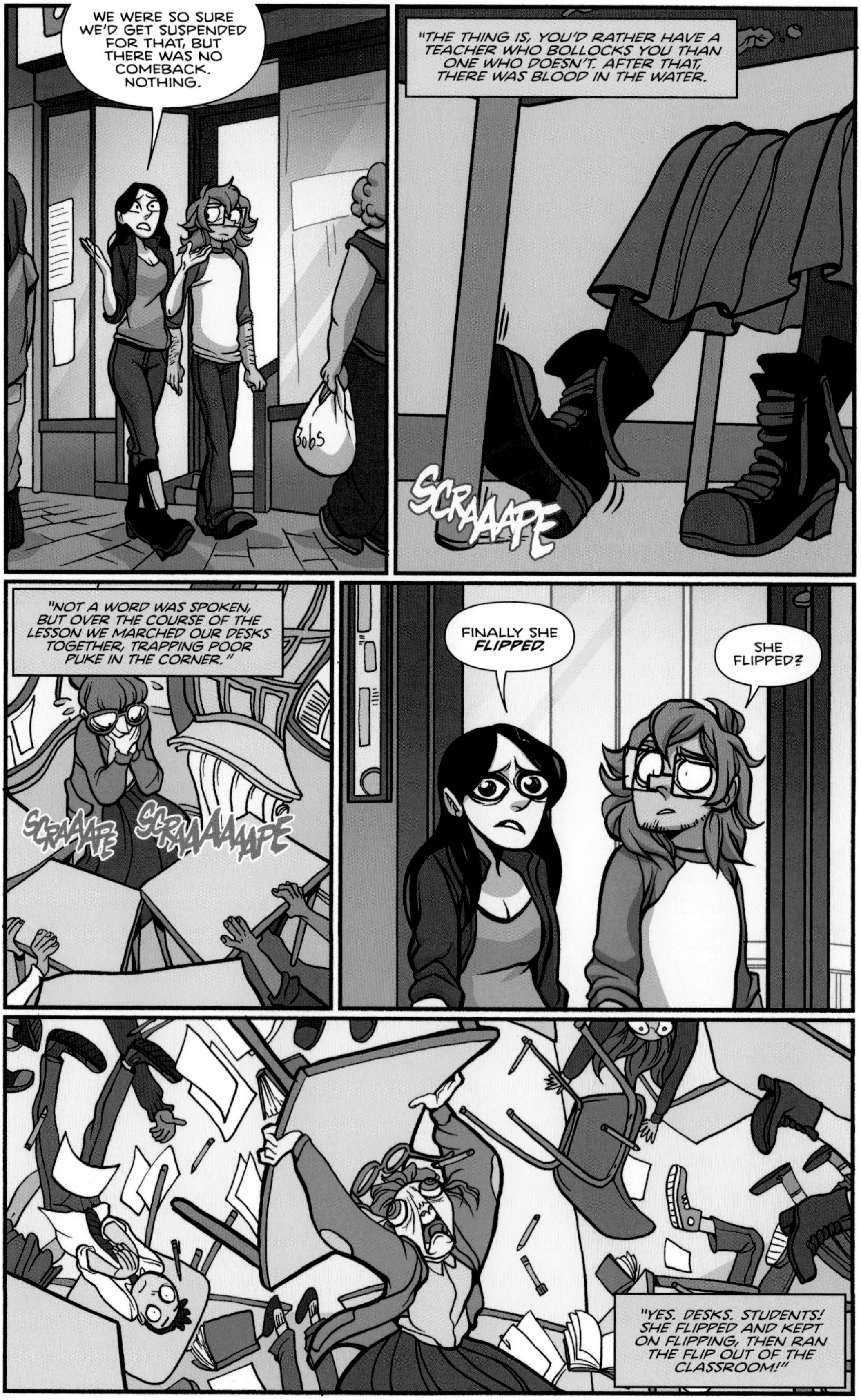
WE WERE SO SURE WE'D GET SUSPENDED FOR THAT, BUT THERE WAS NO COMEBACK. NOTHING.
Bobs
"THE THING IS, YOU'D RATHER HAVE A TEACHER WHO BOLLOCKS YOU THAN ONE WHO DOESN'T. AFTER THAT, THERE WAS BLOOD IN THE WATER.
SCRAAAPE
"NOT A WORD WAS SPOKEN, BUT OVER THE COURSE OF THE LESSON WE MARCHED OUR DESKS TOGETHER, TRAPPING POOR PUKE IN THE CORNER."
SCRAAAPE
SCRAAAAAAPE
FINALLY SHE FLIPPED.
SHE FLIPPED?
"YES. DESKS. STUDENTS! SHE FLIPPED AND KEPT ON FLIPPING, THEN RAN THE FLIP OUT OF THE CLASSROOM!"

PUB #5

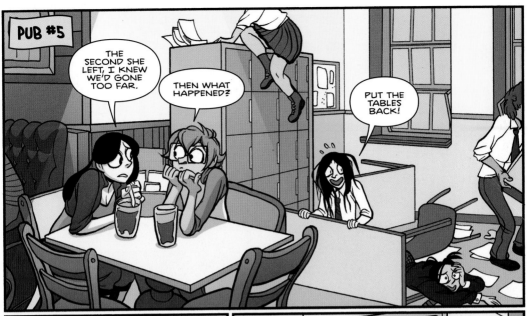

THE SECOND SHE LEFT, I KNEW WE'D GONE TOO FAR.

THEN WHAT HAPPENED?

PUT THE TABLES BACK!

"WE SAT THERE RIGHT TO THE END OF DOUBLE MATHS, NO ONE SAYING ANYTHING.

"AT THE END OF THE LESSON, MR. KNOTT CAME IN AND SPOKE TO US. I THOUGHT HE WAS GOING TO SUSPEND EVERYBODY.

"BUT INSTEAD HE JUST SAID, VERY QUIETLY--"

MRS. PUGH WILL NOT BE COMING BACK.

SARAH SAW HER IN THE SUPERMARKET A COUPLE OF YEARS LATER.

TRYING TO BUY A SINGLE EGG.

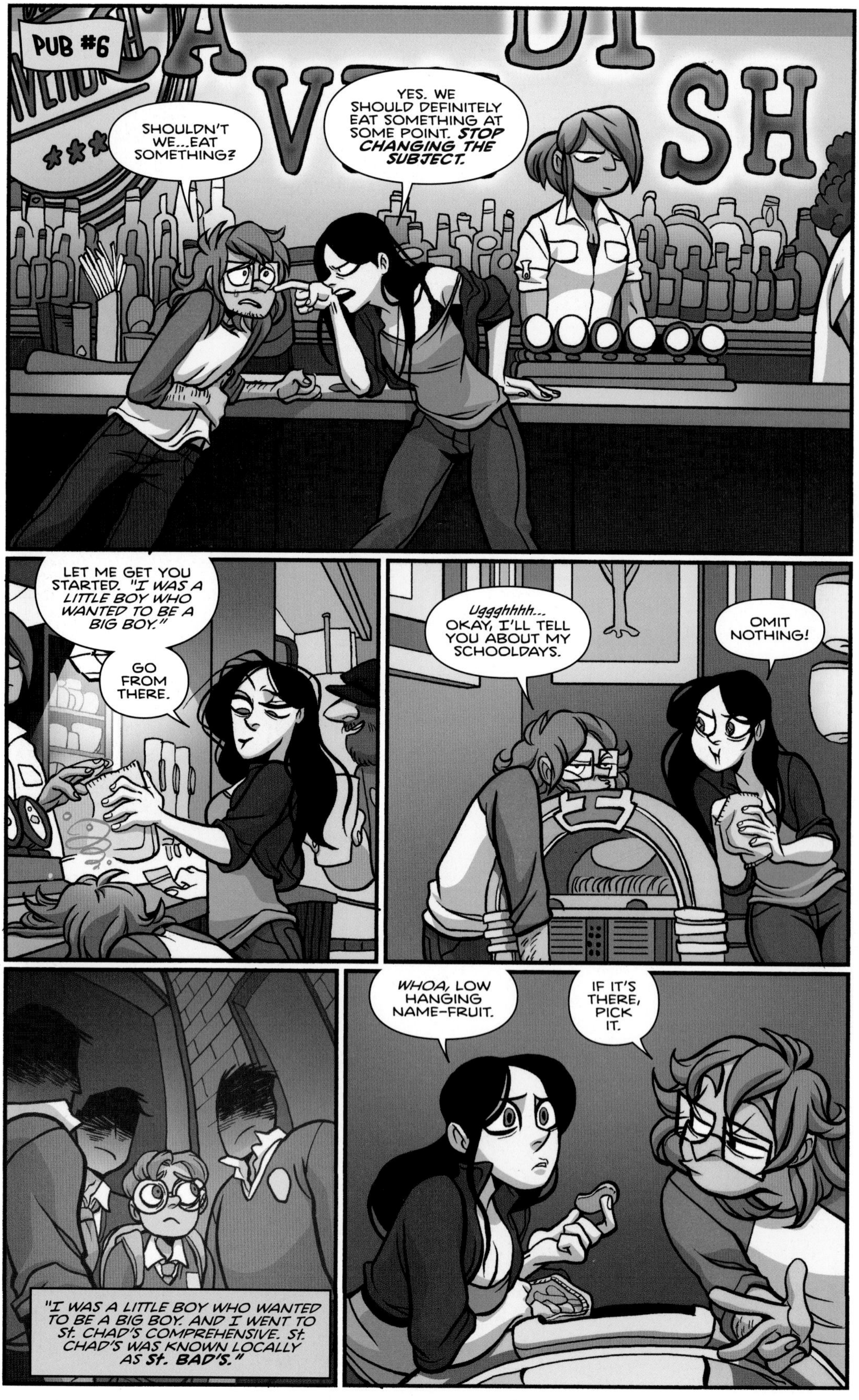
PUB #6
SHOULDN'T WE...EAT SOMETHING?
YES. WE SHOULD DEFINITELY EAT SOMETHING AT SOME POINT. STOP CHANGING THE SUBJECT.
LET ME GET YOU STARTED. "I WAS A LITTLE BOY WHO WANTED TO BE A BIG BOY."
GO FROM THERE.
Uggghhhh... OKAY, I'LL TELL YOU ABOUT MY SCHOOLDAYS.
OMIT NOTHING!
"I WAS A LITTLE BOY WHO WANTED TO BE A BIG BOY. AND I WENT TO St. CHAD'S COMPREHENSIVE. St. CHAD'S WAS KNOWN LOCALLY AS St. BAD'S."
WHOA, LOW HANGING NAME-FRUIT.
IF IT'S THERE, PICK IT.

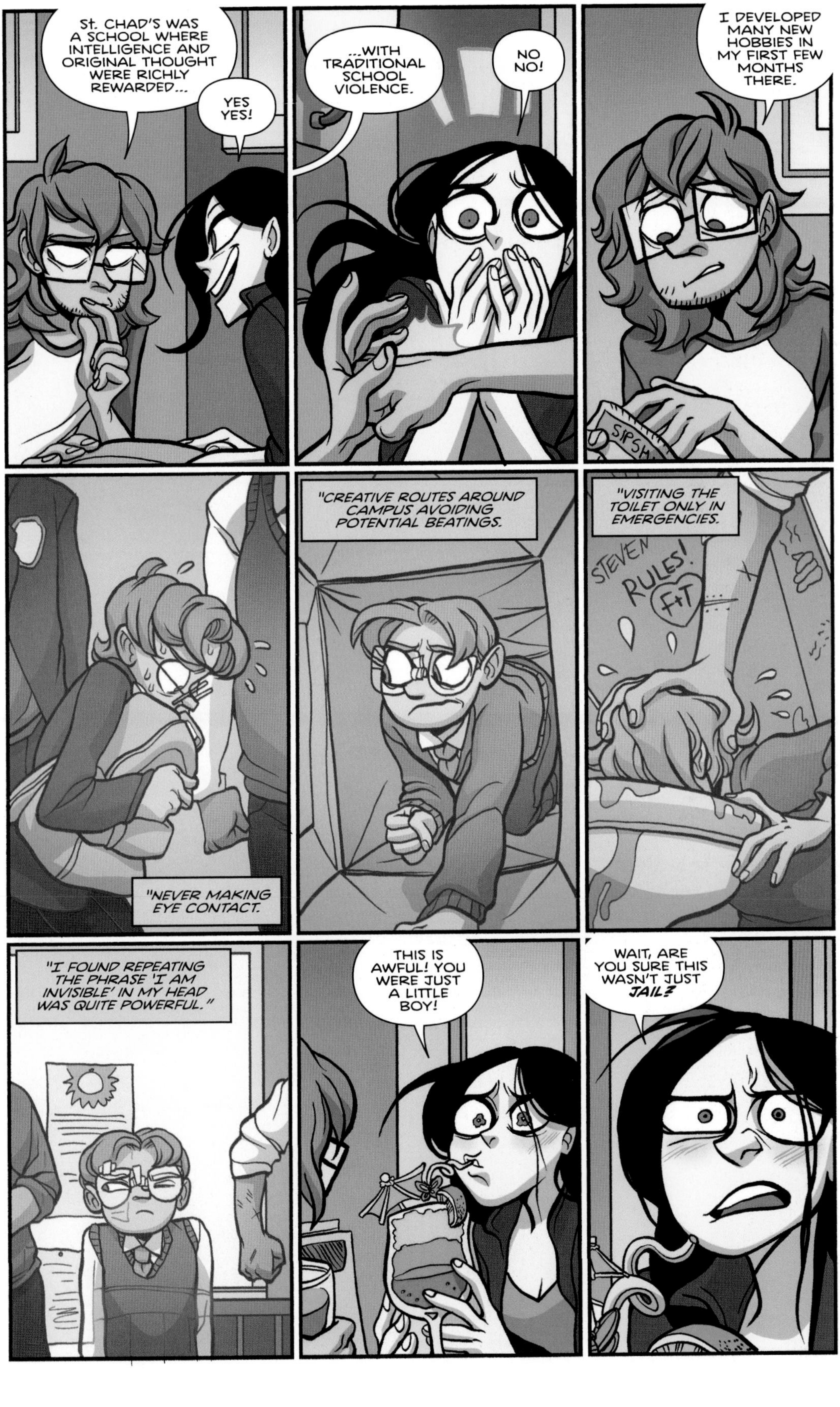
St. CHAD'S WAS A SCHOOL WHERE INTELLIGENCE AND ORIGINAL THOUGHT WERE RICHLY REWARDED...
YES YES!
...WITH TRADITIONAL SCHOOL VIOLENCE.
NO NO!
I DEVELOPED MANY NEW HOBBIES IN MY FIRST FEW MONTHS THERE.
"NEVER MAKING EYE CONTACT.
"CREATIVE ROUTES AROUND CAMPUS AVOIDING POTENTIAL BEATINGS.
"VISITING THE TOILET ONLY IN EMERGENCIES.
STEVEN RULES!
F+T
"I FOUND REPEATING THE PHRASE 'I AM INVISIBLE' IN MY HEAD WAS QUITE POWERFUL."
THIS IS AWFUL! YOU WERE JUST A LITTLE BOY!
WAIT, ARE YOU SURE THIS WASN'T JUST JAIL?

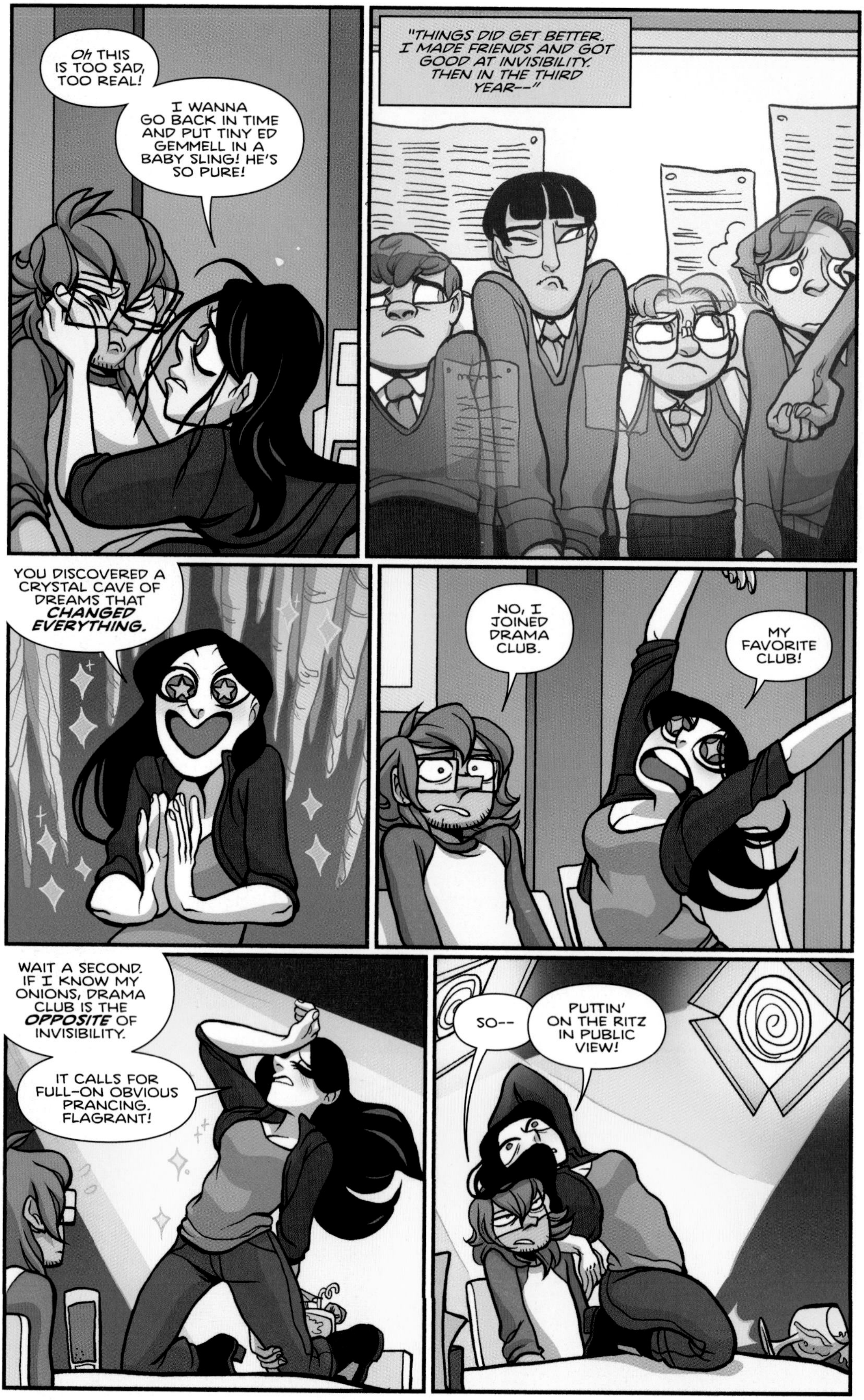
Oh THIS IS TOO SAD, TOO REAL!
I WANNA GO BACK IN TIME AND PUT TINY ED GEMMELL IN A BABY SLING! HE'S SO PURE!
"THINGS DID GET BETTER. I MADE FRIENDS AND GOT GOOD AT INVISIBILITY. THEN IN THE THIRD YEAR--"
YOU DISCOVERED A CRYSTAL CAVE OF DREAMS THAT ***CHANGED EVERYTHING.***
NO, I JOINED DRAMA CLUB.
MY FAVORITE CLUB!
WAIT A SECOND. IF I KNOW MY ONIONS, DRAMA CLUB IS THE ***OPPOSITE*** OF INVISIBILITY.
IT CALLS FOR FULL-ON OBVIOUS PRANCING. FLAGRANT!
SO--
PUTTIN' ON THE RITZ IN PUBLIC VIEW!

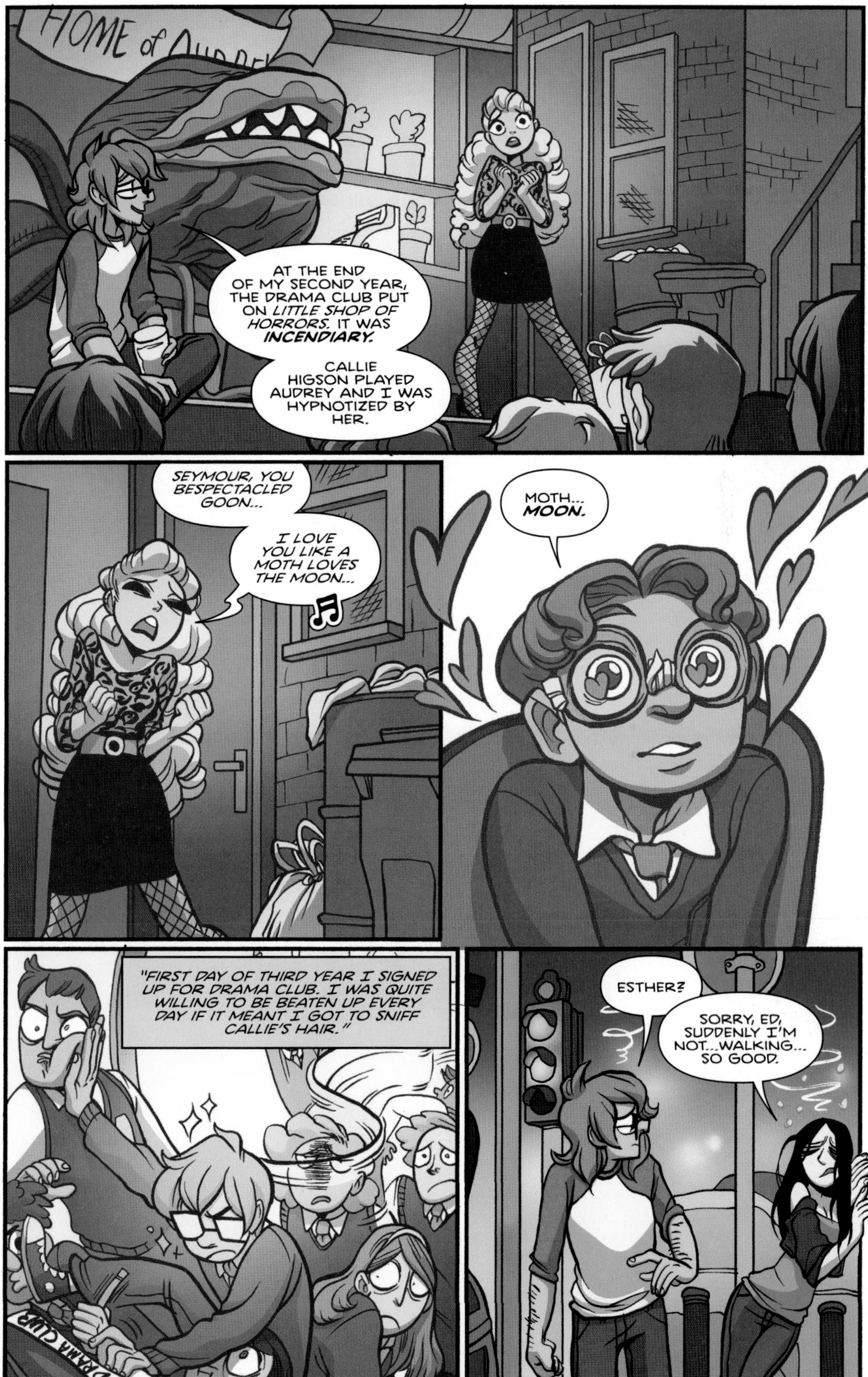
HOME of
AT THE END OF MY SECOND YEAR, THE DRAMA CLUB PUT ON *LITTLE SHOP OF HORRORS.* IT WAS ***INCENDIARY.***
CALLIE HIGSON PLAYED AUDREY AND I WAS HYPNOTIZED BY HER.
SEYMOUR, YOU BESPECTACLED GOON...
I LOVE YOU LIKE A MOTH LOVES THE MOON...
MOTH... ***MOON.***
"FIRST DAY OF THIRD YEAR I SIGNED UP FOR DRAMA CLUB. I WAS QUITE WILLING TO BE BEATEN UP EVERY DAY IF IT MEANT I GOT TO SNIFF CALLIE'S HAIR."
DRAMA CLUB
ESTHER?
SORRY, ED, SUDDENLY I'M NOT...WALKING... SO GOOD.

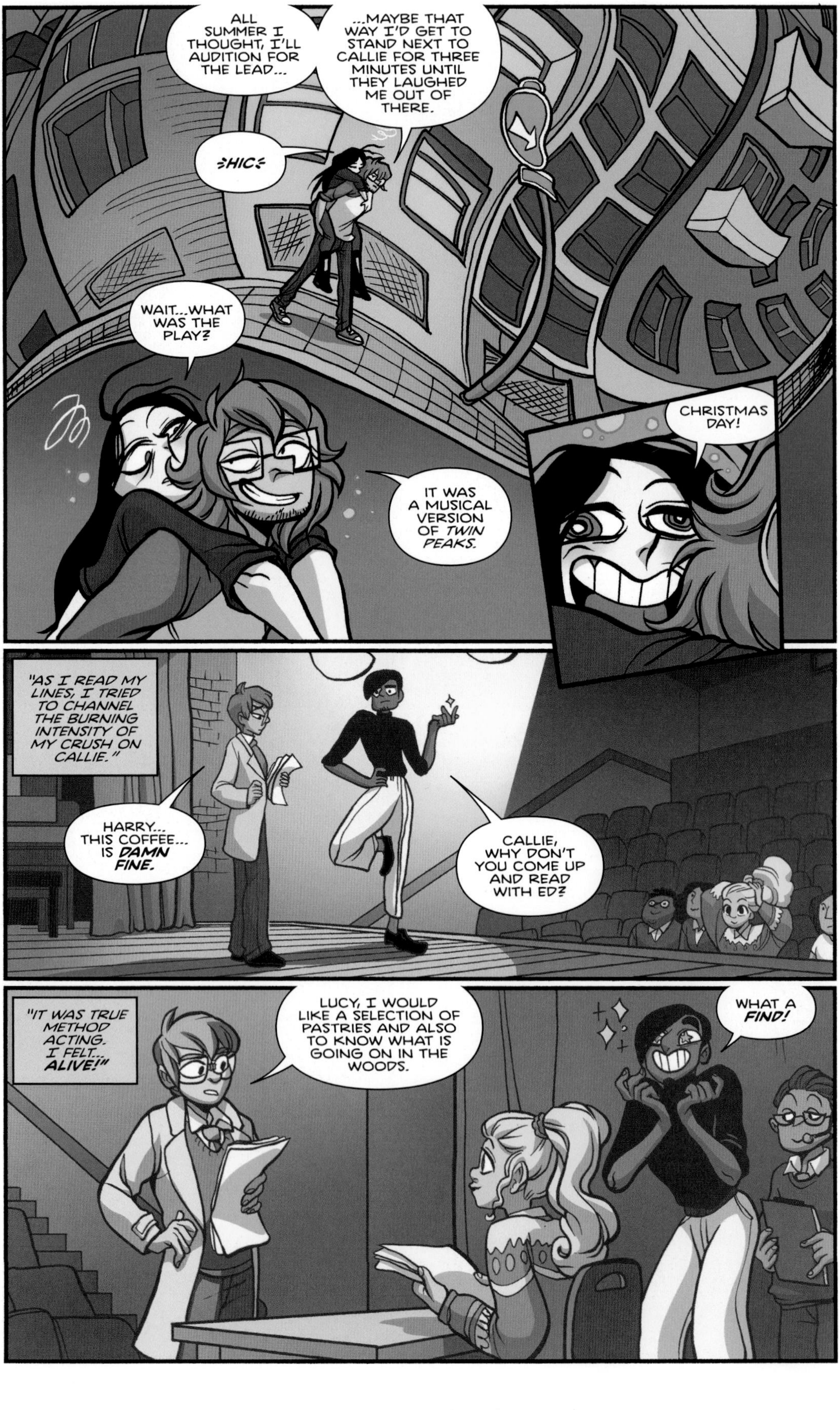
ALL SUMMER I THOUGHT, I'LL AUDITION FOR THE LEAD...
...MAYBE THAT WAY I'D GET TO STAND NEXT TO CALLIE FOR THREE MINUTES UNTIL THEY LAUGHED ME OUT OF THERE.
HIC
WAIT...WHAT WAS THE PLAY?
IT WAS A MUSICAL VERSION OF *TWIN PEAKS.*
CHRISTMAS DAY!
"AS I READ MY LINES, I TRIED TO CHANNEL THE BURNING INTENSITY OF MY CRUSH ON CALLIE."
HARRY... THIS COFFEE... IS **DAMN FINE.**
CALLIE, WHY DON'T YOU COME UP AND READ WITH ED?
"IT WAS TRUE METHOD ACTING. I FELT... **ALIVE!**"
LUCY, I WOULD LIKE A SELECTION OF PASTRIES AND ALSO TO KNOW WHAT IS GOING ON IN THE WOODS.
WHAT A **FIND!**

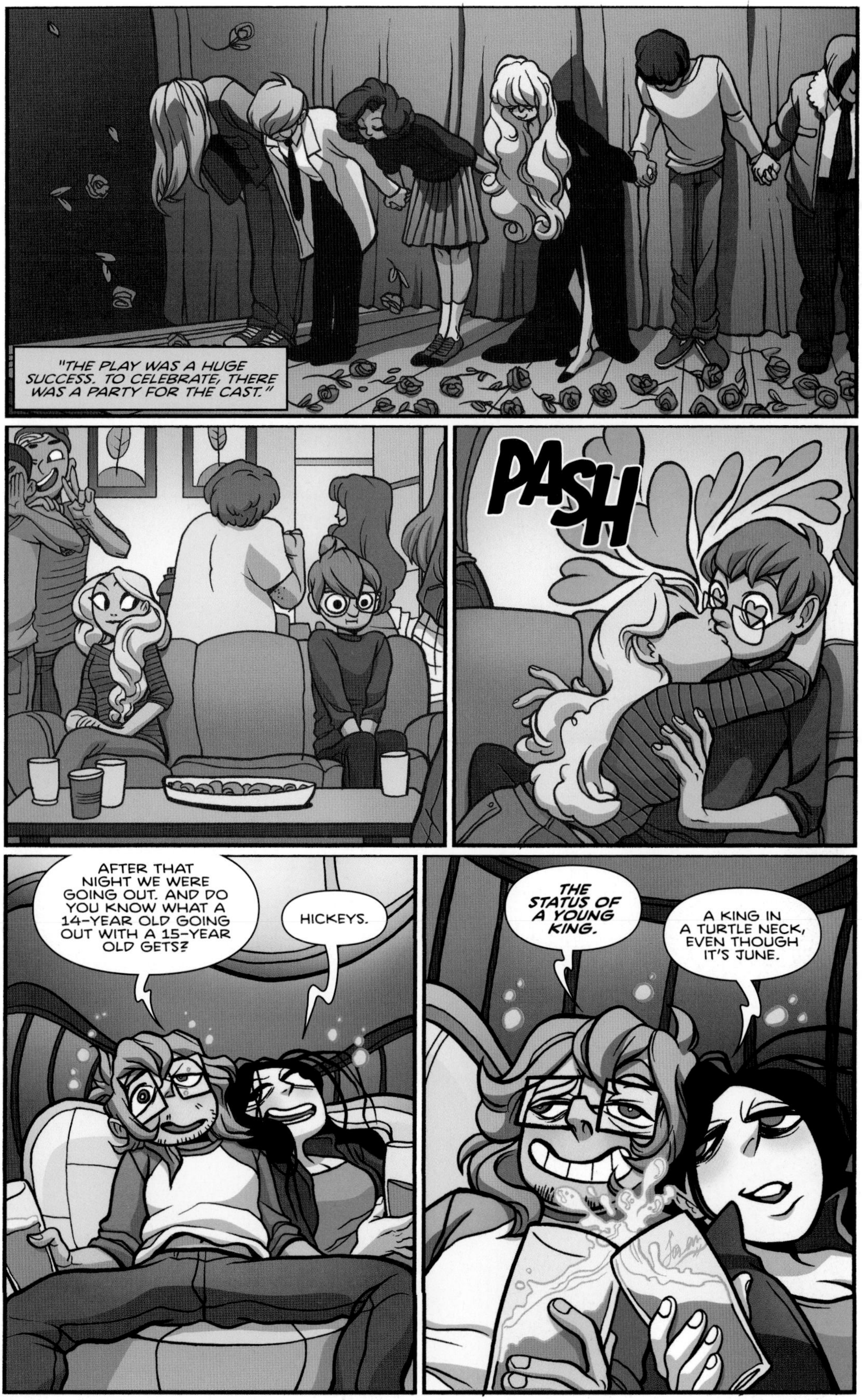
"THE PLAY WAS A HUGE SUCCESS. TO CELEBRATE, THERE WAS A PARTY FOR THE CAST."
PASH
AFTER THAT NIGHT WE WERE GOING OUT. AND DO YOU KNOW WHAT A 14-YEAR OLD GOING OUT WITH A 15-YEAR OLD GETS?
HICKEYS.
THE STATUS OF A YOUNG KING.
A KING IN A TURTLE NECK, EVEN THOUGH IT'S JUNE.

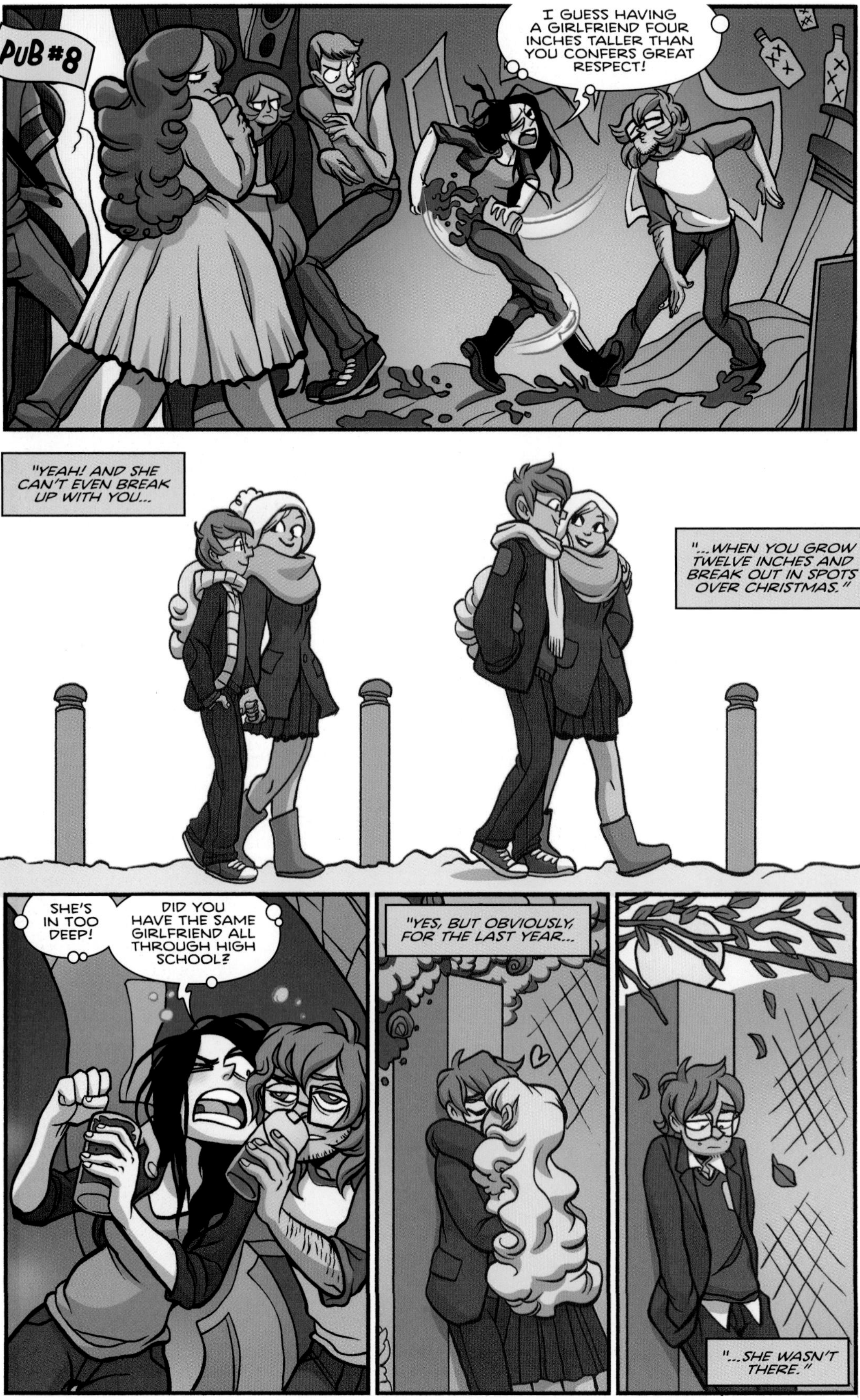
PUB #8
I GUESS HAVING A GIRLFRIEND FOUR INCHES TALLER THAN YOU CONFERS GREAT RESPECT!
"YEAH! AND SHE CAN'T EVEN BREAK UP WITH YOU...
"...WHEN YOU GROW TWELVE INCHES AND BREAK OUT IN SPOTS OVER CHRISTMAS."
SHE'S IN TOO DEEP!
DID YOU HAVE THE SAME GIRLFRIEND ALL THROUGH HIGH SCHOOL?
"YES, BUT OBVIOUSLY, FOR THE LAST YEAR...
"...SHE WASN'T THERE."

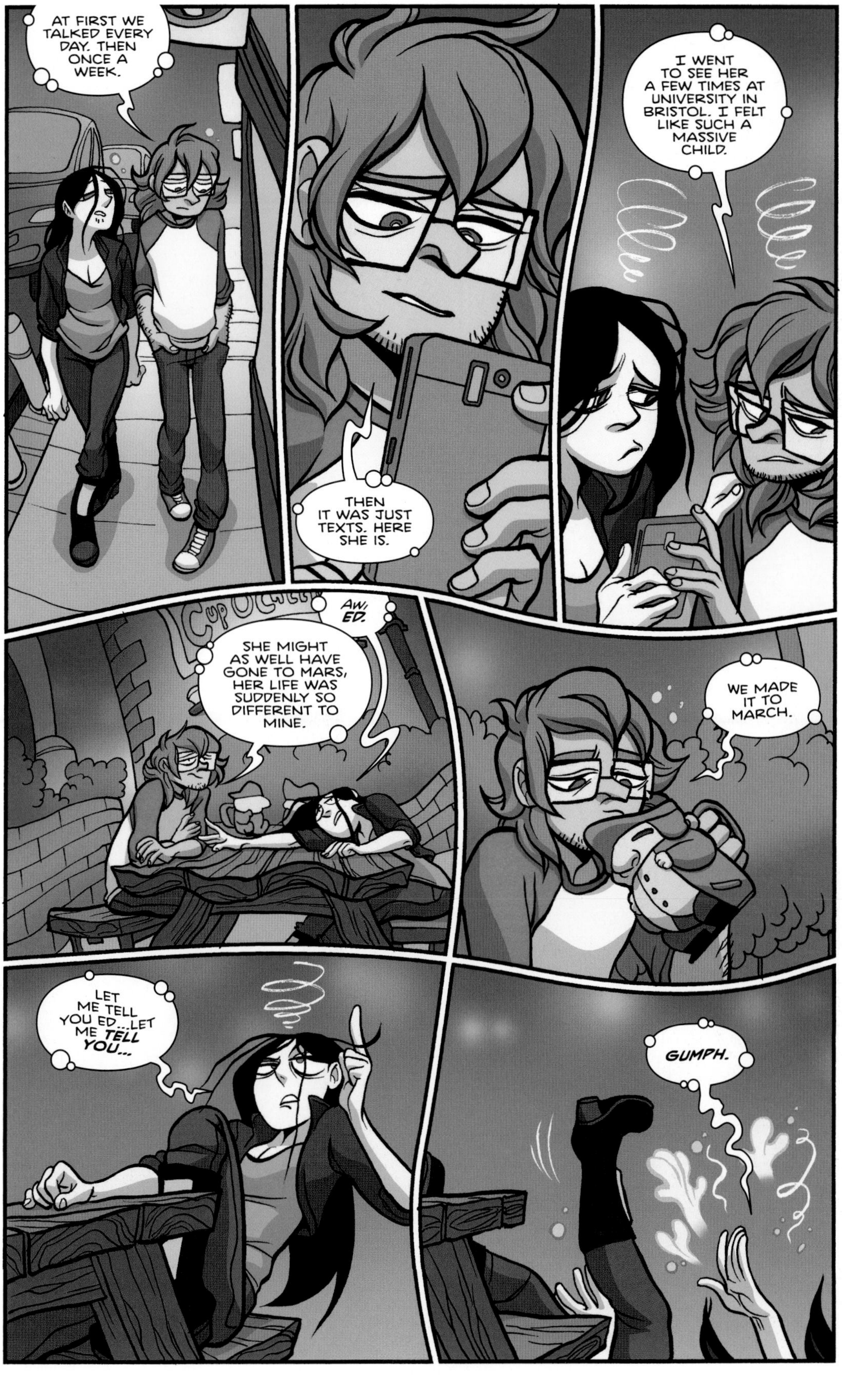
AT FIRST WE TALKED EVERY DAY. THEN ONCE A WEEK.
THEN IT WAS JUST TEXTS. HERE SHE IS.
I WENT TO SEE HER A FEW TIMES AT UNIVERSITY IN BRISTOL. I FELT LIKE SUCH A MASSIVE CHILD.
SHE MIGHT AS WELL HAVE GONE TO MARS, HER LIFE WAS SUDDENLY SO DIFFERENT TO MINE.
AW, ED.
WE MADE IT TO MARCH.
LET ME TELL YOU ED...LET ME TELL YOU...
GUMPH.

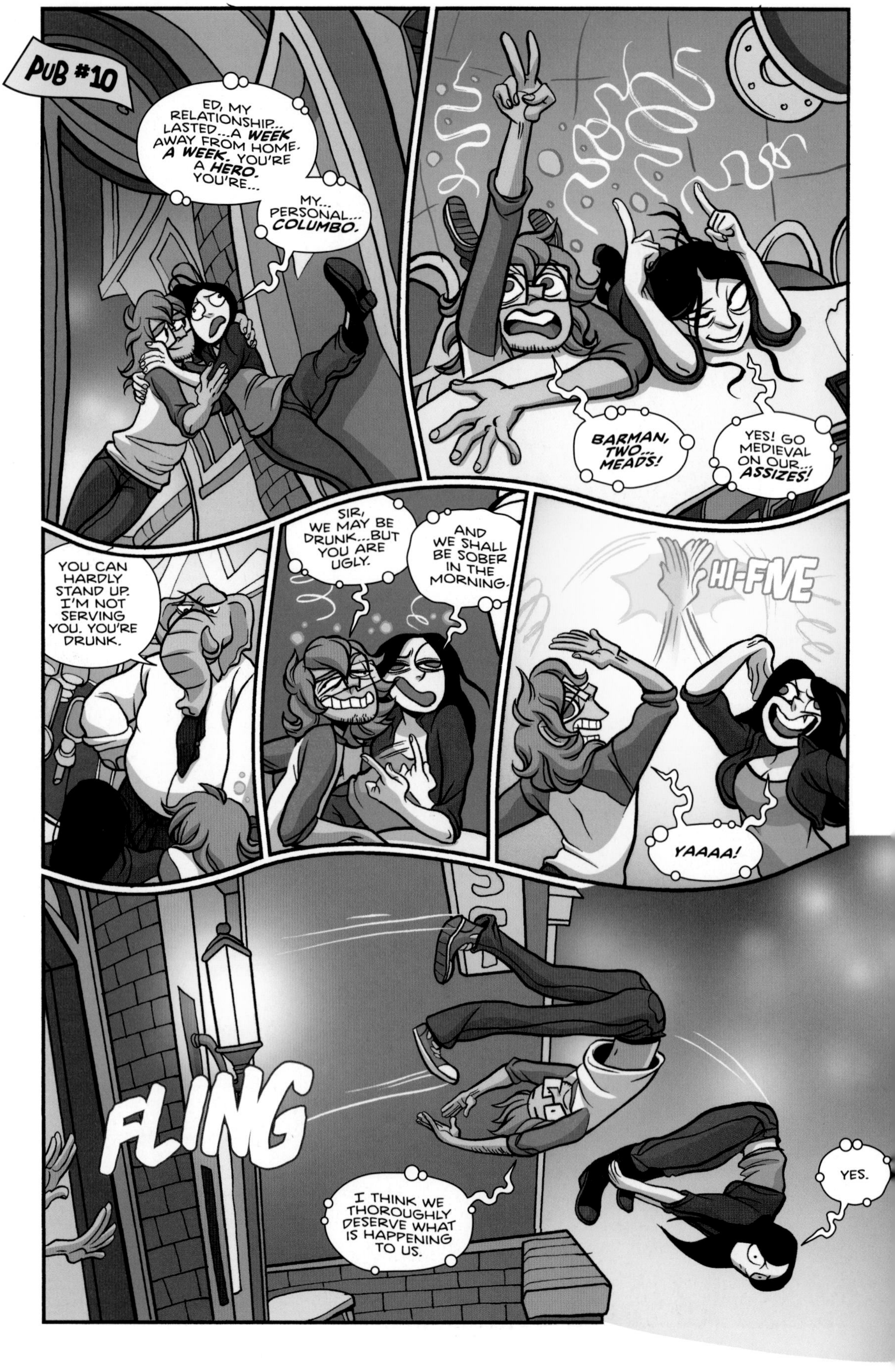
PUB #10
ED, MY RELATIONSHIP... LASTED...A WEEK AWAY FROM HOME. A WEEK. YOU'RE A HERO. YOU'RE...
MY... PERSONAL... COLUMBO.
BARMAN, TWO... MEADS!
YES! GO MEDIEVAL ON OUR... ASSIZES!
YOU CAN HARDLY STAND UP. I'M NOT SERVING YOU. YOU'RE DRUNK.
SIR, WE MAY BE DRUNK...BUT YOU ARE UGLY.
AND WE SHALL BE SOBER IN THE MORNING.
HI-FIVE
YAAAA!
FLING
I THINK WE THOROUGHLY DESERVE WHAT IS HAPPENING TO US.
YES.

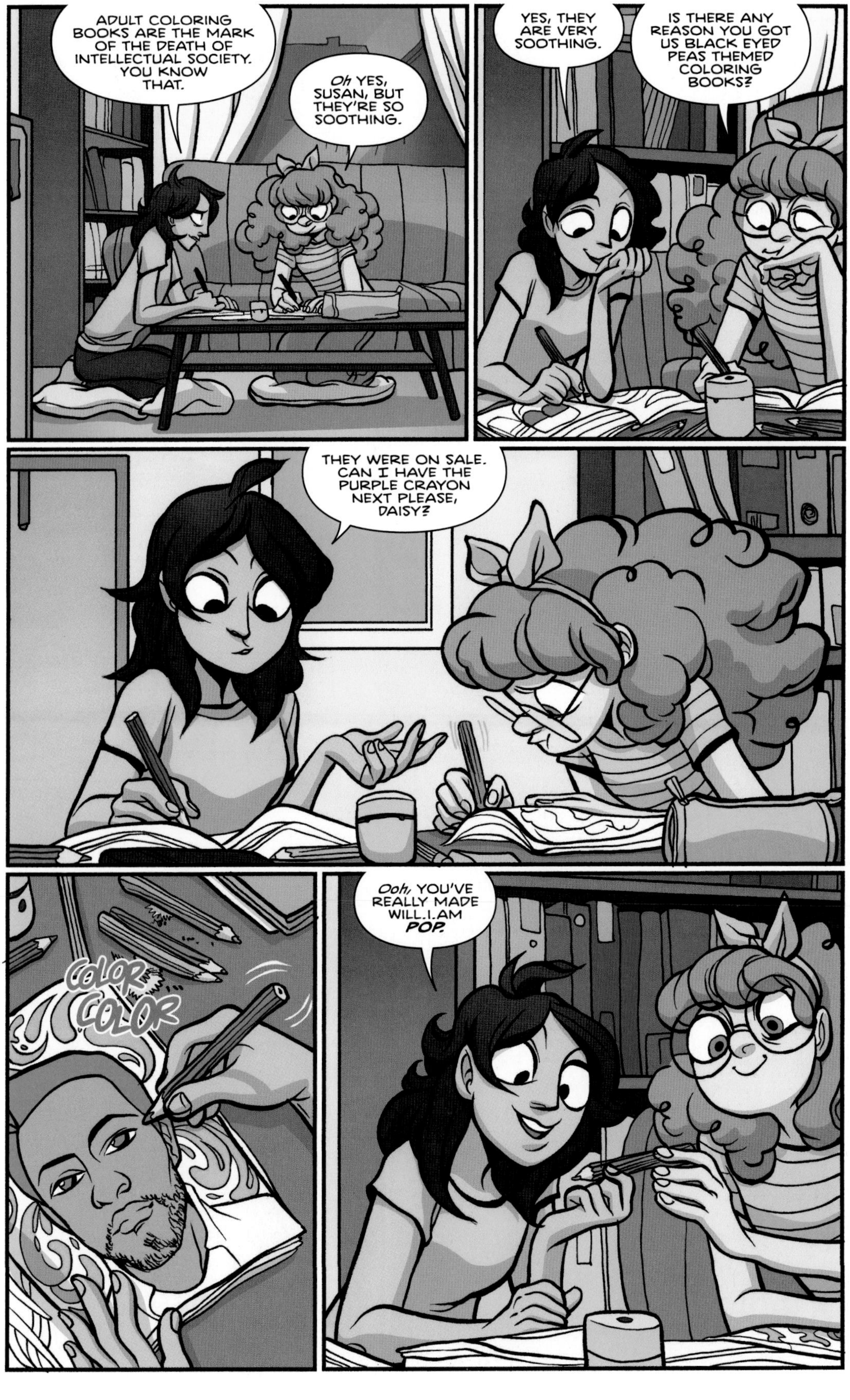
ADULT COLORING BOOKS ARE THE MARK OF THE DEATH OF INTELLECTUAL SOCIETY. YOU KNOW THAT.
Oh YES, SUSAN, BUT THEY'RE SO SOOTHING.
YES, THEY ARE VERY SOOTHING.
IS THERE ANY REASON YOU GOT US BLACK EYED PEAS THEMED COLORING BOOKS?
THEY WERE ON SALE. CAN I HAVE THE PURPLE CRAYON NEXT PLEASE, DAISY?
COLOR
COLOR
Ooh, YOU'VE REALLY MADE WILL.I.AM ***POP.***

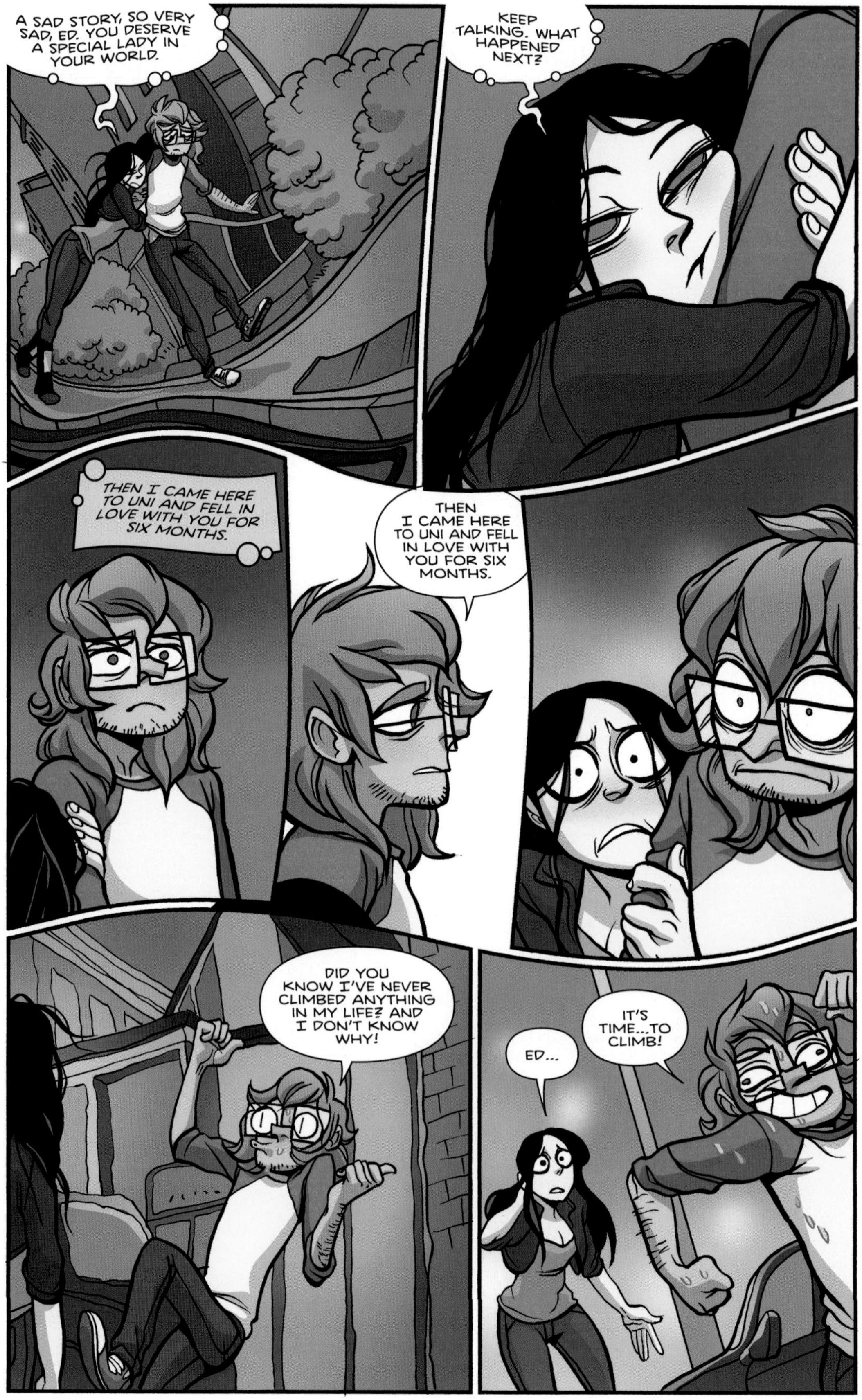

A SAD STORY, SO VERY SAD, ED. YOU DESERVE A SPECIAL LADY IN YOUR WORLD.
KEEP TALKING. WHAT HAPPENED NEXT?
THEN I CAME HERE TO UNI AND FELL IN LOVE WITH YOU FOR SIX MONTHS.
THEN I CAME HERE TO UNI AND FELL IN LOVE WITH YOU FOR SIX MONTHS.
DID YOU KNOW I'VE NEVER CLIMBED ANYTHING IN MY LIFE? AND I DON'T KNOW WHY!
ED...
IT'S TIME...TO CLIMB!

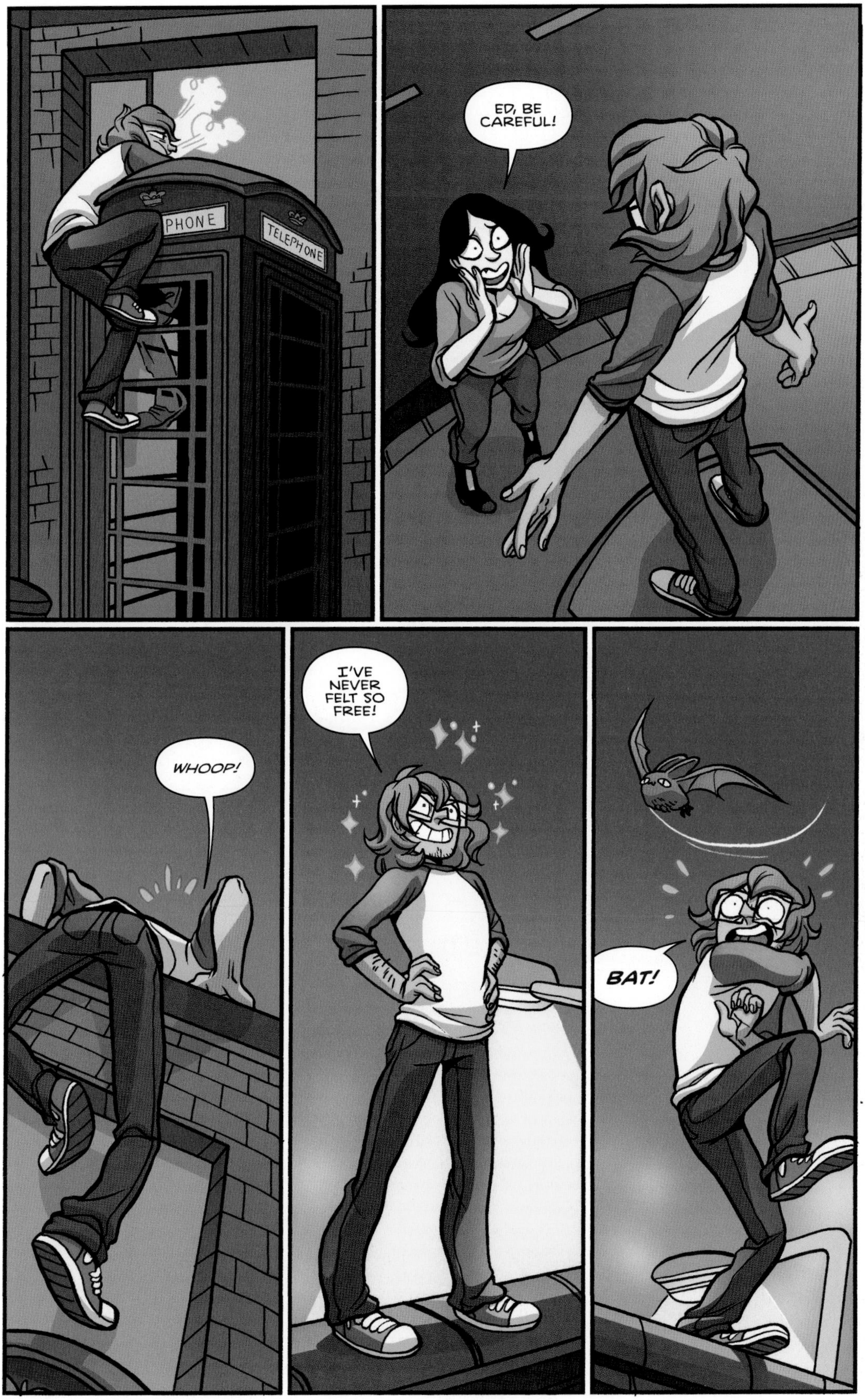
PHONE
TELEPHONE
ED, BE CAREFUL!
WHOOP!
I'VE NEVER FELT SO FREE!
BAT!

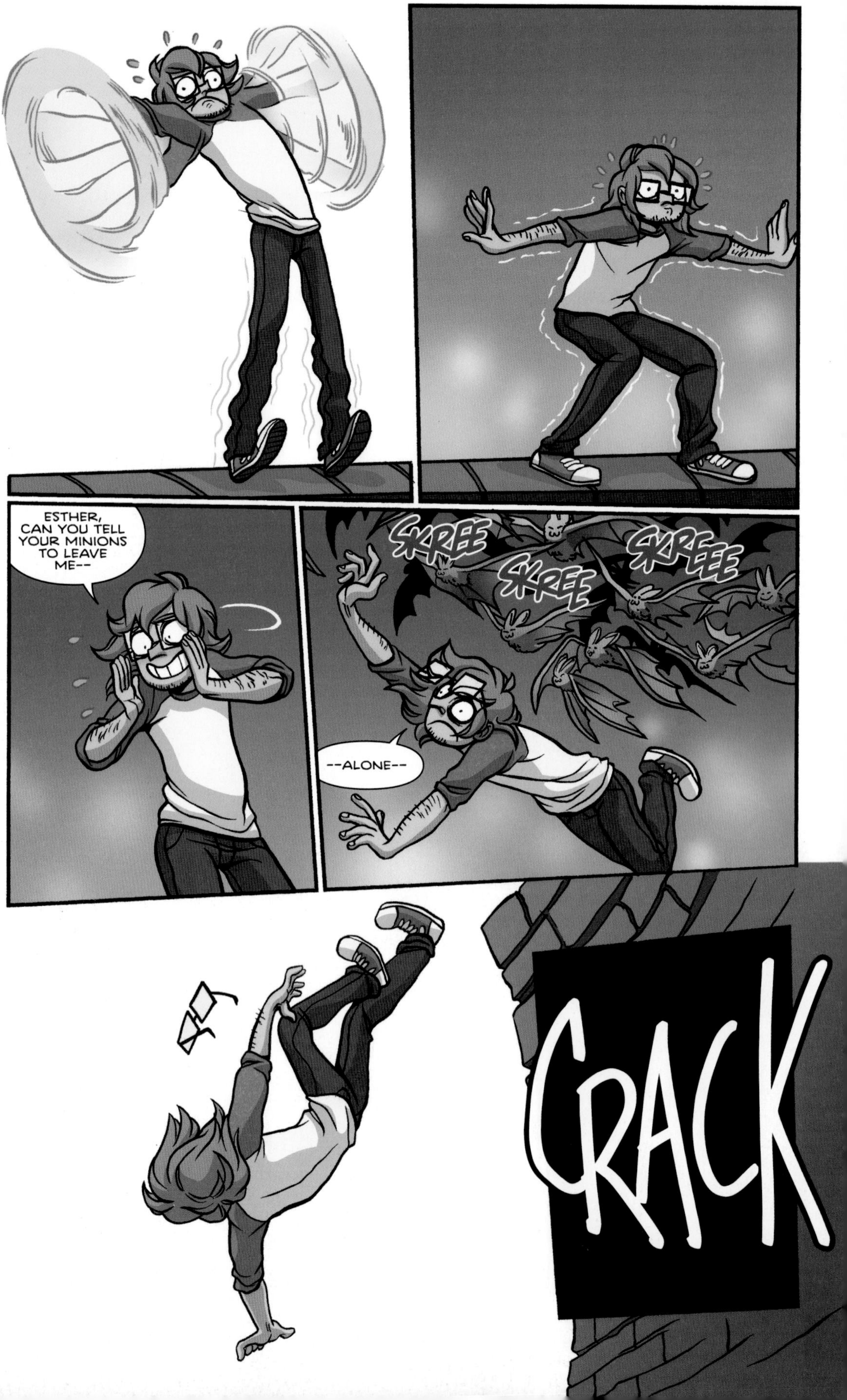
ESTHER, CAN YOU TELL YOUR MINIONS TO LEAVE ME--
SKREE
SKREE
SKREEEE
--ALONE--
CRACK

CHAPTER
THIRTY-FIVE

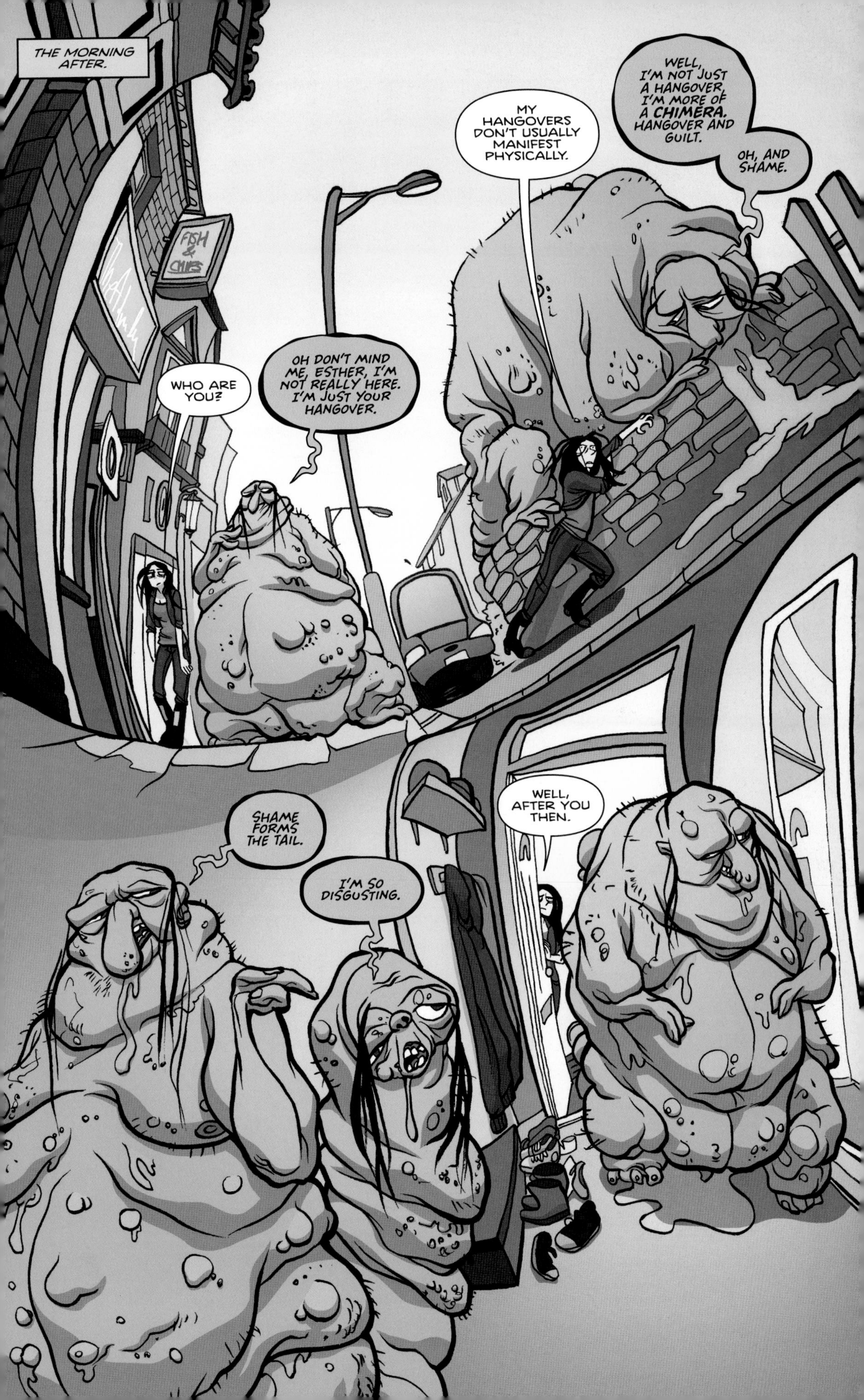
THE MORNING AFTER.
WHO ARE YOU?
OH DON'T MIND ME, ESTHER, I'M NOT REALLY HERE. I'M JUST YOUR HANGOVER.
MY HANGOVERS DON'T USUALLY MANIFEST PHYSICALLY.
WELL, I'M NOT JUST A HANGOVER, I'M MORE OF A CHIMERA. HANGOVER AND GUILT.
OH, AND SHAME.
SHAME FORMS THE TAIL.
I'M SO DISGUSTING.
WELL, AFTER YOU THEN.
FISH & CHIPS

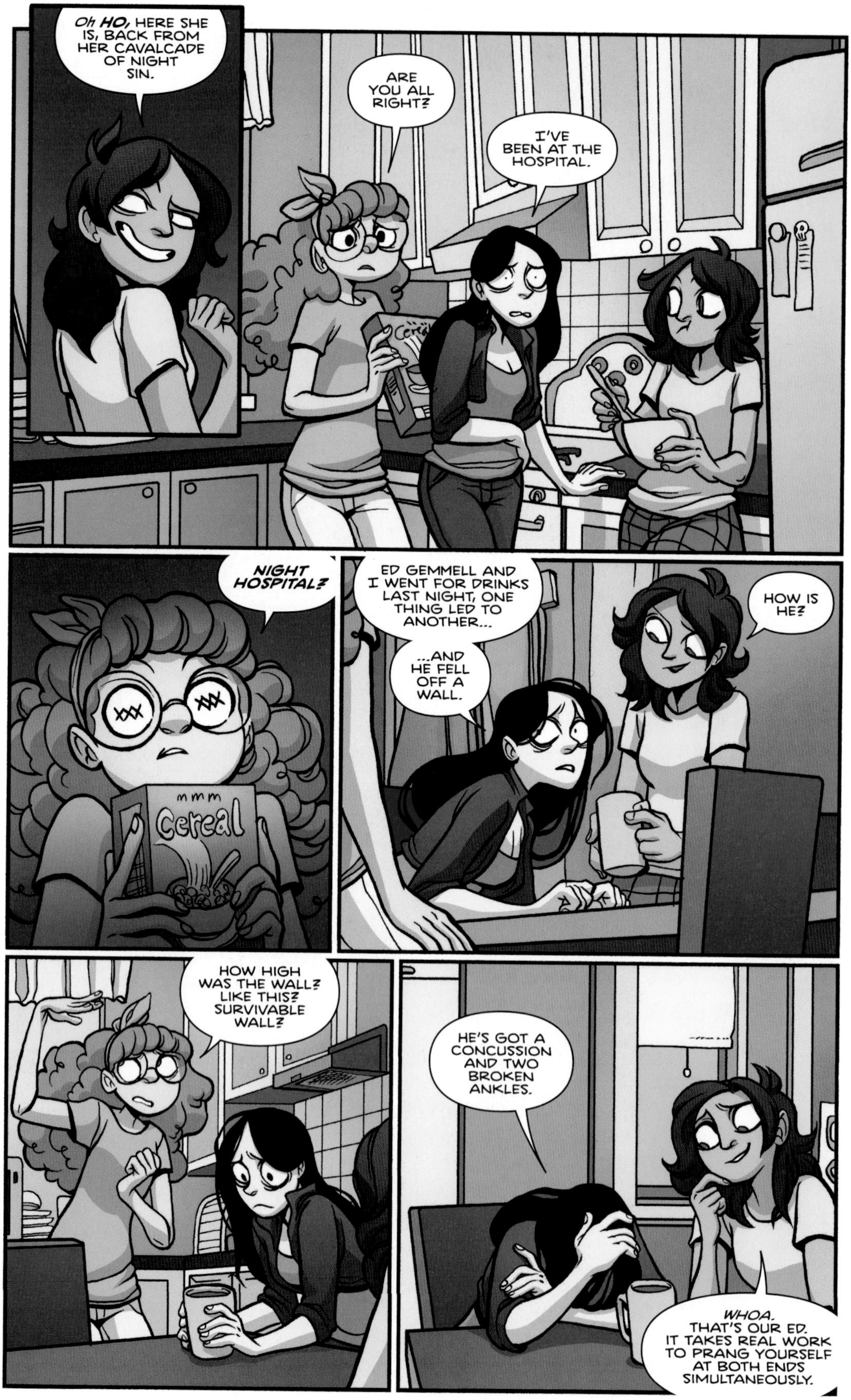
Oh HO, HERE SHE IS, BACK FROM HER CAVALCADE OF NIGHT SIN.
ARE YOU ALL RIGHT?
I'VE BEEN AT THE HOSPITAL.
NIGHT HOSPITAL?
mmm
Cereal
ED GEMMELL AND I WENT FOR DRINKS LAST NIGHT, ONE THING LED TO ANOTHER...
...AND HE FELL OFF A WALL.
HOW IS HE?
HOW HIGH WAS THE WALL? LIKE THIS? SURVIVABLE WALL?
HE'S GOT A CONCUSSION AND TWO BROKEN ANKLES.
WHOA. THAT'S OUR ED. IT TAKES REAL WORK TO PRANG YOURSELF AT BOTH ENDS SIMULTANEOUSLY.

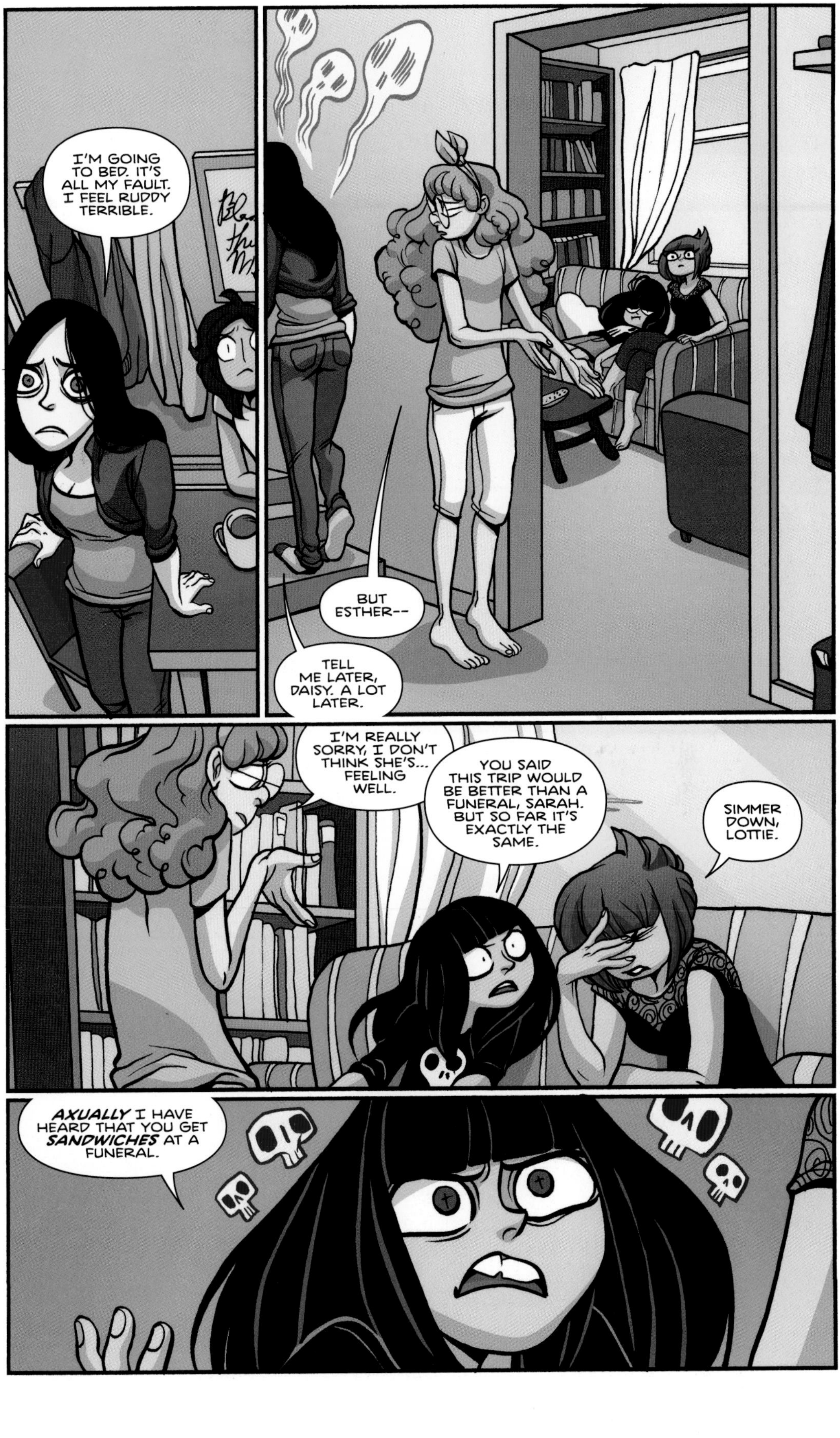
I'M GOING TO BED. IT'S ALL MY FAULT. I FEEL RUDDY TERRIBLE.
BUT ESTHER--
TELL ME LATER, DAISY. A LOT LATER.
I'M REALLY SORRY, I DON'T THINK SHE'S... FEELING WELL.
YOU SAID THIS TRIP WOULD BE BETTER THAN A FUNERAL, SARAH. BUT SO FAR IT'S EXACTLY THE SAME.
SIMMER DOWN, LOTTIE.
AXUALLY I HAVE HEARD THAT YOU GET SANDWICHES AT A FUNERAL.

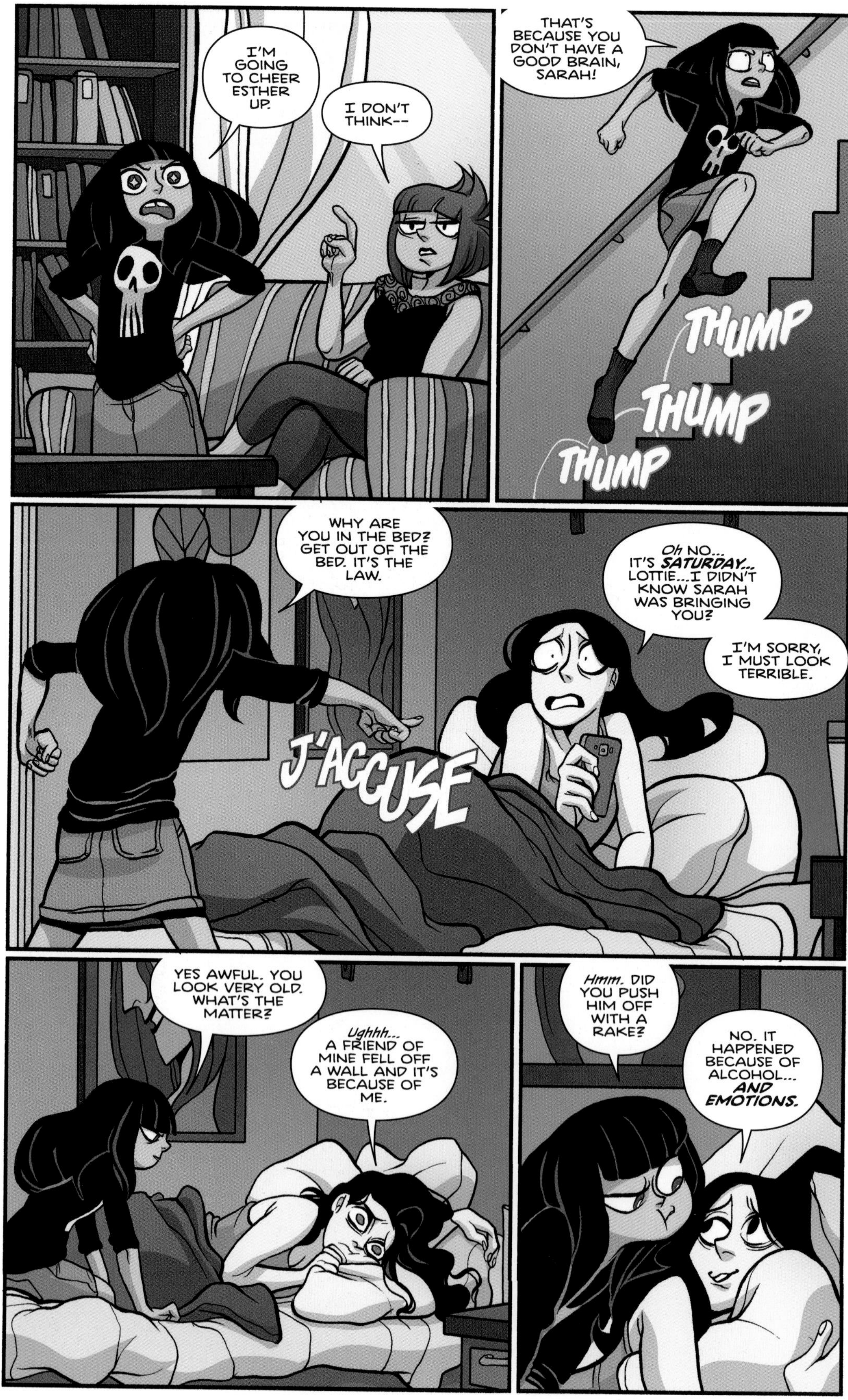
I'M GOING TO CHEER ESTHER UP.
I DON'T THINK--
THAT'S BECAUSE YOU DON'T HAVE A GOOD BRAIN, SARAH!
THUMP
THUMP
THUMP
WHY ARE YOU IN THE BED? GET OUT OF THE BED. IT'S THE LAW.
J'ACCUSE
Oh NO... IT'S ***SATURDAY...*** LOTTIE... I DIDN'T KNOW SARAH WAS BRINGING YOU?
I'M SORRY, I MUST LOOK TERRIBLE.
YES AWFUL. YOU LOOK VERY OLD. WHAT'S THE MATTER?
Ughhh... A FRIEND OF MINE FELL OFF A WALL AND IT'S BECAUSE OF ME.
Hmm. DID YOU PUSH HIM OFF WITH A RAKE?
NO. IT HAPPENED BECAUSE OF ALCOHOL... ***AND EMOTIONS.***

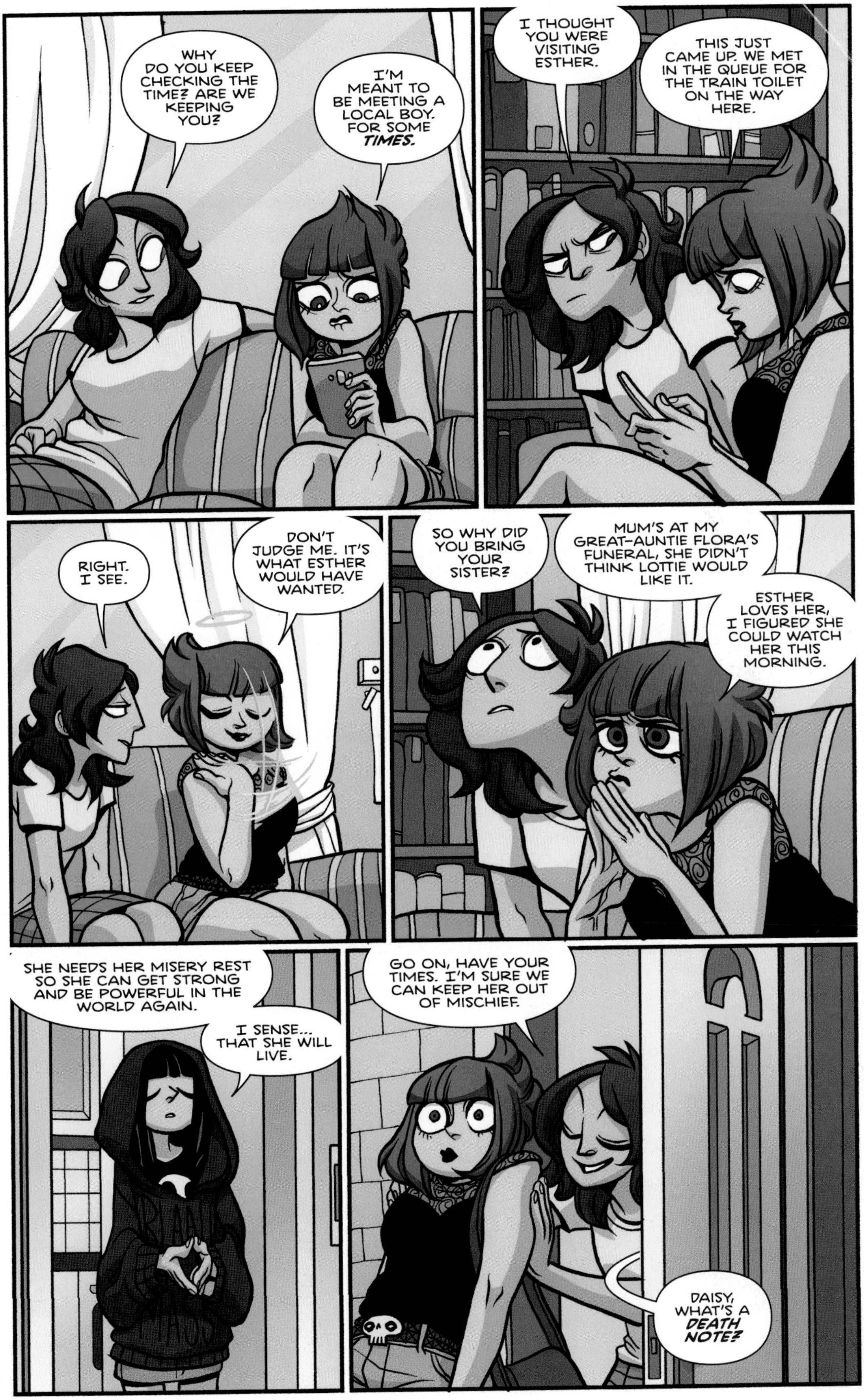
WHY DO YOU KEEP CHECKING THE TIME? ARE WE KEEPING YOU?
I'M MEANT TO BE MEETING A LOCAL BOY. FOR SOME *TIMES.*
I THOUGHT YOU WERE VISITING ESTHER.
THIS JUST CAME UP. WE MET IN THE QUEUE FOR THE TRAIN TOILET ON THE WAY HERE.
RIGHT. I SEE.
DON'T JUDGE ME. IT'S WHAT ESTHER WOULD HAVE WANTED.
SO WHY DID YOU BRING YOUR SISTER?
MUM'S AT MY GREAT-AUNTIE FLORA'S FUNERAL, SHE DIDN'T THINK LOTTIE WOULD LIKE IT.
ESTHER LOVES HER, I FIGURED SHE COULD WATCH HER THIS MORNING.
SHE NEEDS HER MISERY REST SO SHE CAN GET STRONG AND BE POWERFUL IN THE WORLD AGAIN.
I SENSE... THAT SHE WILL LIVE.
GO ON, HAVE YOUR TIMES. I'M SURE WE CAN KEEP HER OUT OF MISCHIEF.
DAISY, WHAT'S A *DEATH NOTE?*

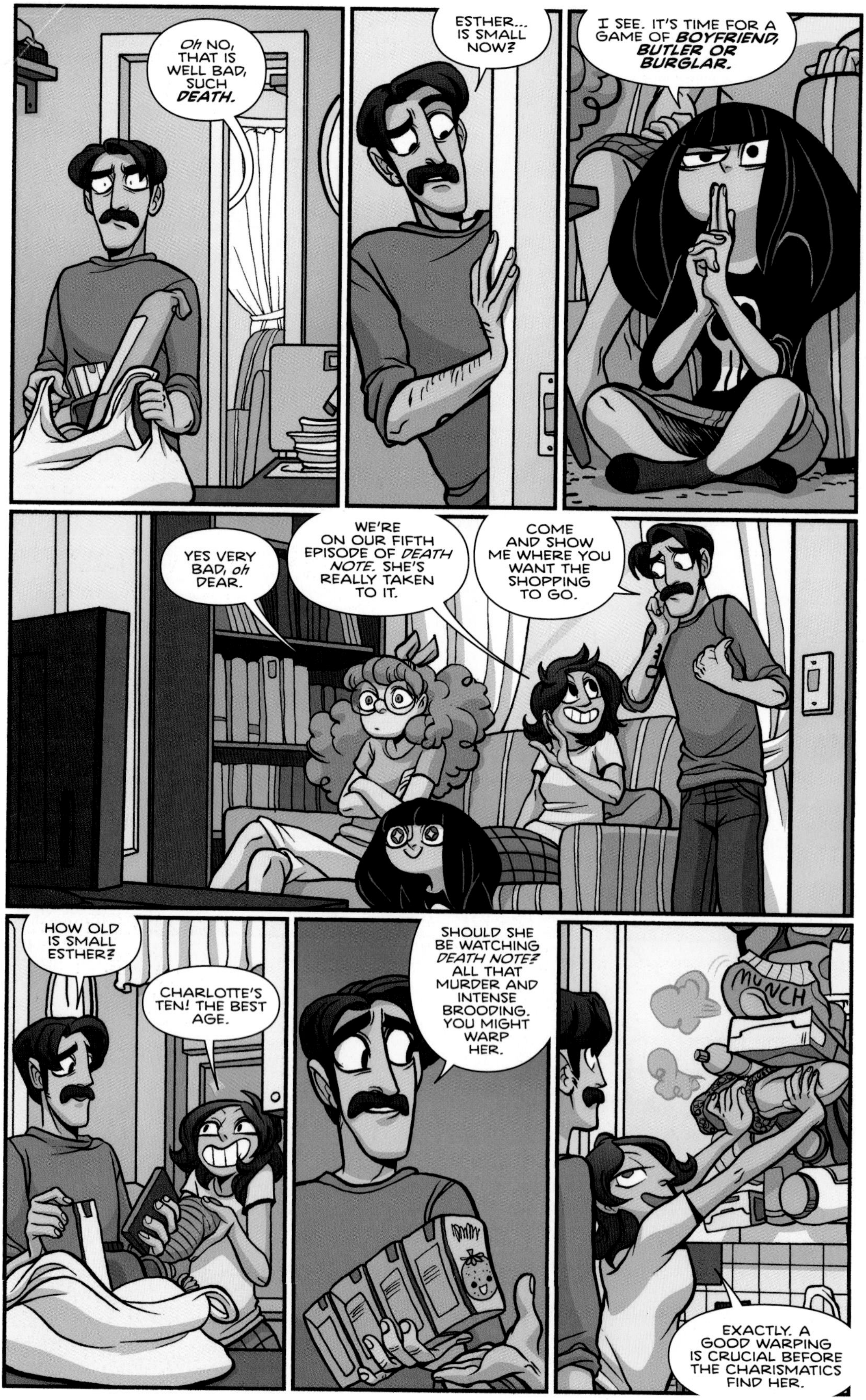

Oh NO, THAT IS WELL BAD, SUCH DEATH.
ESTHER... IS SMALL NOW?
I SEE. IT'S TIME FOR A GAME OF BOYFRIEND, BUTLER OR BURGLAR.
YES VERY BAD, oh DEAR.
WE'RE ON OUR FIFTH EPISODE OF DEATH NOTE. SHE'S REALLY TAKEN TO IT.
COME AND SHOW ME WHERE YOU WANT THE SHOPPING TO GO.
HOW OLD IS SMALL ESTHER?
CHARLOTTE'S TEN! THE BEST AGE.
SHOULD SHE BE WATCHING DEATH NOTE? ALL THAT MURDER AND INTENSE BROODING. YOU MIGHT WARP HER.
MUNCH
EXACTLY. A GOOD WARPING IS CRUCIAL BEFORE THE CHARISMATICS FIND HER.

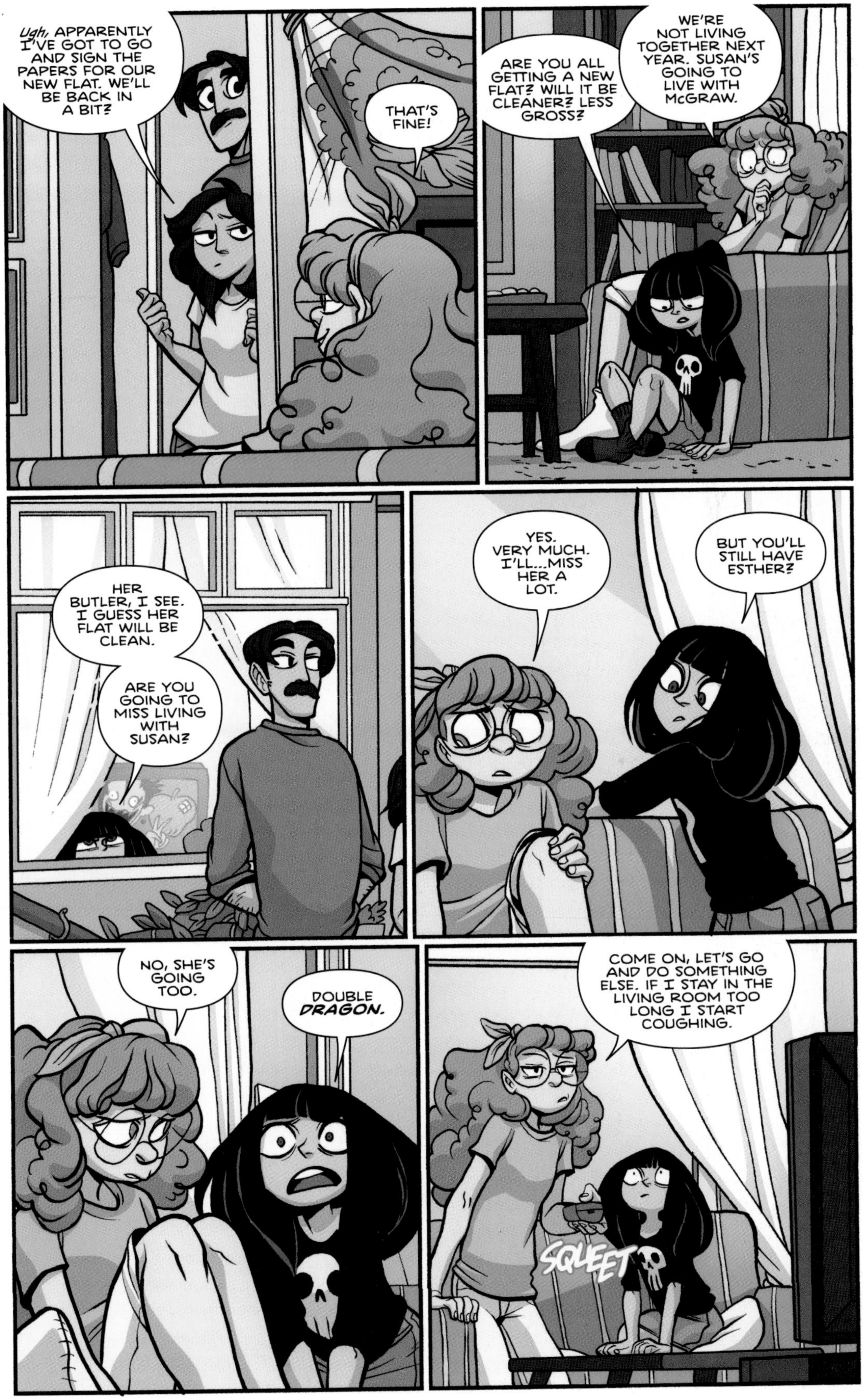
Ugh, APPARENTLY I'VE GOT TO GO AND SIGN THE PAPERS FOR OUR NEW FLAT. WE'LL BE BACK IN A BIT?
THAT'S FINE!
ARE YOU ALL GETTING A NEW FLAT? WILL IT BE CLEANER? LESS GROSS?
WE'RE NOT LIVING TOGETHER NEXT YEAR. SUSAN'S GOING TO LIVE WITH McGRAW.
HER BUTLER, I SEE. I GUESS HER FLAT WILL BE CLEAN.
ARE YOU GOING TO MISS LIVING WITH SUSAN?
YES. VERY MUCH. I'LL...MISS HER A LOT.
BUT YOU'LL STILL HAVE ESTHER?
NO, SHE'S GOING TOO.
DOUBLE DRAGON.
COME ON, LET'S GO AND DO SOMETHING ELSE. IF I STAY IN THE LIVING ROOM TOO LONG I START COUGHING.
SQUEET

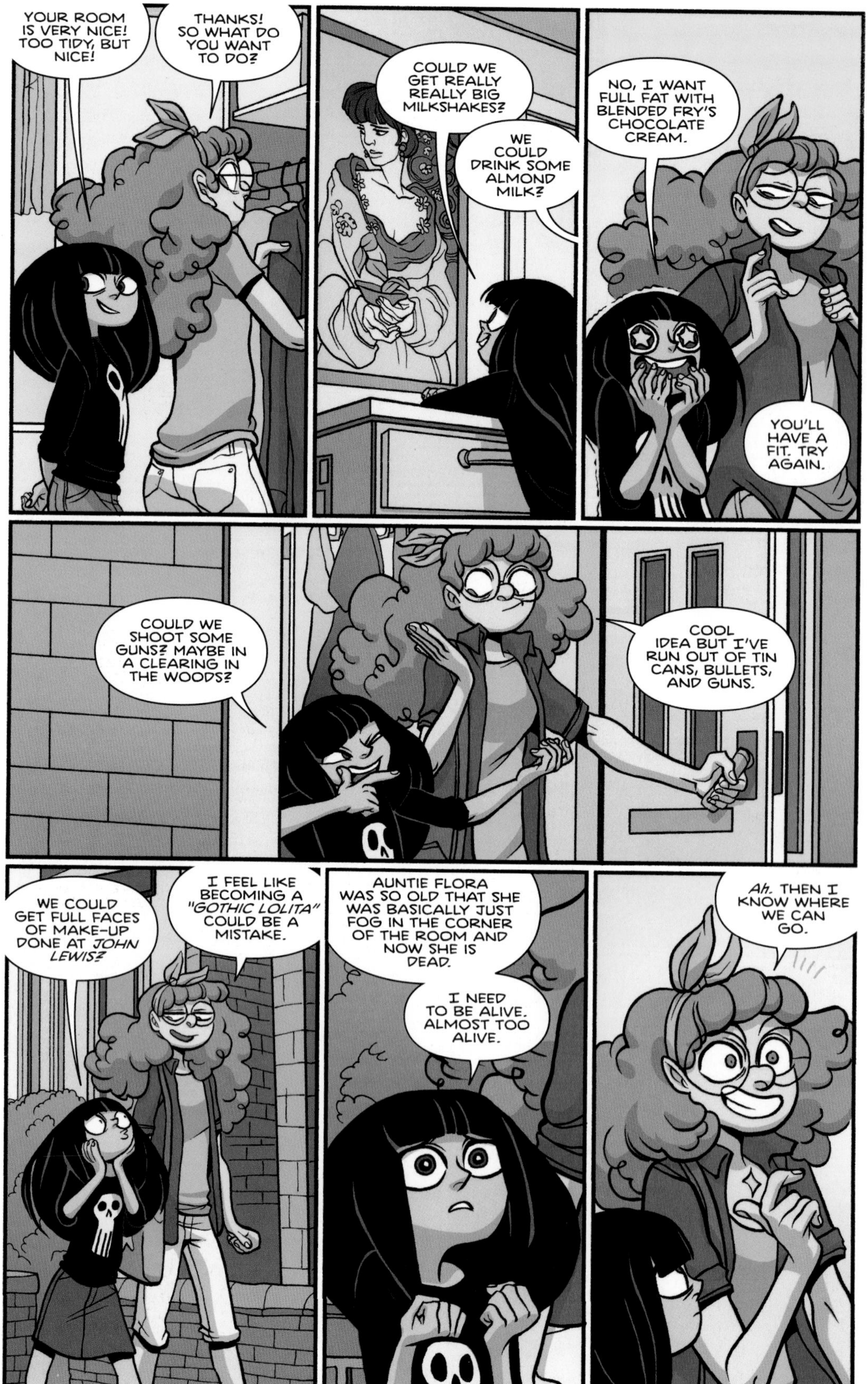
YOUR ROOM IS VERY NICE! TOO TIDY, BUT NICE!
THANKS! SO WHAT DO YOU WANT TO DO?
COULD WE GET REALLY REALLY BIG MILKSHAKES?
WE COULD DRINK SOME ALMOND MILK?
NO, I WANT FULL FAT WITH BLENDED FRY'S CHOCOLATE CREAM.
YOU'LL HAVE A FIT. TRY AGAIN.
COULD WE SHOOT SOME GUNS? MAYBE IN A CLEARING IN THE WOODS?
COOL IDEA BUT I'VE RUN OUT OF TIN CANS, BULLETS, AND GUNS.
WE COULD GET FULL FACES OF MAKE-UP DONE AT *JOHN LEWIS*?
I FEEL LIKE BECOMING A "*GOTHIC LOLITA*" COULD BE A MISTAKE.
AUNTIE FLORA WAS SO OLD THAT SHE WAS BASICALLY JUST FOG IN THE CORNER OF THE ROOM AND NOW SHE IS DEAD.
I NEED TO BE ALIVE. ALMOST TOO ALIVE.
Ah. THEN I KNOW WHERE WE CAN GO.

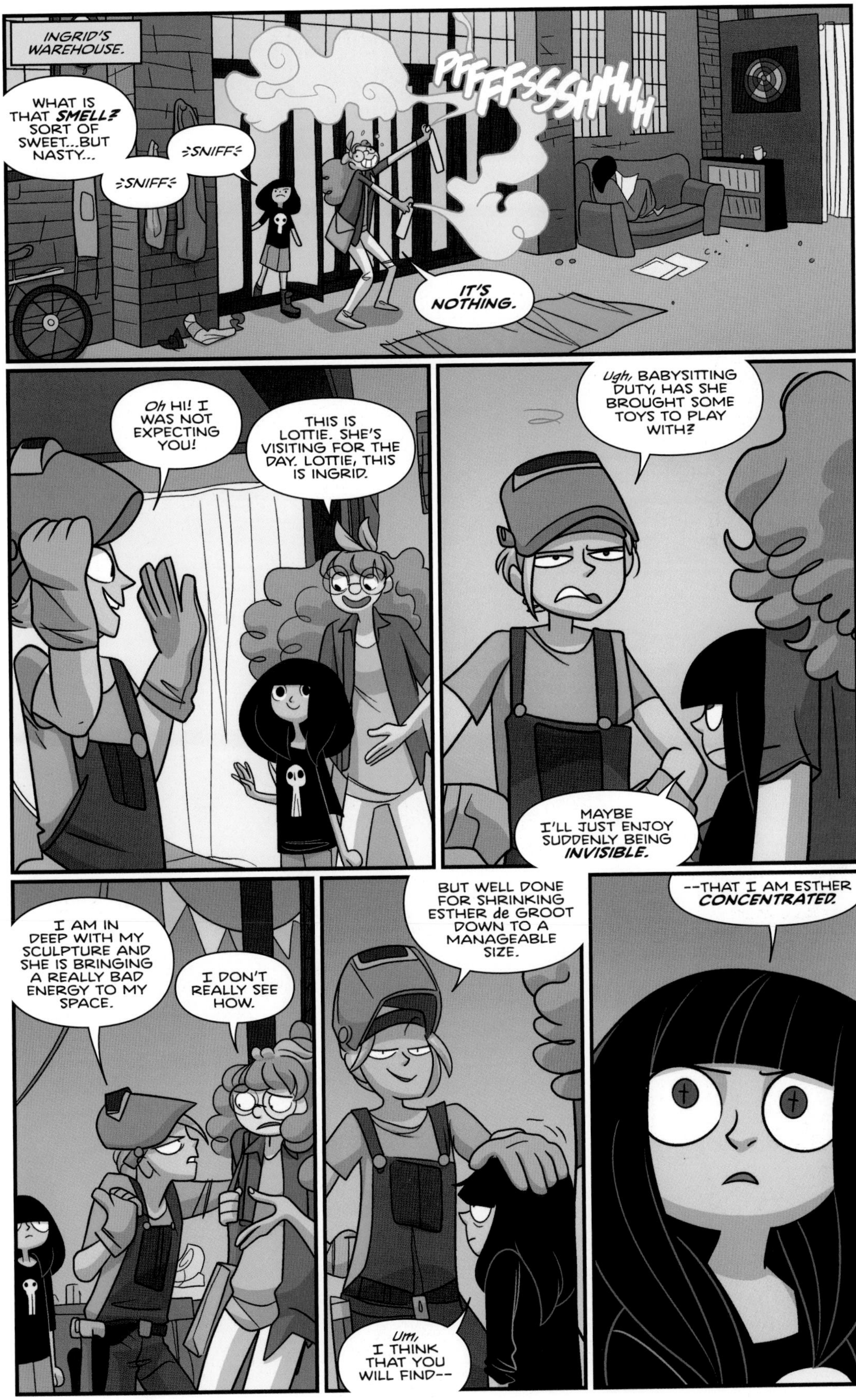
INGRID'S WAREHOUSE.
WHAT IS THAT SMELL? SORT OF SWEET...BUT NASTY...
SNIFF
SNIFF
PFFFFSSSHHHH
IT'S NOTHING.
Oh HI! I WAS NOT EXPECTING YOU!
THIS IS LOTTIE. SHE'S VISITING FOR THE DAY. LOTTIE, THIS IS INGRID.
Ugh, BABYSITTING DUTY, HAS SHE BROUGHT SOME TOYS TO PLAY WITH?
MAYBE I'LL JUST ENJOY SUDDENLY BEING INVISIBLE.
I AM IN DEEP WITH MY SCULPTURE AND SHE IS BRINGING A REALLY BAD ENERGY TO MY SPACE.
I DON'T REALLY SEE HOW.
BUT WELL DONE FOR SHRINKING ESTHER de GROOT DOWN TO A MANAGEABLE SIZE.
Um, I THINK THAT YOU WILL FIND--
--THAT I AM ESTHER CONCENTRATED.

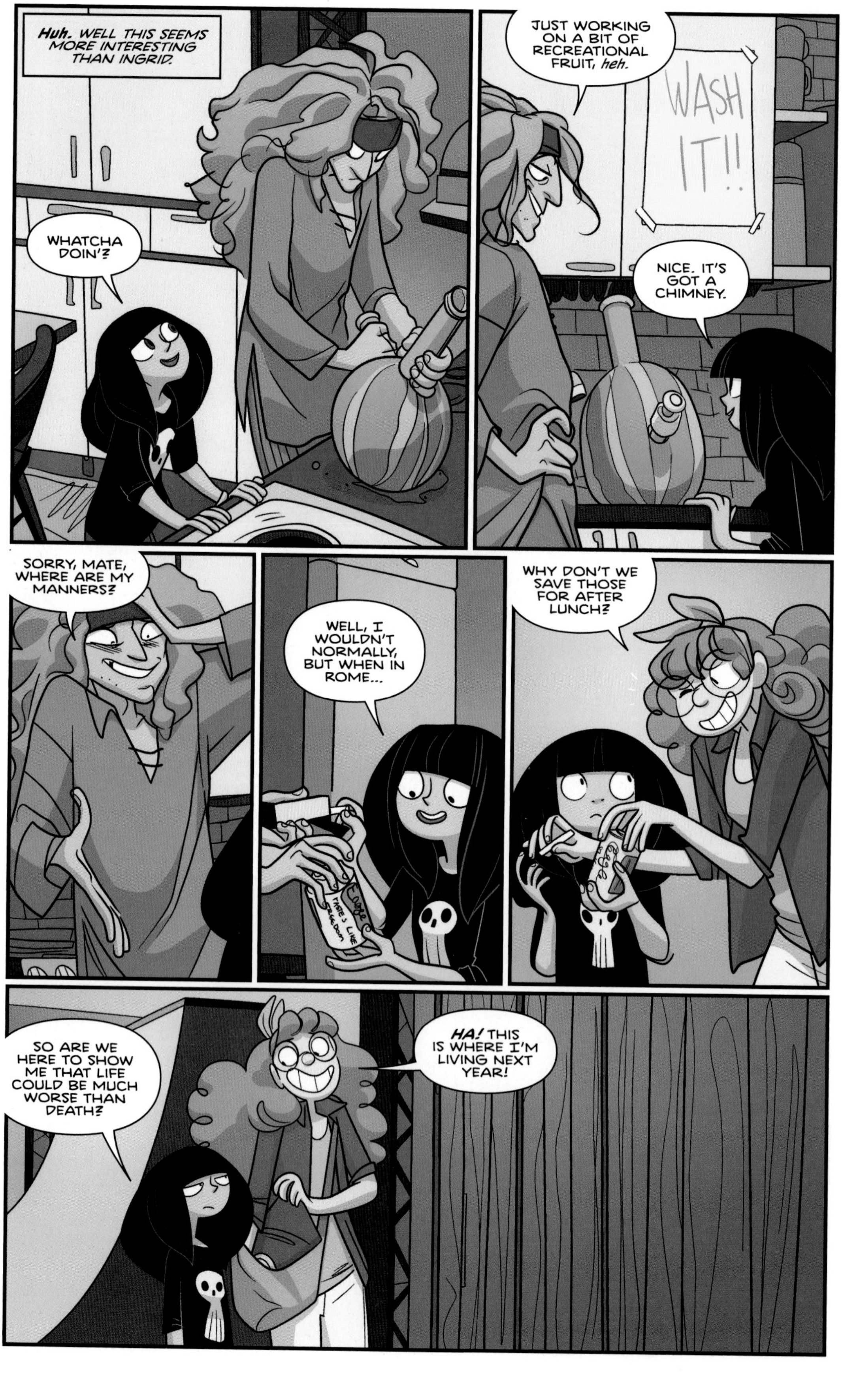
Huh. WELL THIS SEEMS MORE INTERESTING THAN INGRID.
WHATCHA DOIN'?
JUST WORKING ON A BIT OF RECREATIONAL FRUIT, heh.
WASH IT!!
NICE. IT'S GOT A CHIMNEY.
SORRY, MATE, WHERE ARE MY MANNERS?
WELL, I WOULDN'T NORMALLY, BUT WHEN IN ROME...
WHY DON'T WE SAVE THOSE FOR AFTER LUNCH?
SO ARE WE HERE TO SHOW ME THAT LIFE COULD BE MUCH WORSE THAN DEATH?
HA! THIS IS WHERE I'M LIVING NEXT YEAR!

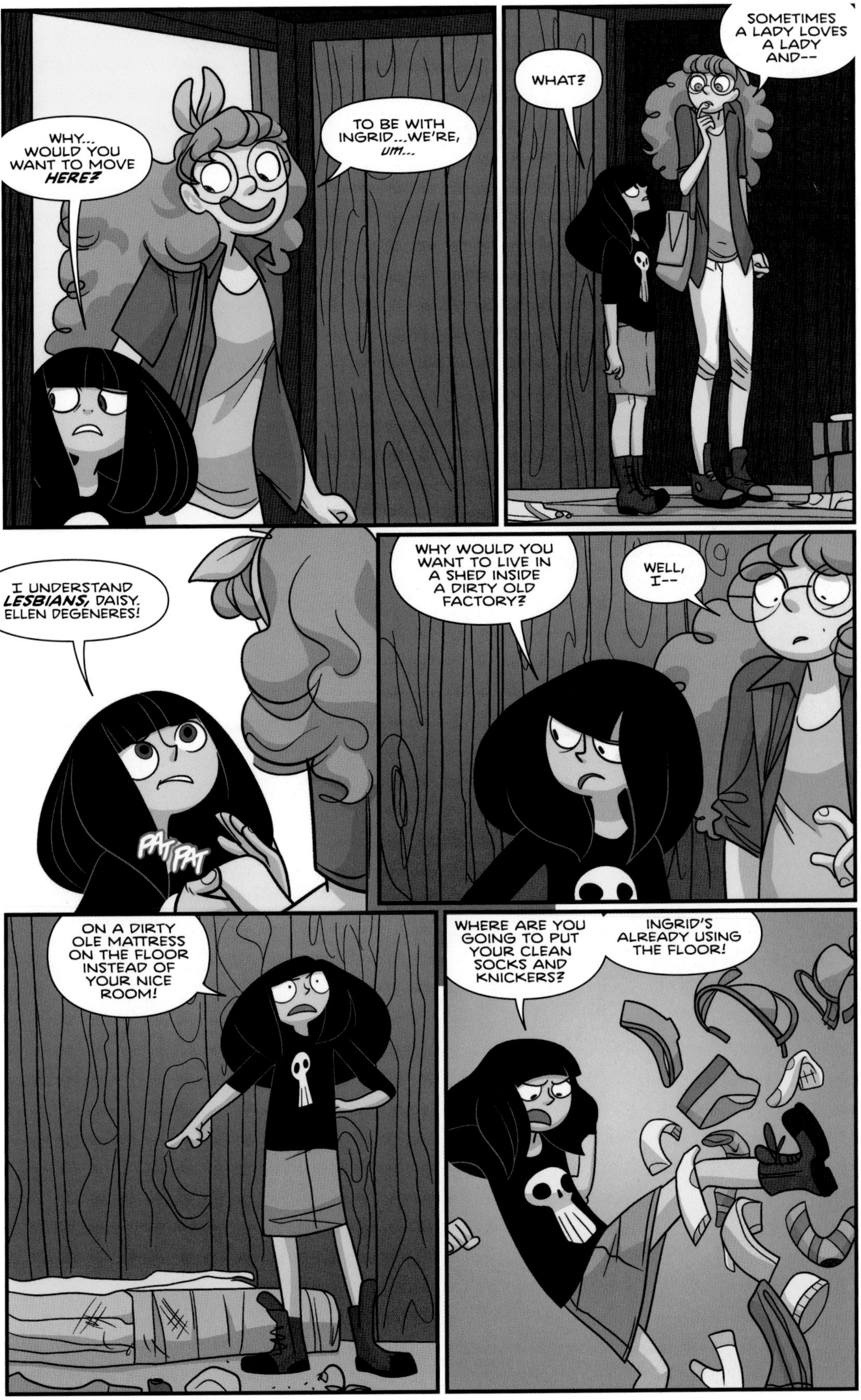
WHY... WOULD YOU WANT TO MOVE *HERE?*
TO BE WITH INGRID...WE'RE, *UM...*
WHAT?
SOMETIMES A LADY LOVES A LADY AND--
I UNDERSTAND *LESBIANS,* DAISY. ELLEN DEGENERES!
PAT PAT
WHY WOULD YOU WANT TO LIVE IN A SHED INSIDE A DIRTY OLD FACTORY?
WELL, I--
ON A DIRTY OLE MATTRESS ON THE FLOOR INSTEAD OF YOUR NICE ROOM!
WHERE ARE YOU GOING TO PUT YOUR CLEAN SOCKS AND KNICKERS?
INGRID'S ALREADY USING THE FLOOR!

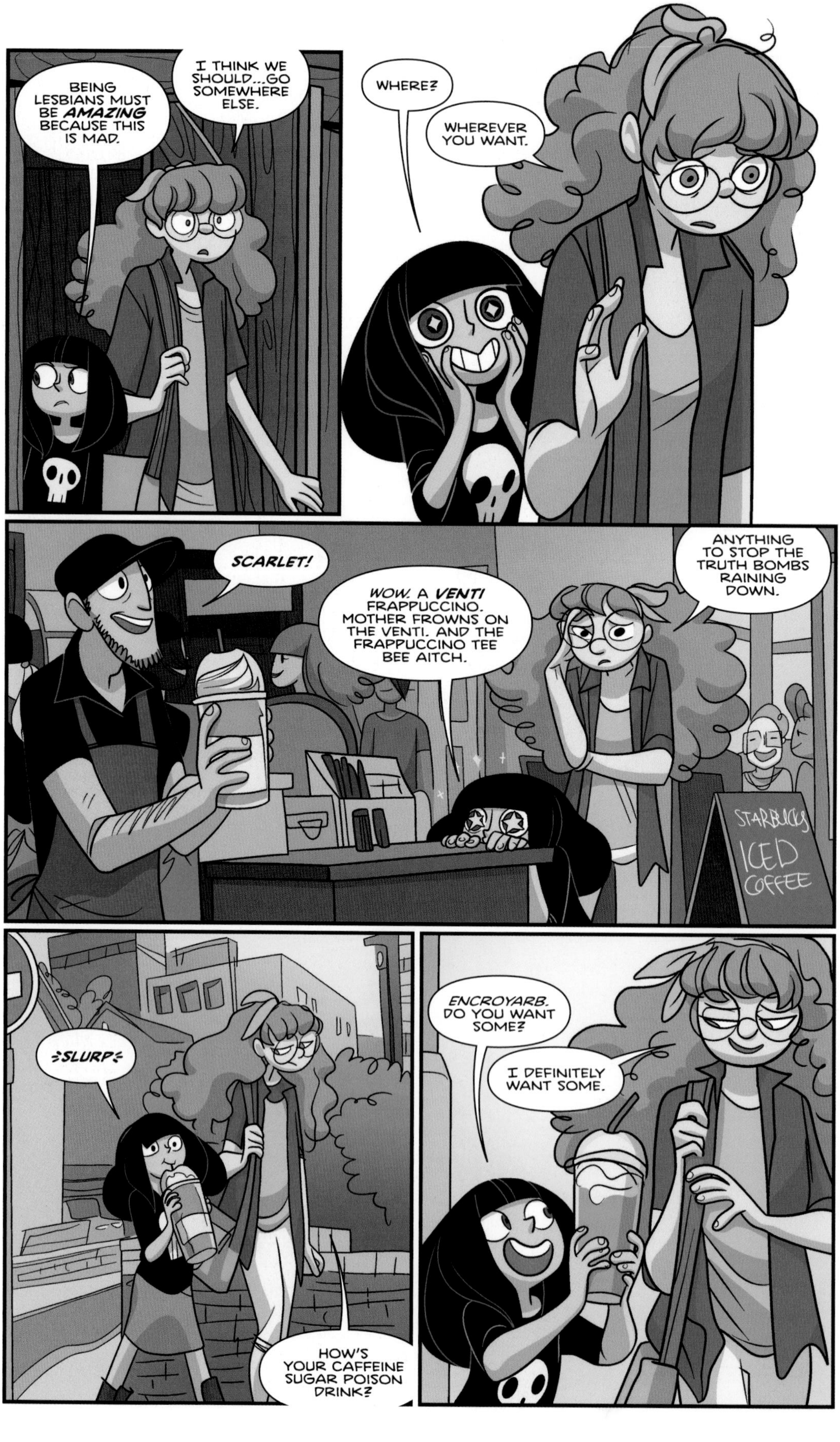
BEING LESBIANS MUST BE *AMAZING* BECAUSE THIS IS MAD.
I THINK WE SHOULD...GO SOMEWHERE ELSE.
WHERE?
WHEREVER YOU WANT.
SCARLET!
WOW. A *VENTI* FRAPPUCCINO. MOTHER FROWNS ON THE VENTI. AND THE FRAPPUCCINO TEE BEE AITCH.
ANYTHING TO STOP THE TRUTH BOMBS RAINING DOWN.
STARBUCKS
ICED COFFEE
SLURP
HOW'S YOUR CAFFEINE SUGAR POISON DRINK?
ENCROYARB. DO YOU WANT SOME?
I DEFINITELY WANT SOME.

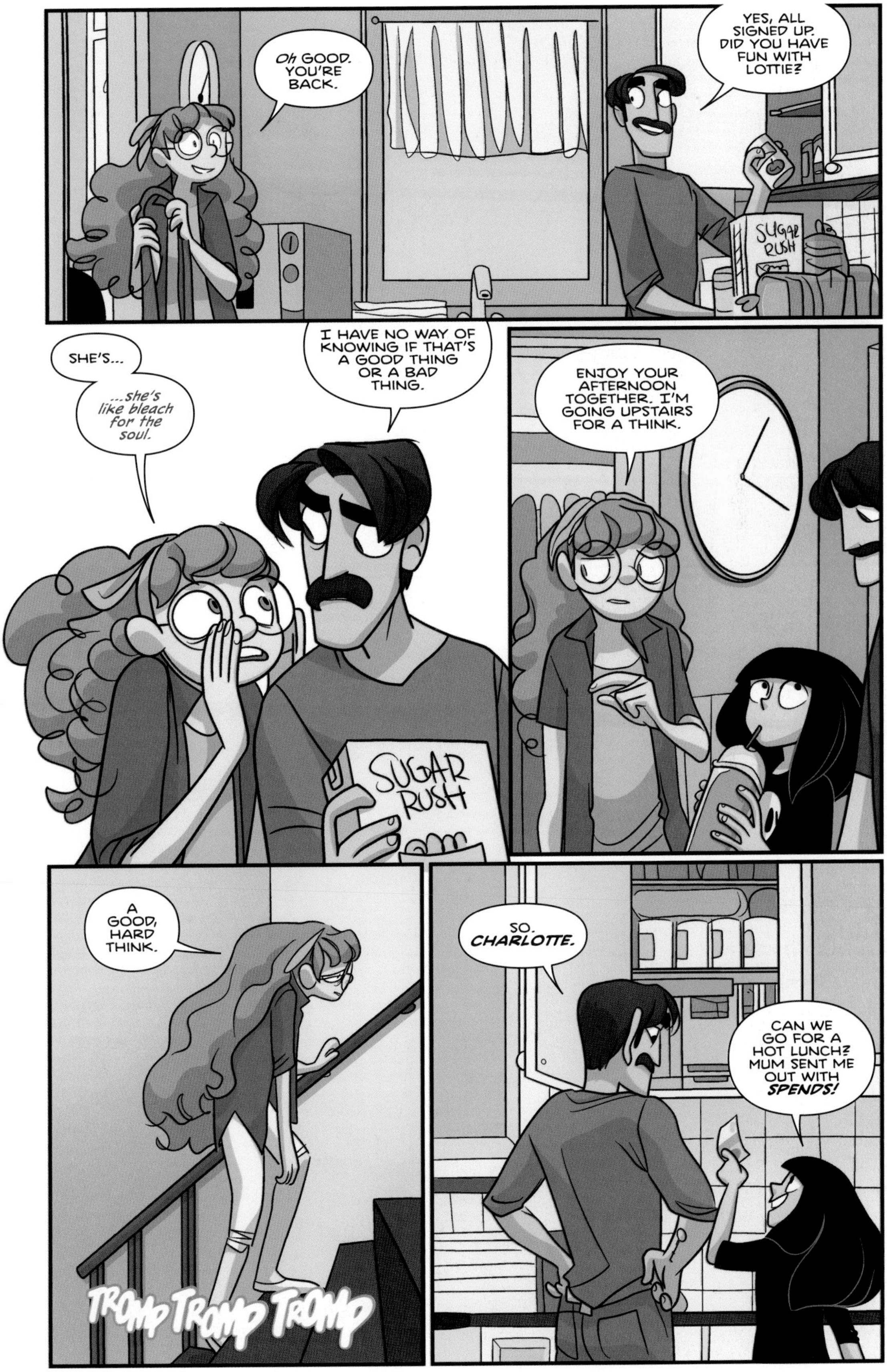

Oh GOOD. YOU'RE BACK.
YES, ALL SIGNED UP. DID YOU HAVE FUN WITH LOTTIE?
SUGAR RUSH
SHE'S...
...she's like bleach for the soul.
I HAVE NO WAY OF KNOWING IF THAT'S A GOOD THING OR A BAD THING.
SUGAR RUSH
ENJOY YOUR AFTERNOON TOGETHER. I'M GOING UPSTAIRS FOR A THINK.
A GOOD, HARD THINK.
TROMP TROMP TROMP
SO. CHARLOTTE.
CAN WE GO FOR A HOT LUNCH? MUM SENT ME OUT WITH SPENDS!

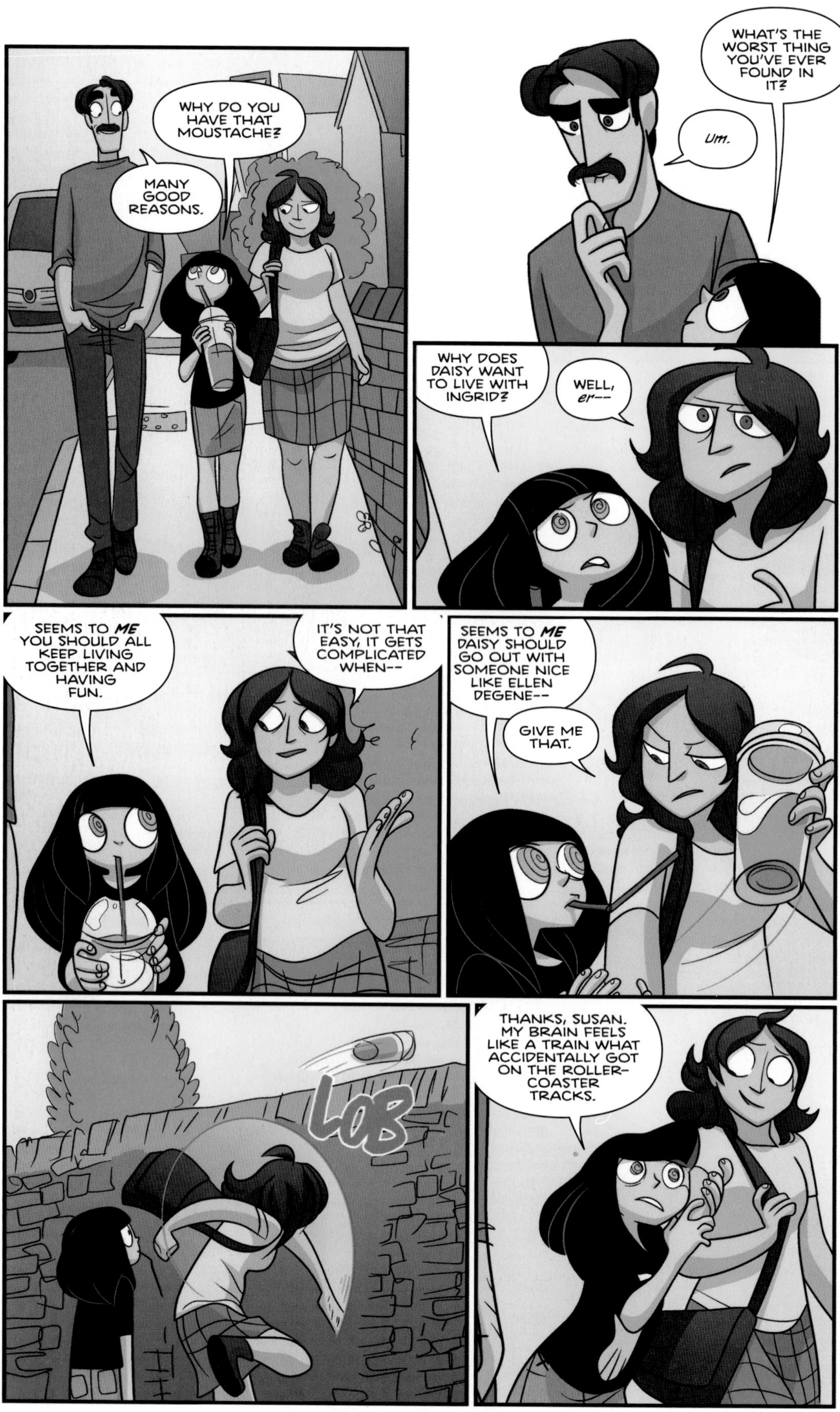
WHY DO YOU HAVE THAT MOUSTACHE?
MANY GOOD REASONS.
WHAT'S THE WORST THING YOU'VE EVER FOUND IN IT?
Um.
WHY DOES DAISY WANT TO LIVE WITH INGRID?
WELL, er--
SEEMS TO ME YOU SHOULD ALL KEEP LIVING TOGETHER AND HAVING FUN.
IT'S NOT THAT EASY, IT GETS COMPLICATED WHEN--
SEEMS TO ME DAISY SHOULD GO OUT WITH SOMEONE NICE LIKE ELLEN DEGENE--
GIVE ME THAT.
LOB
THANKS, SUSAN. MY BRAIN FEELS LIKE A TRAIN WHAT ACCIDENTALLY GOT ON THE ROLLER-COASTER TRACKS.

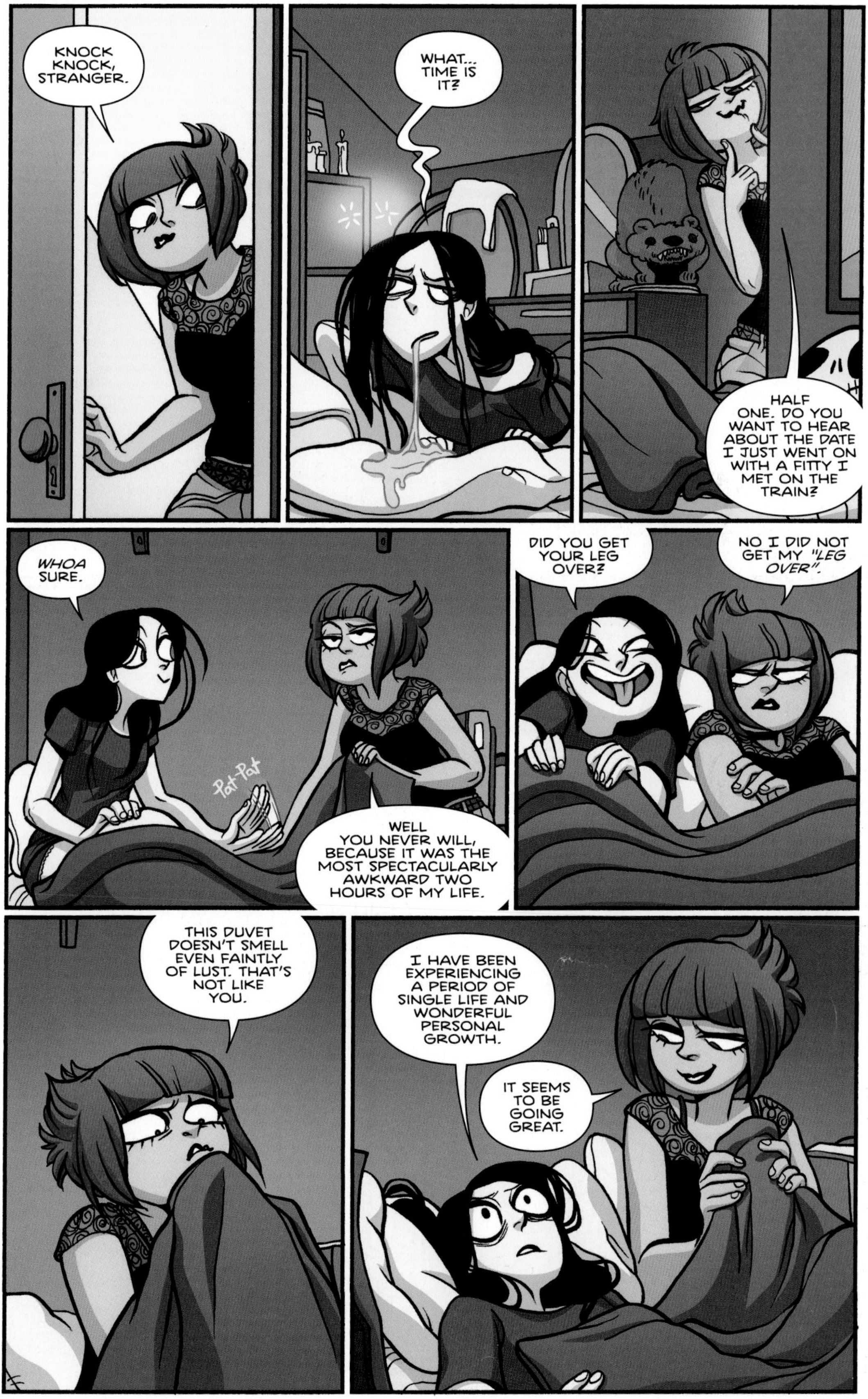
KNOCK KNOCK, STRANGER.
WHAT... TIME IS IT?
HALF ONE. DO YOU WANT TO HEAR ABOUT THE DATE I JUST WENT ON WITH A FITTY I MET ON THE TRAIN?
WHOA SURE.
Pat-Pat
WELL YOU NEVER WILL, BECAUSE IT WAS THE MOST SPECTACULARLY AWKWARD TWO HOURS OF MY LIFE.
DID YOU GET YOUR LEG OVER?
NO I DID NOT GET MY "LEG OVER".
THIS DUVET DOESN'T SMELL EVEN FAINTLY OF LUST. THAT'S NOT LIKE YOU.
I HAVE BEEN EXPERIENCING A PERIOD OF SINGLE LIFE AND WONDERFUL PERSONAL GROWTH.
IT SEEMS TO BE GOING GREAT.

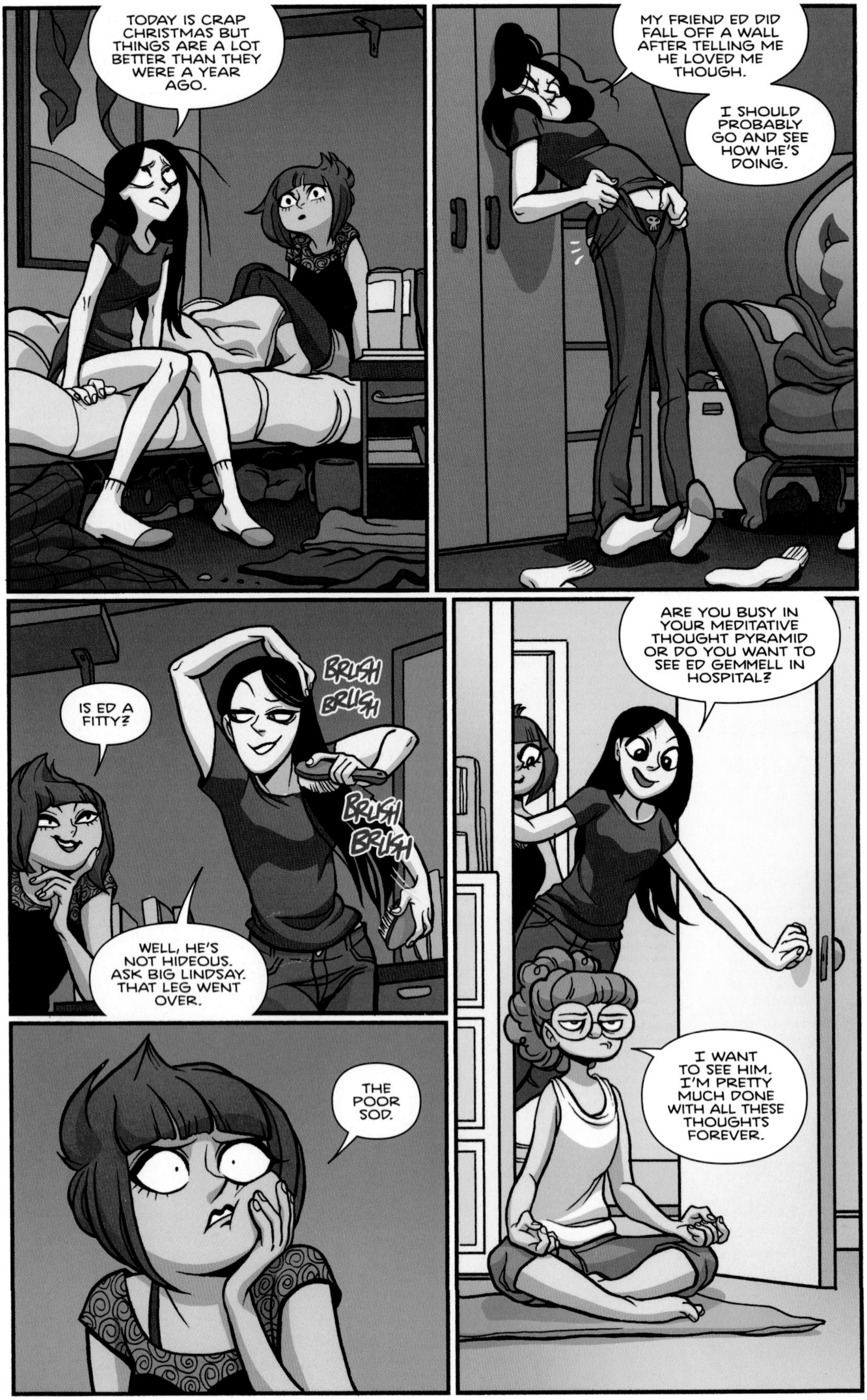
TODAY IS CRAP CHRISTMAS BUT THINGS ARE A LOT BETTER THAN THEY WERE A YEAR AGO.
MY FRIEND ED DID FALL OFF A WALL AFTER TELLING ME HE LOVED ME THOUGH.
I SHOULD PROBABLY GO AND SEE HOW HE'S DOING.
IS ED A FITTY?
BRUSH BRUSH
BRUSH BRUSH
WELL, HE'S NOT HIDEOUS. ASK BIG LINDSAY. THAT LEG WENT OVER.
THE POOR SOD.
ARE YOU BUSY IN YOUR MEDITATIVE THOUGHT PYRAMID OR DO YOU WANT TO SEE ED GEMMELL IN HOSPITAL?
I WANT TO SEE HIM. I'M PRETTY MUCH DONE WITH ALL THESE THOUGHTS FOREVER.

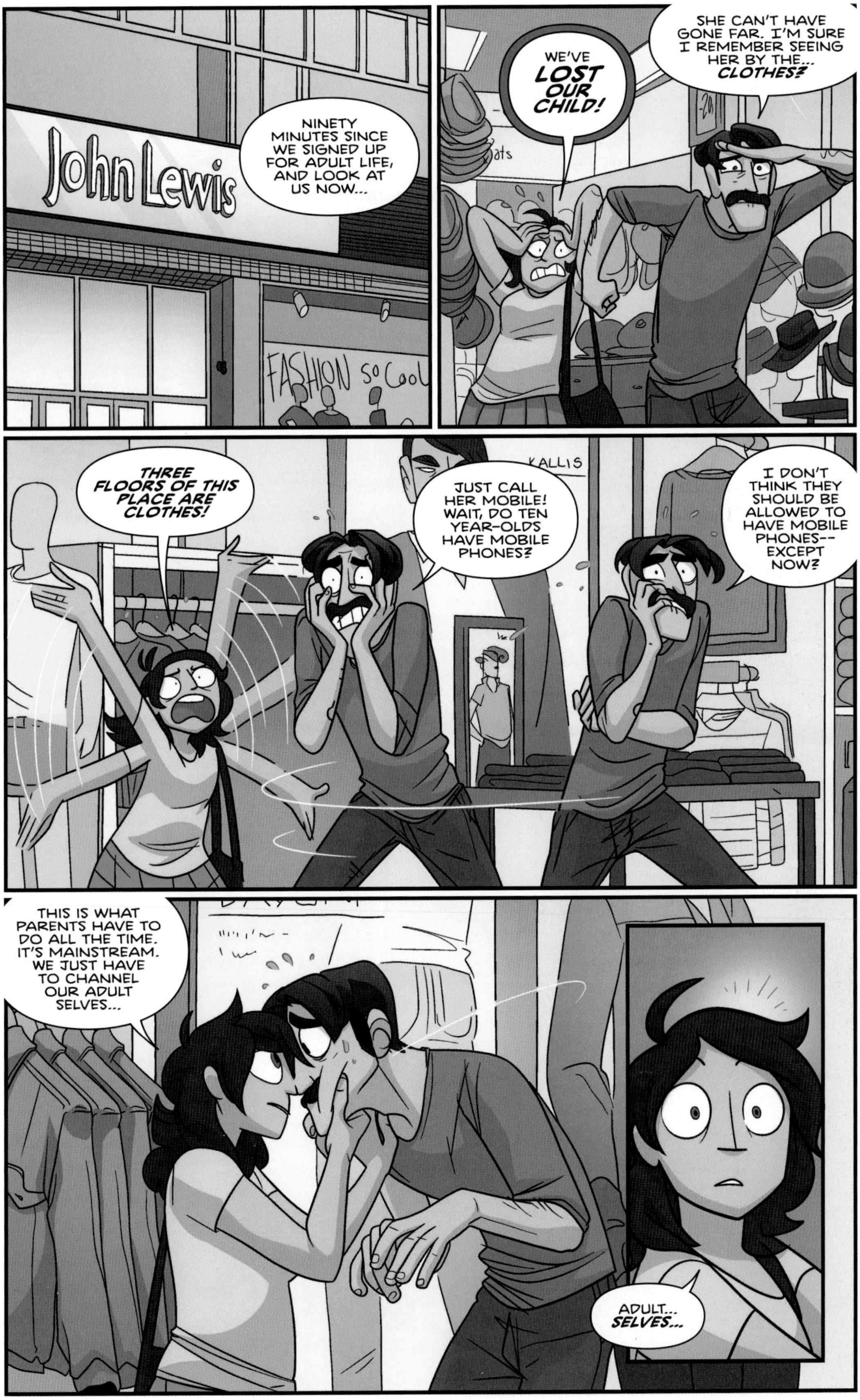
John Lewis
NINETY MINUTES SINCE WE SIGNED UP FOR ADULT LIFE, AND LOOK AT US NOW...
FASHION So Cool
WE'VE *LOST OUR CHILD!*
SHE CAN'T HAVE GONE FAR. I'M SURE I REMEMBER SEEING HER BY THE... *CLOTHES?*
THREE FLOORS OF THIS PLACE ARE CLOTHES!
KALLIS
JUST CALL HER MOBILE! WAIT, DO TEN YEAR-OLDS HAVE MOBILE PHONES?
I DON'T THINK THEY SHOULD BE ALLOWED TO HAVE MOBILE PHONES-- EXCEPT NOW?
THIS IS WHAT PARENTS HAVE TO DO ALL THE TIME. IT'S MAINSTREAM. WE JUST HAVE TO CHANNEL OUR ADULT SELVES...
ADULT... *SELVES...*

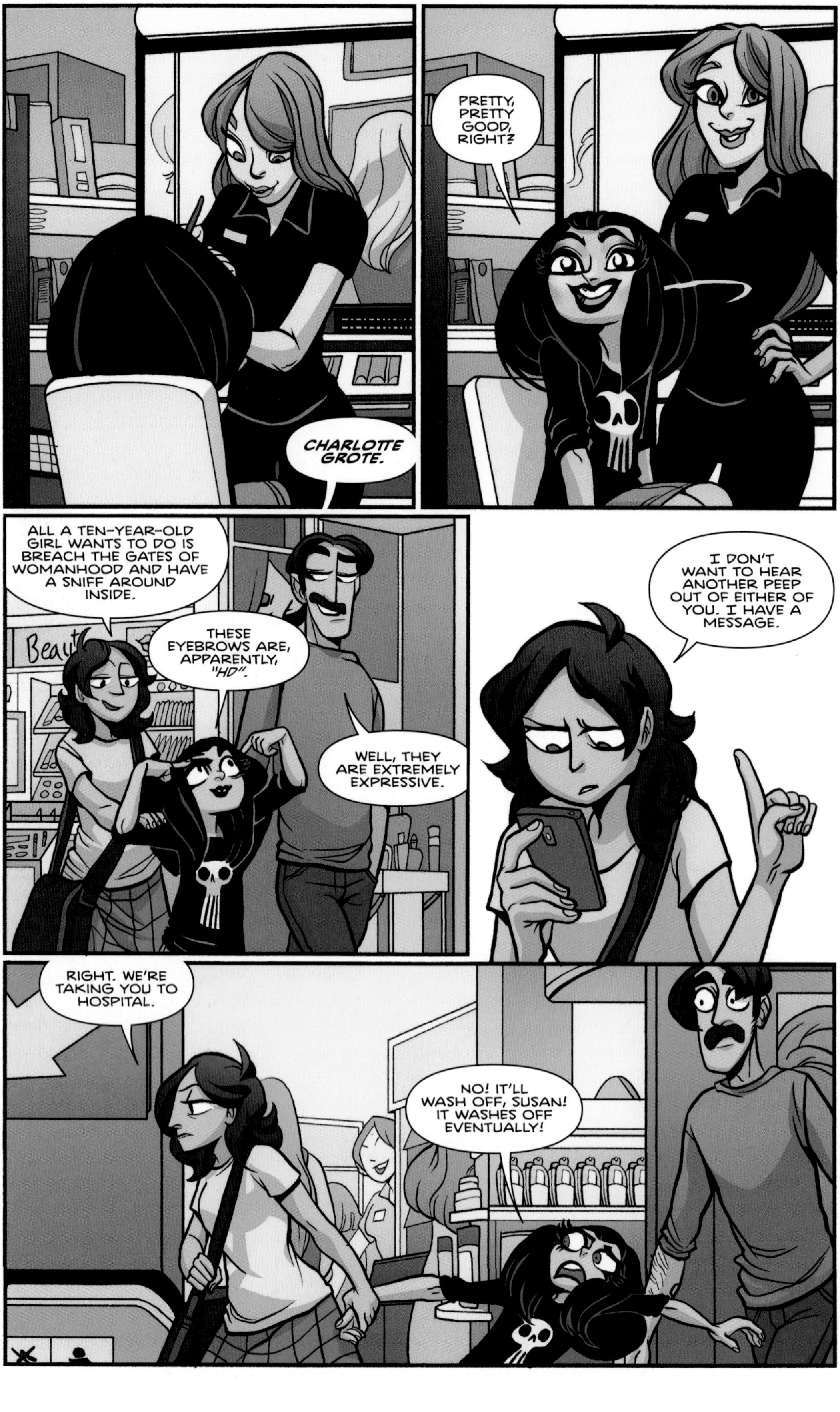

CHARLOTTE GROTE.
PRETTY, PRETTY GOOD, RIGHT?
ALL A TEN-YEAR-OLD GIRL WANTS TO DO IS BREACH THE GATES OF WOMANHOOD AND HAVE A SNIFF AROUND INSIDE.
THESE EYEBROWS ARE, APPARENTLY, "HD".
WELL, THEY ARE EXTREMELY EXPRESSIVE.
I DON'T WANT TO HEAR ANOTHER PEEP OUT OF EITHER OF YOU. I HAVE A MESSAGE.
RIGHT. WE'RE TAKING YOU TO HOSPITAL.
NO! IT'LL WASH OFF, SUSAN! IT WASHES OFF EVENTUALLY!

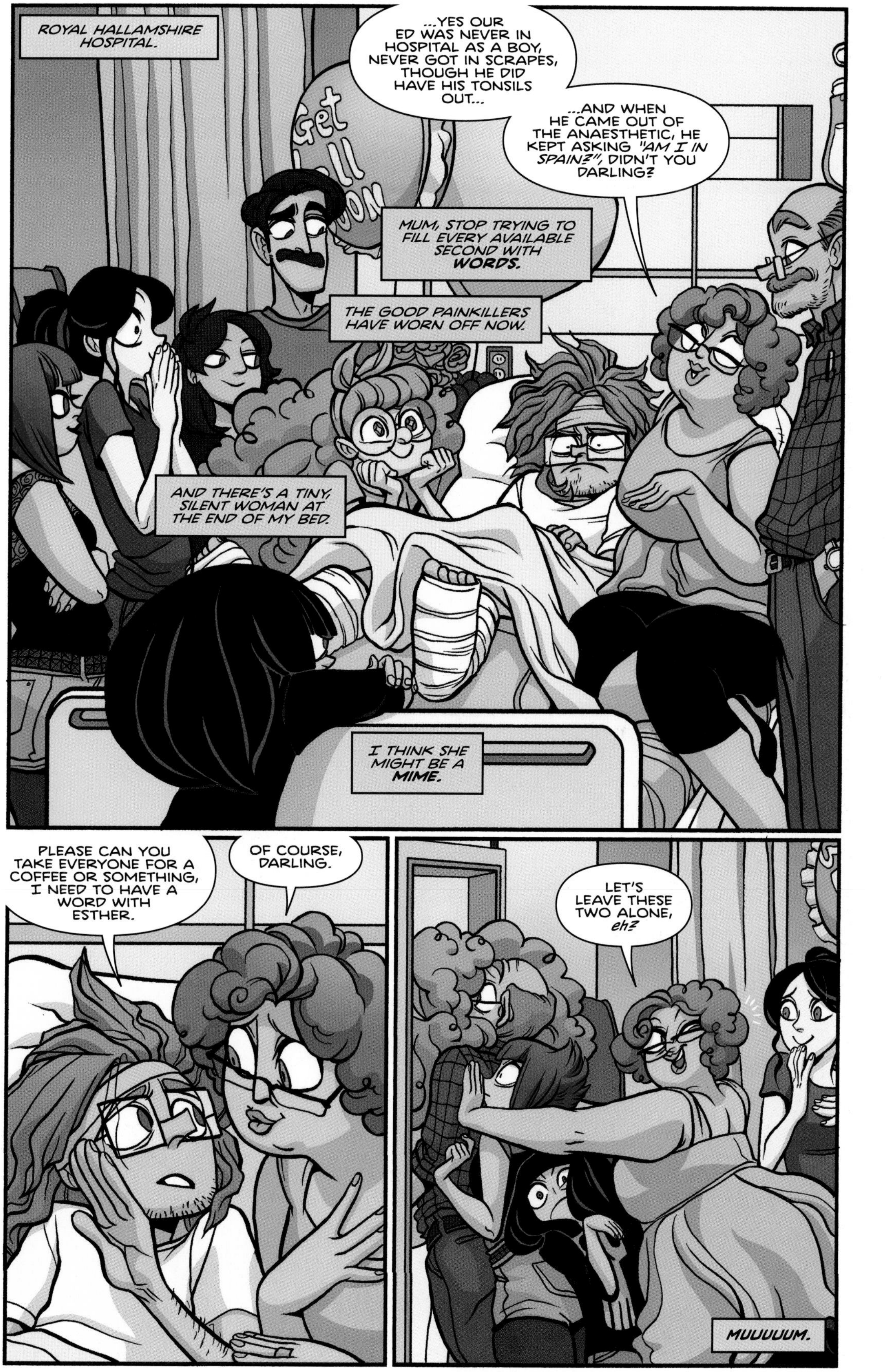
ROYAL HALLAMSHIRE HOSPITAL.
...YES OUR ED WAS NEVER IN HOSPITAL AS A BOY, NEVER GOT IN SCRAPES, THOUGH HE DID HAVE HIS TONSILS OUT...
...AND WHEN HE CAME OUT OF THE ANAESTHETIC, HE KEPT ASKING "AM I IN SPAIN?", DIDN'T YOU DARLING?
MUM, STOP TRYING TO FILL EVERY AVAILABLE SECOND WITH WORDS.
THE GOOD PAINKILLERS HAVE WORN OFF NOW.
AND THERE'S A TINY, SILENT WOMAN AT THE END OF MY BED.
I THINK SHE MIGHT BE A MIME.
PLEASE CAN YOU TAKE EVERYONE FOR A COFFEE OR SOMETHING, I NEED TO HAVE A WORD WITH ESTHER.
OF COURSE, DARLING.
LET'S LEAVE THESE TWO ALONE, eh?
MUUUUUM.

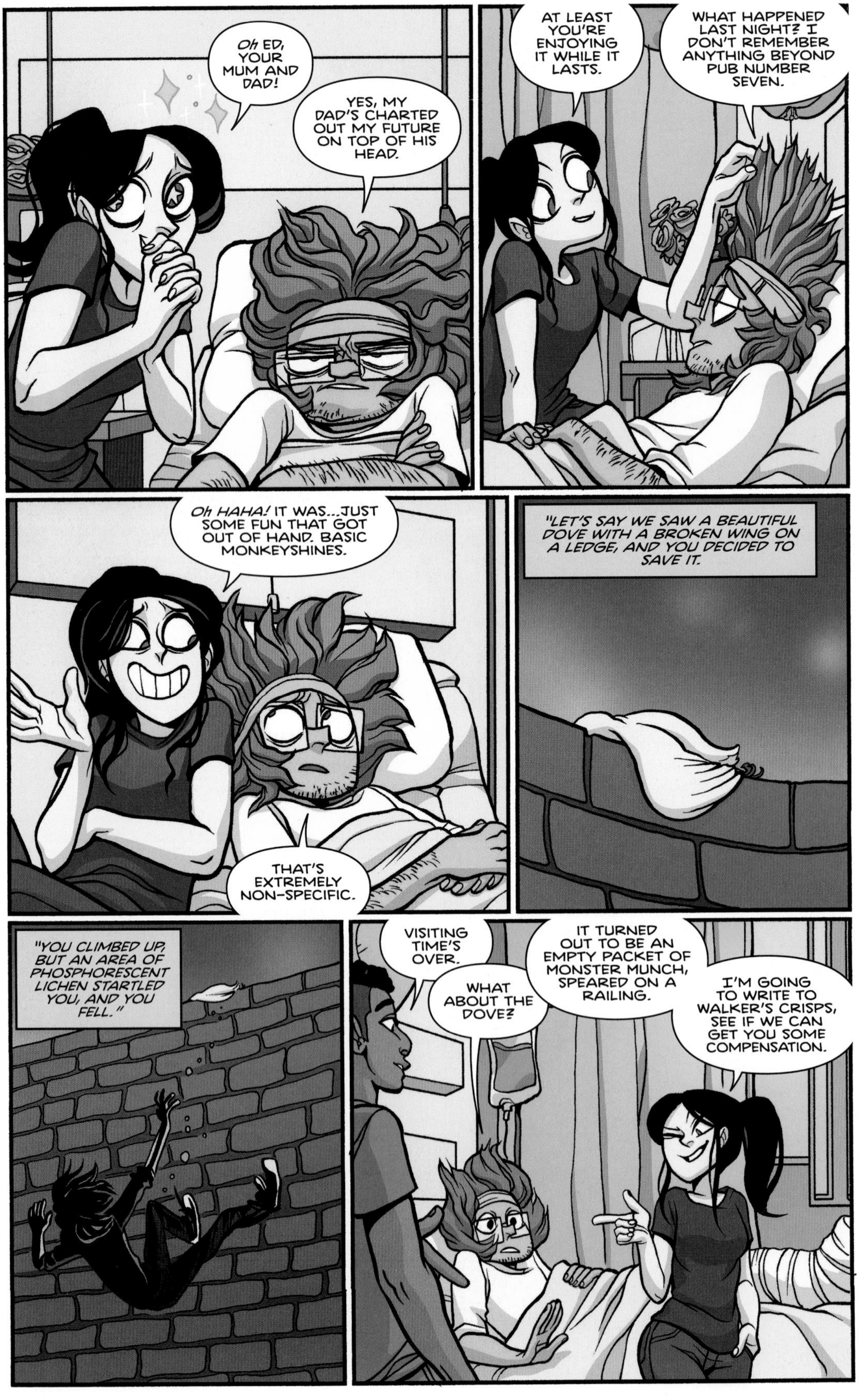

Oh ED, YOUR MUM AND DAD!
YES, MY DAD'S CHARTED OUT MY FUTURE ON TOP OF HIS HEAD.
AT LEAST YOU'RE ENJOYING IT WHILE IT LASTS.
WHAT HAPPENED LAST NIGHT? I DON'T REMEMBER ANYTHING BEYOND PUB NUMBER SEVEN.
Oh HAHA! IT WAS...JUST SOME FUN THAT GOT OUT OF HAND. BASIC MONKEYSHINES.
THAT'S EXTREMELY NON-SPECIFIC.
"LET'S SAY WE SAW A BEAUTIFUL DOVE WITH A BROKEN WING ON A LEDGE, AND YOU DECIDED TO SAVE IT.
"YOU CLIMBED UP, BUT AN AREA OF PHOSPHORESCENT LICHEN STARTLED YOU, AND YOU FELL."
VISITING TIME'S OVER.
WHAT ABOUT THE DOVE?
IT TURNED OUT TO BE AN EMPTY PACKET OF MONSTER MUNCH, SPEARED ON A RAILING.
I'M GOING TO WRITE TO WALKER'S CRISPS, SEE IF WE CAN GET YOU SOME COMPENSATION.

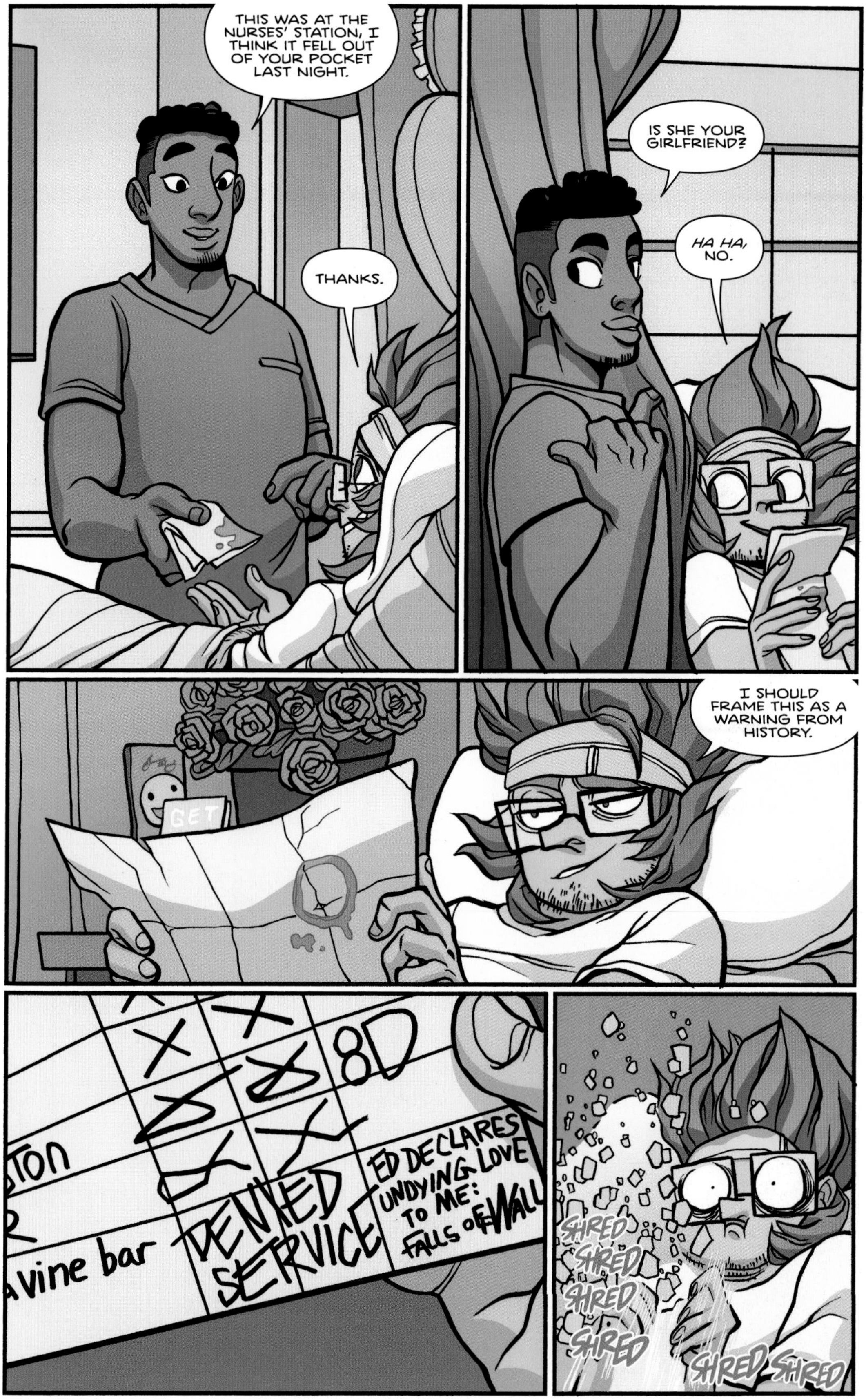
THIS WAS AT THE NURSES' STATION, I THINK IT FELL OUT OF YOUR POCKET LAST NIGHT.
THANKS.
IS SHE YOUR GIRLFRIEND?
HA HA, NO.
I SHOULD FRAME THIS AS A WARNING FROM HISTORY.
GET
8D
vine bar
DENIED SERVICE
ED DECLARES UNDYING LOVE TO ME: FALLS OFF WALL
SHRED SHRED SHRED SHRED SHRED SHRED

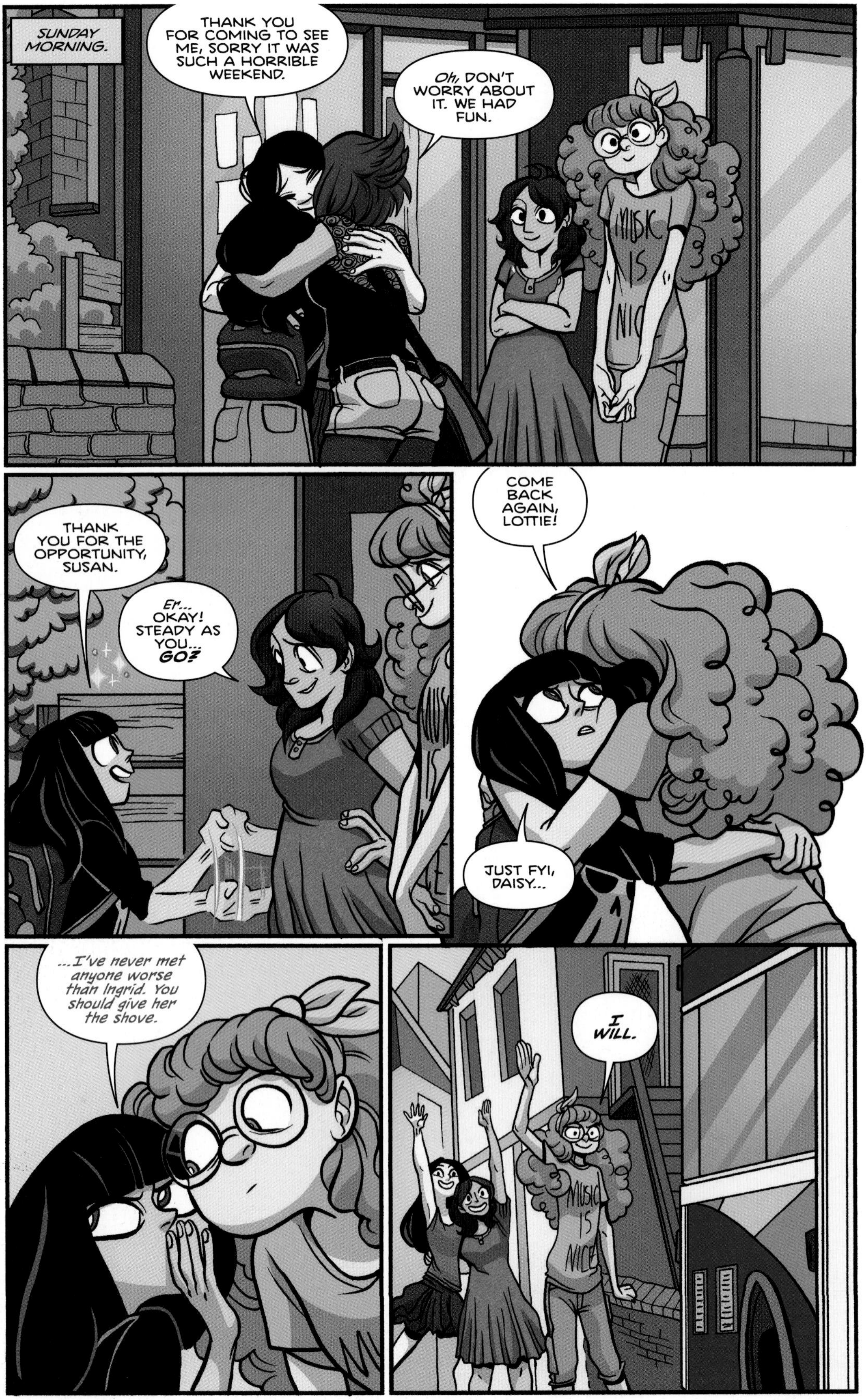
SUNDAY MORNING.
THANK YOU FOR COMING TO SEE ME, SORRY IT WAS SUCH A HORRIBLE WEEKEND.
Oh, DON'T WORRY ABOUT IT. WE HAD FUN.
MUSIC IS NIC
THANK YOU FOR THE OPPORTUNITY, SUSAN.
Er... OKAY! STEADY AS YOU... GO?
COME BACK AGAIN, LOTTIE!
JUST FYI, DAISY...
...I've never met anyone worse than Ingrid. You should give her the shove.
I WILL.
MUSIC IS NICE

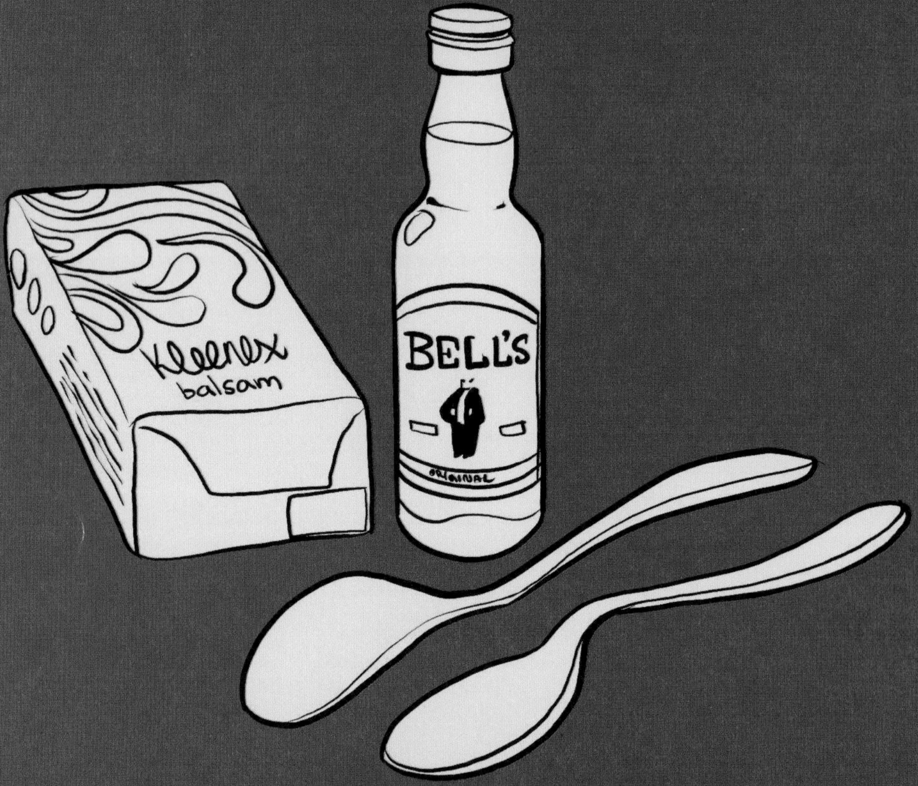
Kleenex
balsam
BELL'S
ORIGINAL

CHAPTER THIRTY-SIX

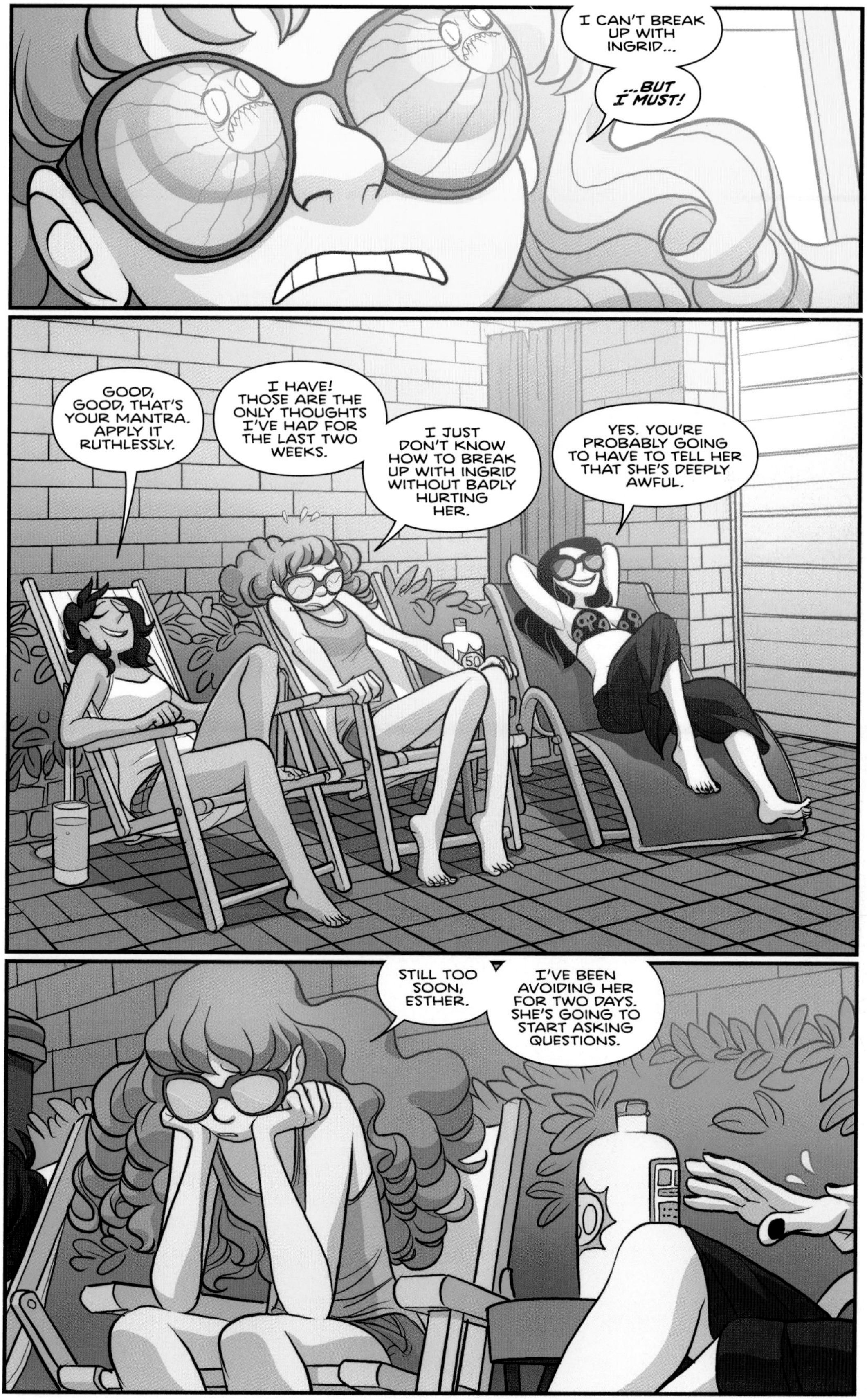
I CAN'T BREAK UP WITH INGRID...
...BUT I MUST!
GOOD, GOOD, THAT'S YOUR MANTRA. APPLY IT RUTHLESSLY.
I HAVE! THOSE ARE THE ONLY THOUGHTS I'VE HAD FOR THE LAST TWO WEEKS.
I JUST DON'T KNOW HOW TO BREAK UP WITH INGRID WITHOUT BADLY HURTING HER.
YES. YOU'RE PROBABLY GOING TO HAVE TO TELL HER THAT SHE'S DEEPLY AWFUL.
STILL TOO SOON, ESTHER.
I'VE BEEN AVOIDING HER FOR TWO DAYS. SHE'S GOING TO START ASKING QUESTIONS.

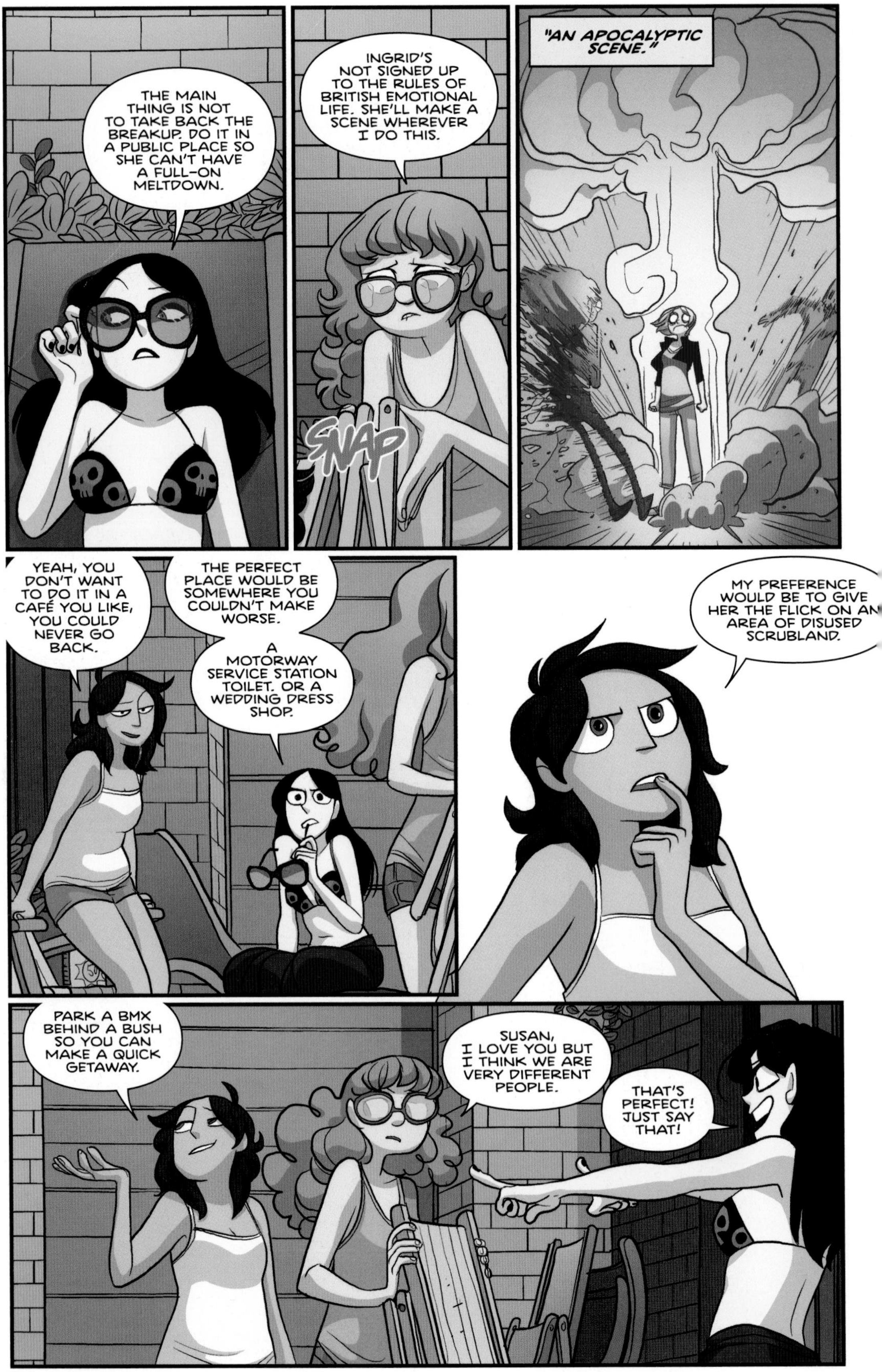
THE MAIN THING IS NOT TO TAKE BACK THE BREAKUP. DO IT IN A PUBLIC PLACE SO SHE CAN'T HAVE A FULL-ON MELTDOWN.
INGRID'S NOT SIGNED UP TO THE RULES OF BRITISH EMOTIONAL LIFE. SHE'LL MAKE A SCENE WHEREVER I DO THIS.
SNAP
"AN APOCALYPTIC SCENE."
YEAH, YOU DON'T WANT TO DO IT IN A CAFÉ YOU LIKE, YOU COULD NEVER GO BACK.
THE PERFECT PLACE WOULD BE SOMEWHERE YOU COULDN'T MAKE WORSE.
A MOTORWAY SERVICE STATION TOILET. OR A WEDDING DRESS SHOP.
MY PREFERENCE WOULD BE TO GIVE HER THE FLICK ON AN AREA OF DISUSED SCRUBLAND.
PARK A BMX BEHIND A BUSH SO YOU CAN MAKE A QUICK GETAWAY.
SUSAN, I LOVE YOU BUT I THINK WE ARE VERY DIFFERENT PEOPLE.
THAT'S PERFECT! JUST SAY THAT!

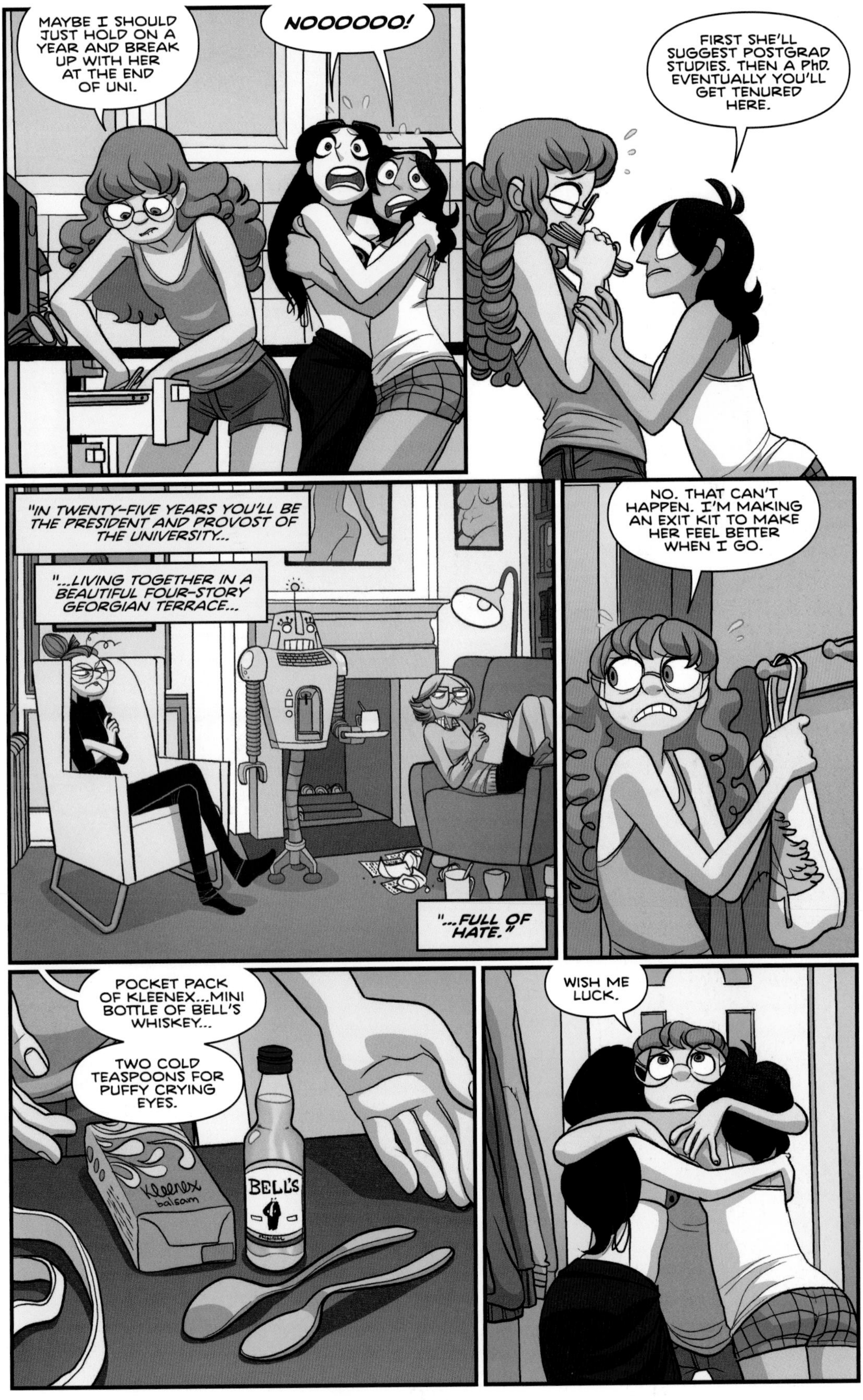
MAYBE I SHOULD JUST HOLD ON A YEAR AND BREAK UP WITH HER AT THE END OF UNI.
NOOOOOO!
FIRST SHE'LL SUGGEST POSTGRAD STUDIES. THEN A PhD. EVENTUALLY YOU'LL GET TENURED HERE.
"IN TWENTY-FIVE YEARS YOU'LL BE THE PRESIDENT AND PROVOST OF THE UNIVERSITY...
"...LIVING TOGETHER IN A BEAUTIFUL FOUR-STORY GEORGIAN TERRACE...
"...FULL OF HATE."
NO. THAT CAN'T HAPPEN. I'M MAKING AN EXIT KIT TO MAKE HER FEEL BETTER WHEN I GO.
POCKET PACK OF KLEENEX...MINI BOTTLE OF BELL'S WHISKEY...
TWO COLD TEASPOONS FOR PUFFY CRYING EYES.
Kleenex
balsam
BELL'S
WISH ME LUCK.

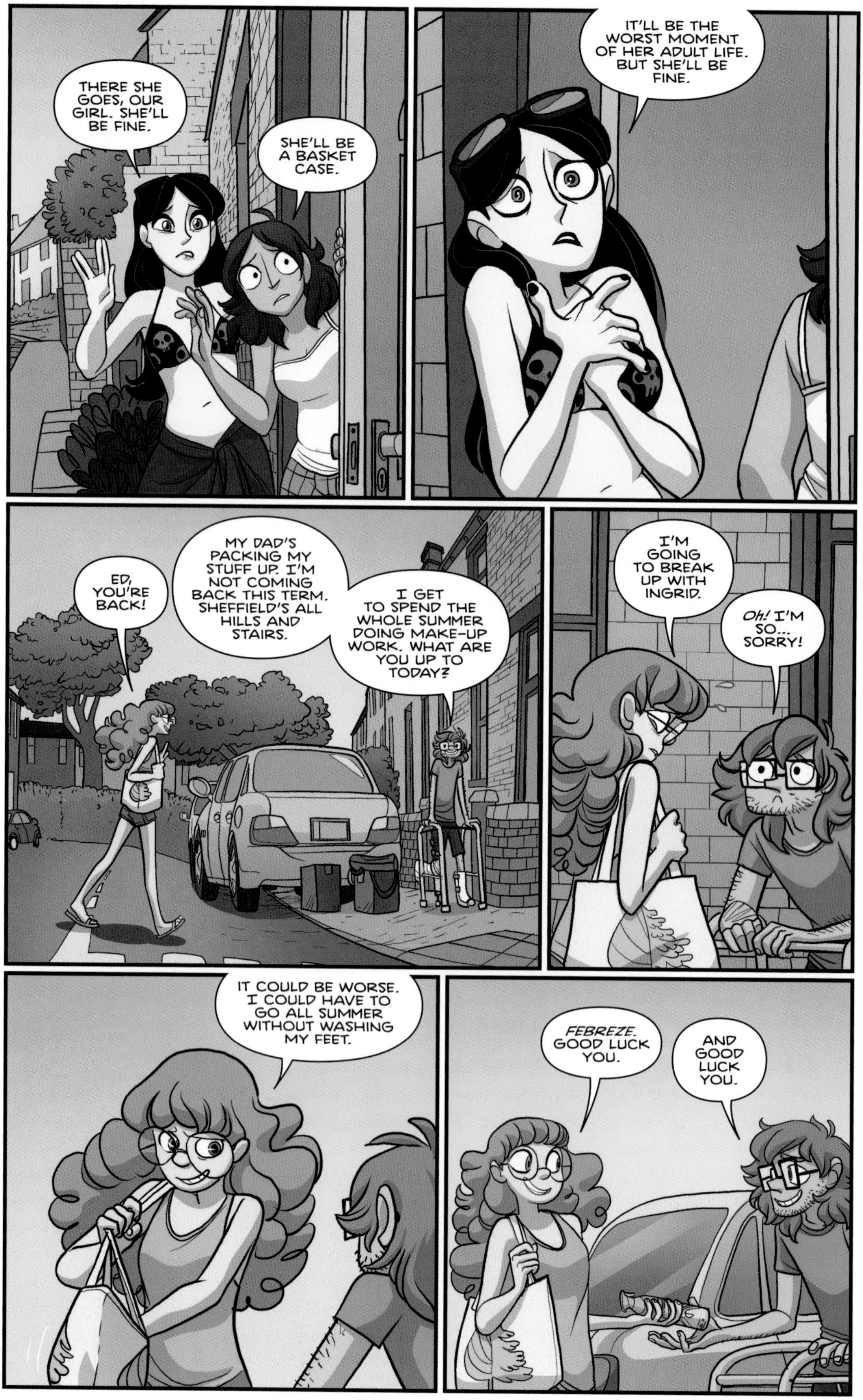
THERE SHE GOES, OUR GIRL. SHE'LL BE FINE.
SHE'LL BE A BASKET CASE.
IT'LL BE THE WORST MOMENT OF HER ADULT LIFE. BUT SHE'LL BE FINE.
ED, YOU'RE BACK!
MY DAD'S PACKING MY STUFF UP. I'M NOT COMING BACK THIS TERM. SHEFFIELD'S ALL HILLS AND STAIRS.
I GET TO SPEND THE WHOLE SUMMER DOING MAKE-UP WORK. WHAT ARE YOU UP TO TODAY?
I'M GOING TO BREAK UP WITH INGRID.
Oh! I'M SO... SORRY!
IT COULD BE WORSE. I COULD HAVE TO GO ALL SUMMER WITHOUT WASHING MY FEET.
FEBREZE. GOOD LUCK YOU.
AND GOOD LUCK YOU.

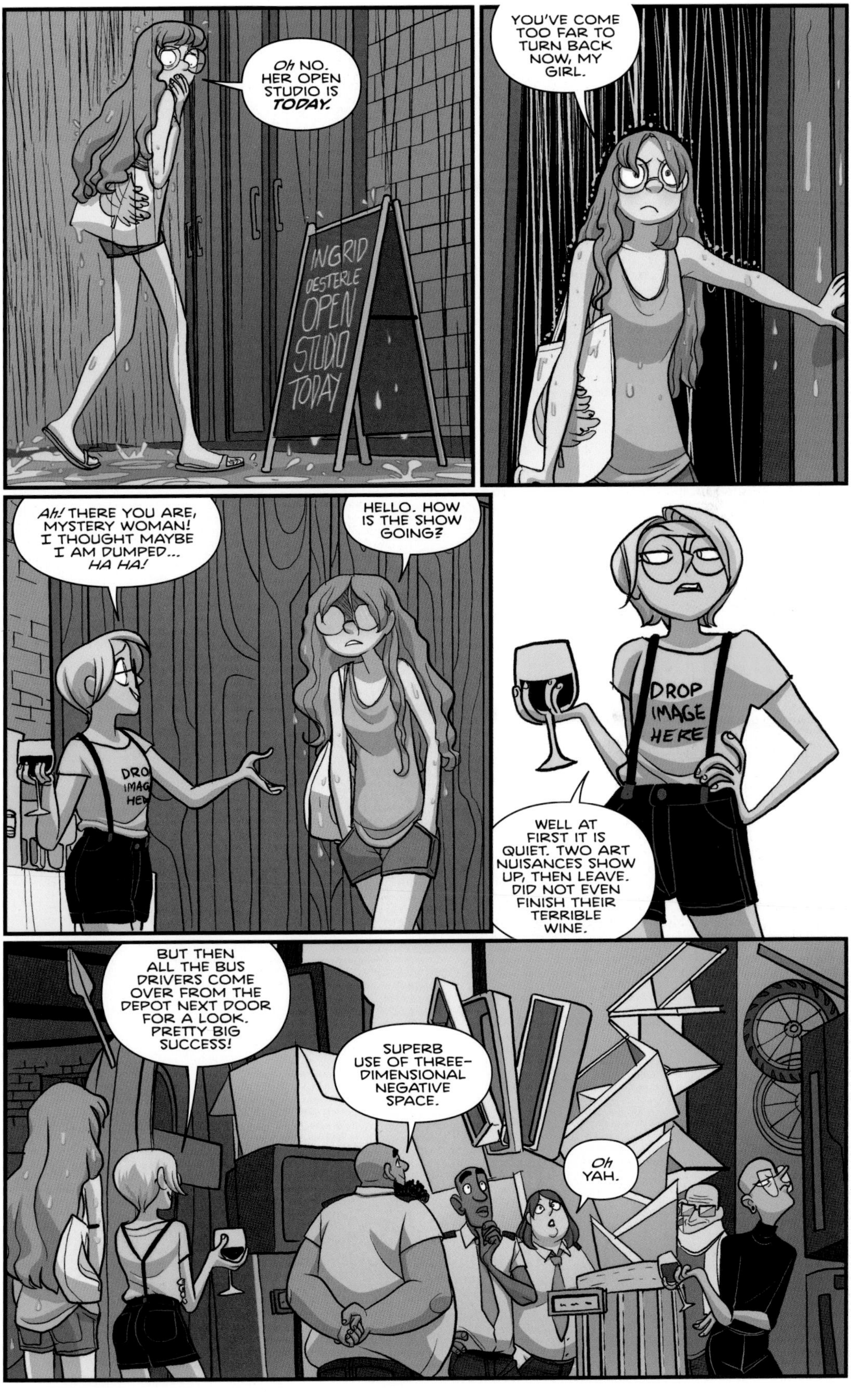

Oh NO. HER OPEN STUDIO IS ***TODAY.***
INGRID OESTERLE OPEN STUDIO TODAY
YOU'VE COME TOO FAR TO TURN BACK NOW, MY GIRL.
Ah! THERE YOU ARE, MYSTERY WOMAN! I THOUGHT MAYBE I AM DUMPED... *HA HA!*
HELLO. HOW IS THE SHOW GOING?
DROP IMAGE HERE
WELL AT FIRST IT IS QUIET. TWO ART NUISANCES SHOW UP, THEN LEAVE. DID NOT EVEN FINISH THEIR TERRIBLE WINE.
BUT THEN ALL THE BUS DRIVERS COME OVER FROM THE DEPOT NEXT DOOR FOR A LOOK. PRETTY BIG SUCCESS!
SUPERB USE OF THREE-DIMENSIONAL NEGATIVE SPACE.
Oh YAH.

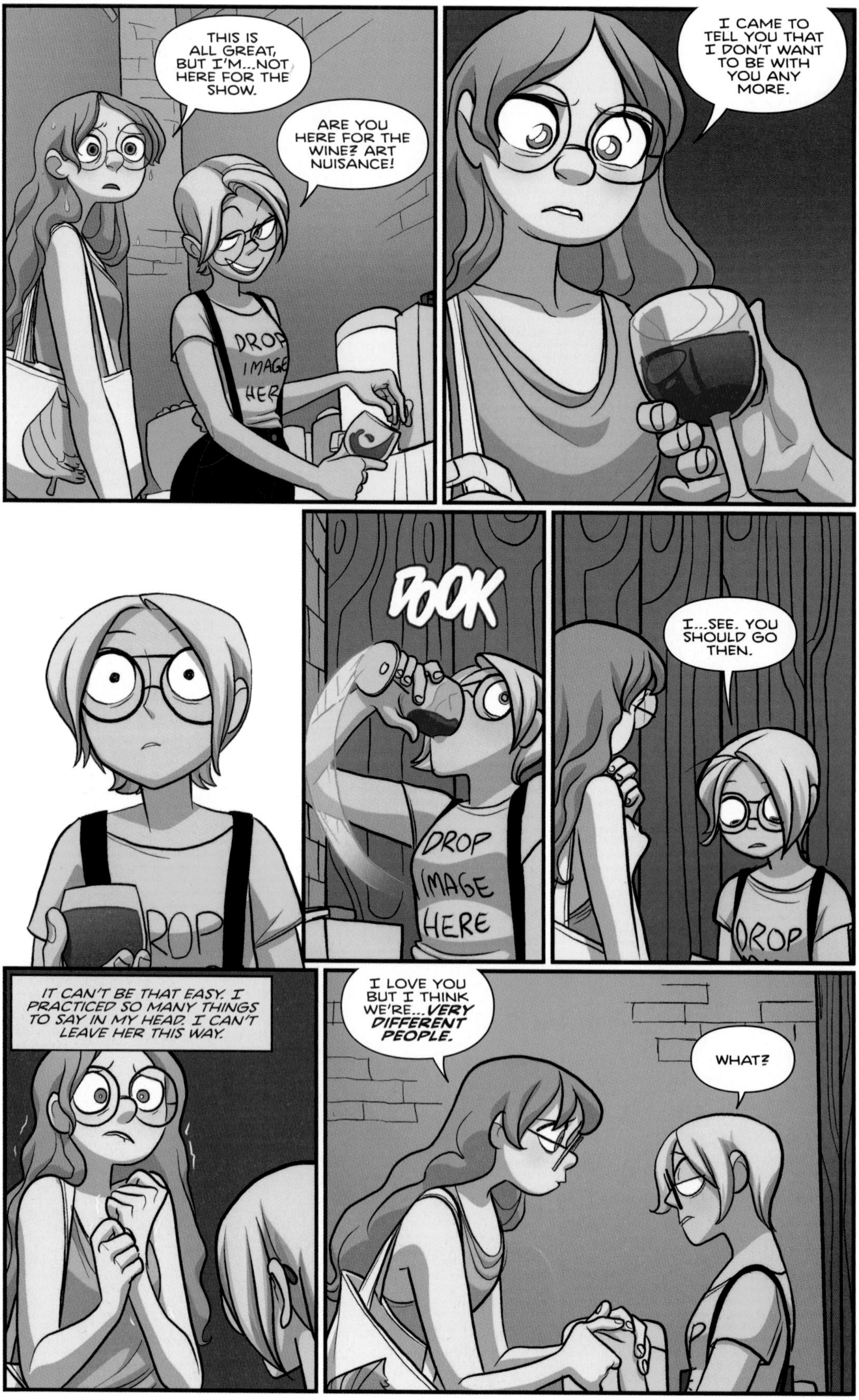
THIS IS ALL GREAT, BUT I'M...NOT HERE FOR THE SHOW.
ARE YOU HERE FOR THE WINE? ART NUISANCE!
DROP IMAGE HERE
I CAME TO TELL YOU THAT I DON'T WANT TO BE WITH YOU ANY MORE.
DOOK
DROP IMAGE HERE
I...SEE. YOU SHOULD GO THEN.
IT CAN'T BE THAT EASY. I PRACTICED SO MANY THINGS TO SAY IN MY HEAD. I CAN'T LEAVE HER THIS WAY.
I LOVE YOU BUT I THINK WE'RE...VERY DIFFERENT PEOPLE.
WHAT?

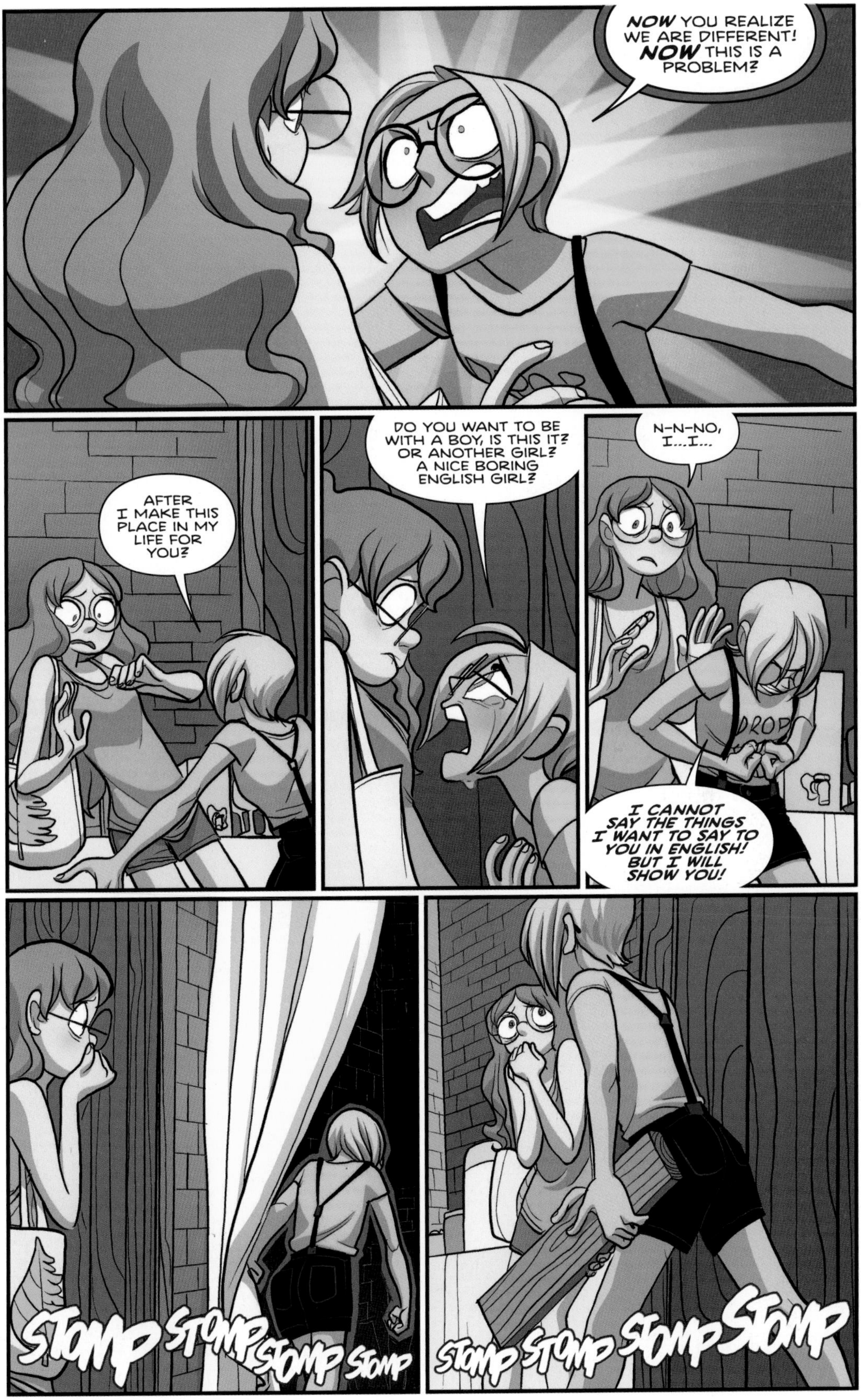

NOW YOU REALIZE WE ARE DIFFERENT! **NOW** THIS IS A PROBLEM?
AFTER I MAKE THIS PLACE IN MY LIFE FOR YOU?
DO YOU WANT TO BE WITH A BOY, IS THIS IT? OR ANOTHER GIRL? A NICE BORING ENGLISH GIRL?
N-N-NO, I...I...
I CANNOT SAY THE THINGS I WANT TO SAY TO YOU IN ENGLISH! BUT I WILL SHOW YOU!
STOMP STOMP STOMP STOMP
STOMP STOMP STOMP STOMP

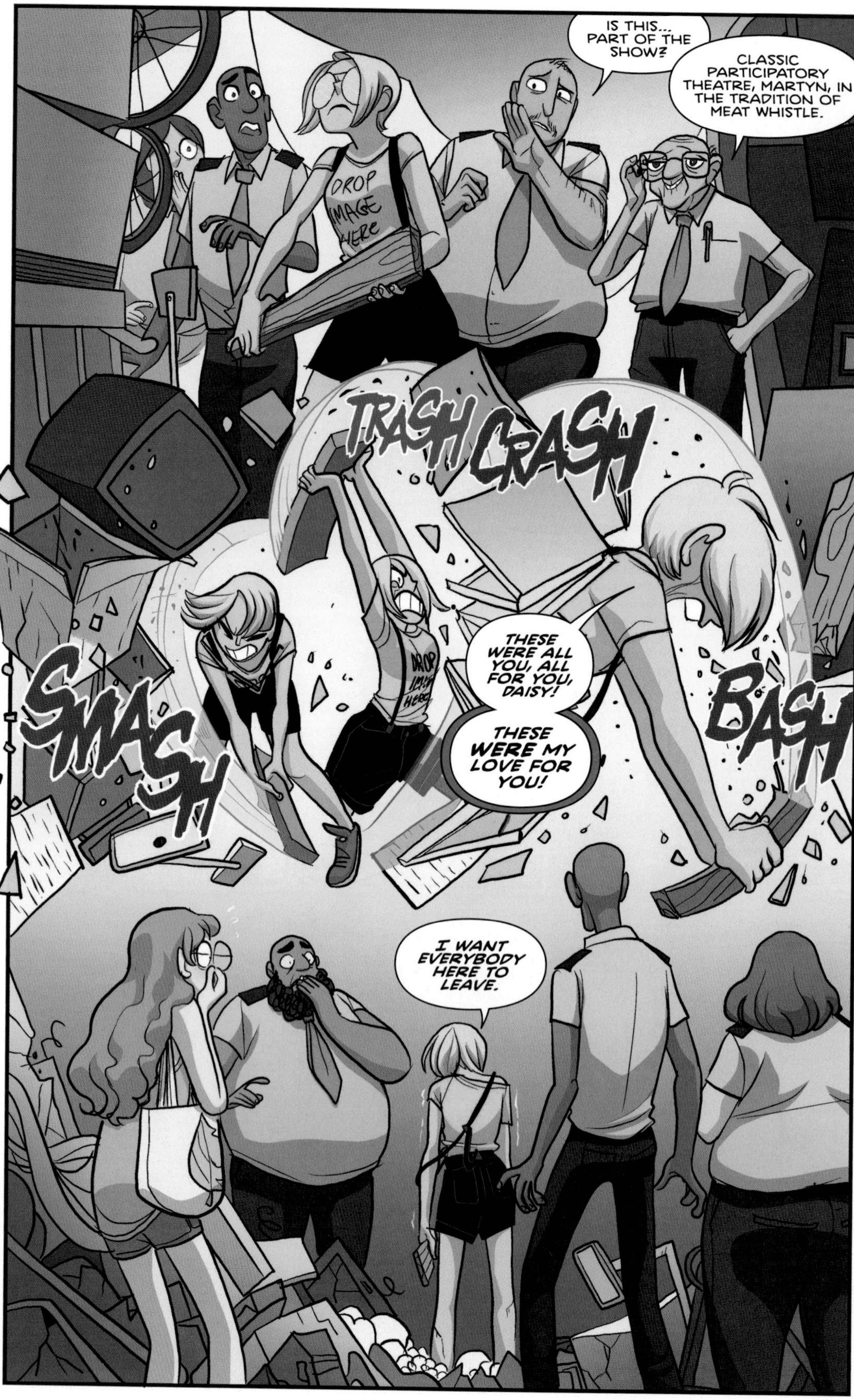
IS THIS... PART OF THE SHOW?
CLASSIC PARTICIPATORY THEATRE, MARTYN, IN THE TRADITION OF MEAT WHISTLE.
DROP IMAGE HERE
TRASH
CRASH
SMASH
THESE WERE ALL YOU, ALL FOR YOU, DAISY!
THESE WERE MY LOVE FOR YOU!
BASH
I WANT EVERYBODY HERE TO LEAVE.

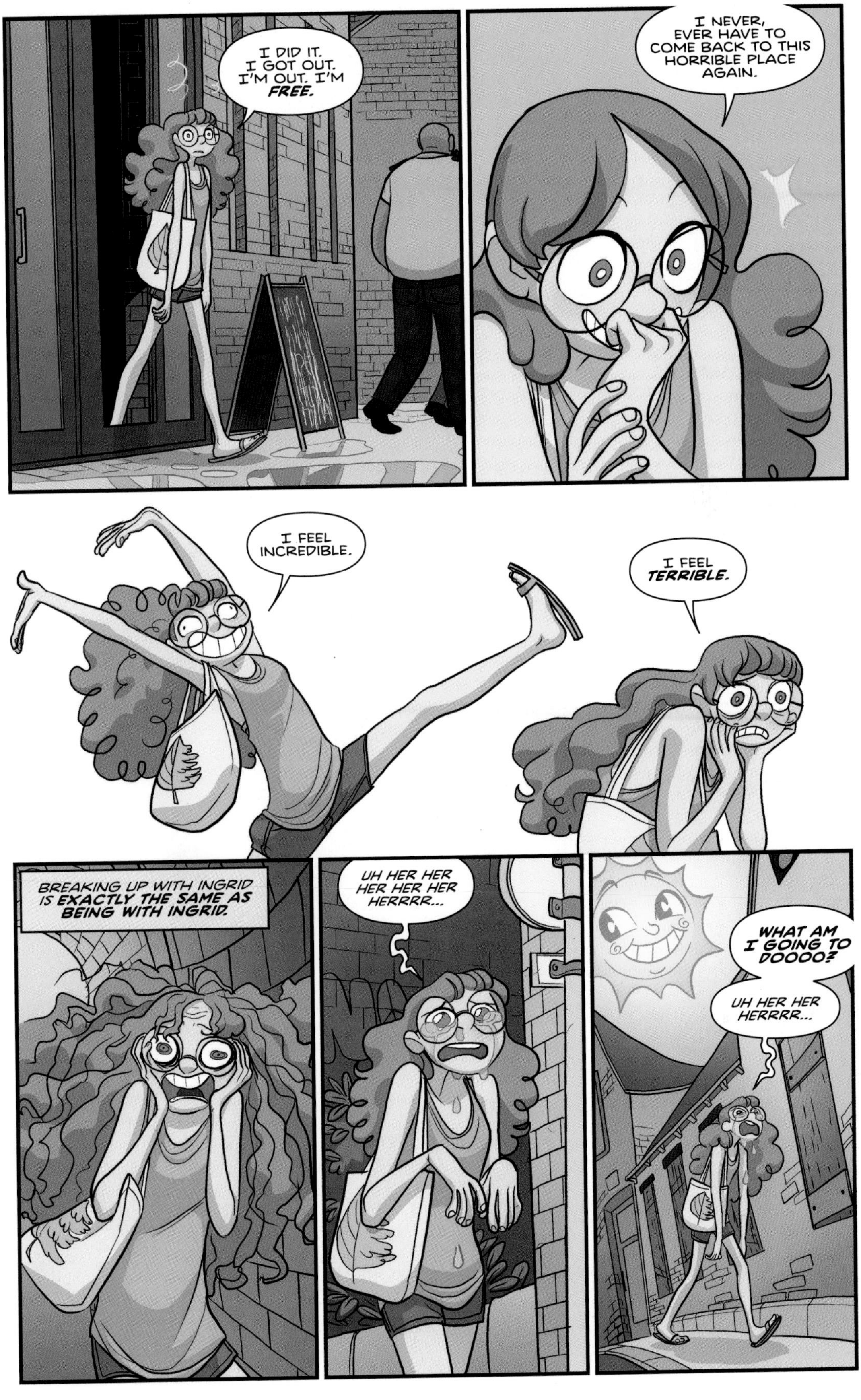
I DID IT. I GOT OUT. I'M OUT. I'M FREE.
I NEVER, EVER HAVE TO COME BACK TO THIS HORRIBLE PLACE AGAIN.
I FEEL INCREDIBLE.
I FEEL TERRIBLE.
BREAKING UP WITH INGRID IS EXACTLY THE SAME AS BEING WITH INGRID.
UH HER HER HER HER HER HERRRR...
WHAT AM I GOING TO DOOOO?
UH HER HER HERRRR...

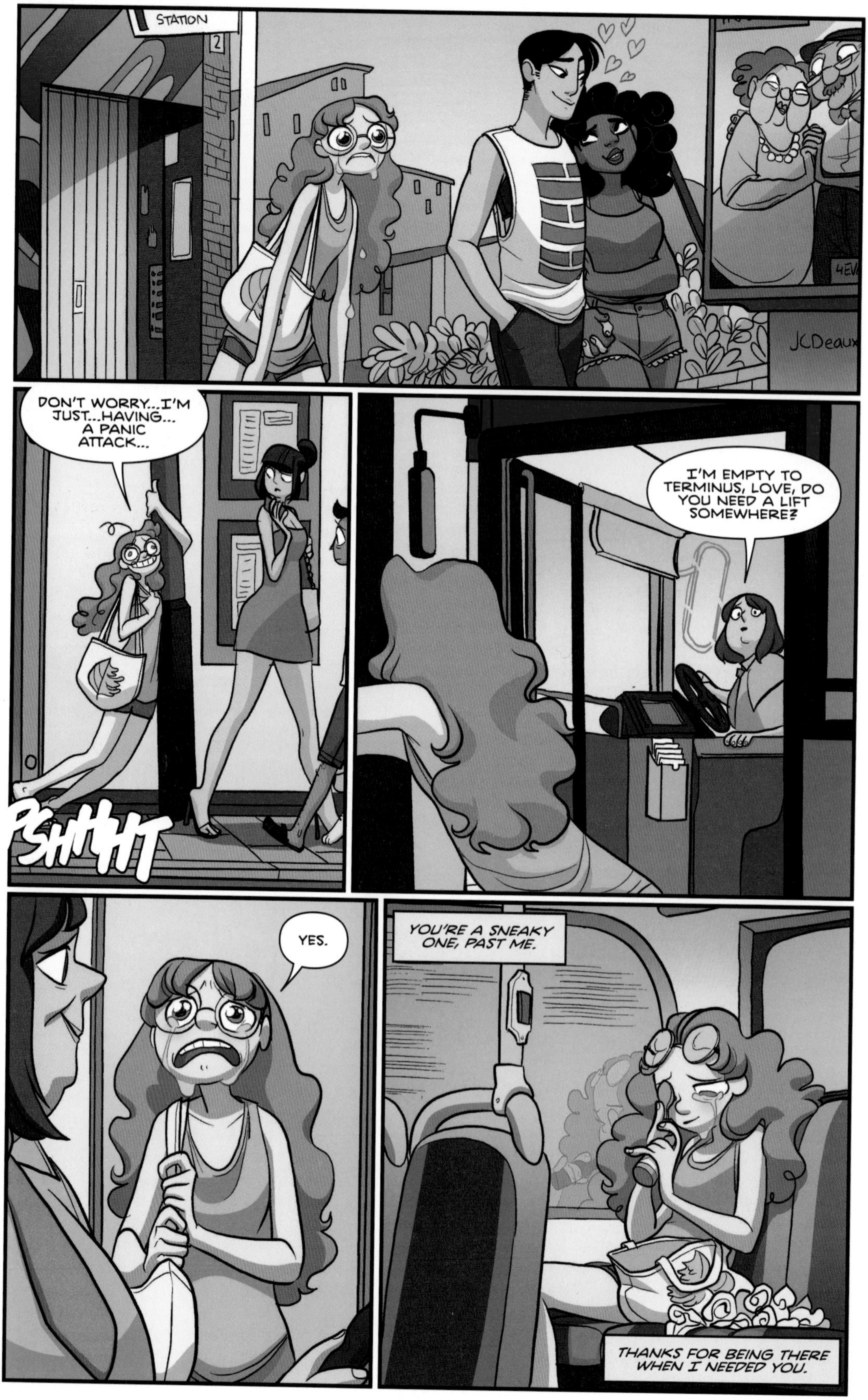
STATION
JCDeaux
DON'T WORRY...I'M JUST...HAVING... A PANIC ATTACK...
PSHHHT
I'M EMPTY TO TERMINUS, LOVE, DO YOU NEED A LIFT SOMEWHERE?
YES.
YOU'RE A SNEAKY ONE, PAST ME.
THANKS FOR BEING THERE WHEN I NEEDED YOU.

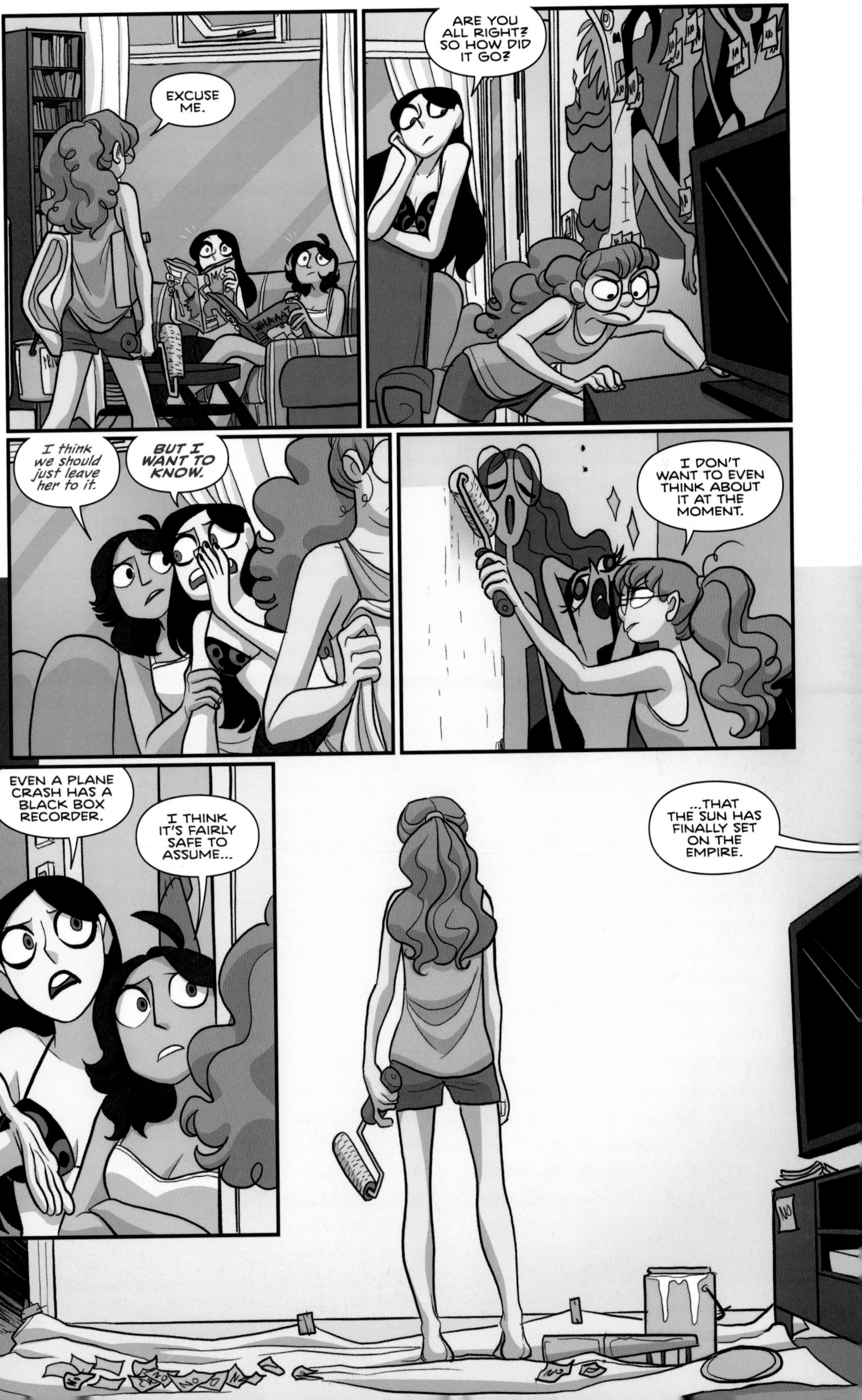
EXCUSE ME.
WHAAAT
ARE YOU ALL RIGHT? SO HOW DID IT GO?
NO
I think we should just leave her to it.
BUT I WANT TO KNOW.
I DON'T WANT TO EVEN THINK ABOUT IT AT THE MOMENT.
EVEN A PLANE CRASH HAS A BLACK BOX RECORDER.
I THINK IT'S FAIRLY SAFE TO ASSUME...
...THAT THE SUN HAS FINALLY SET ON THE EMPIRE.
NO

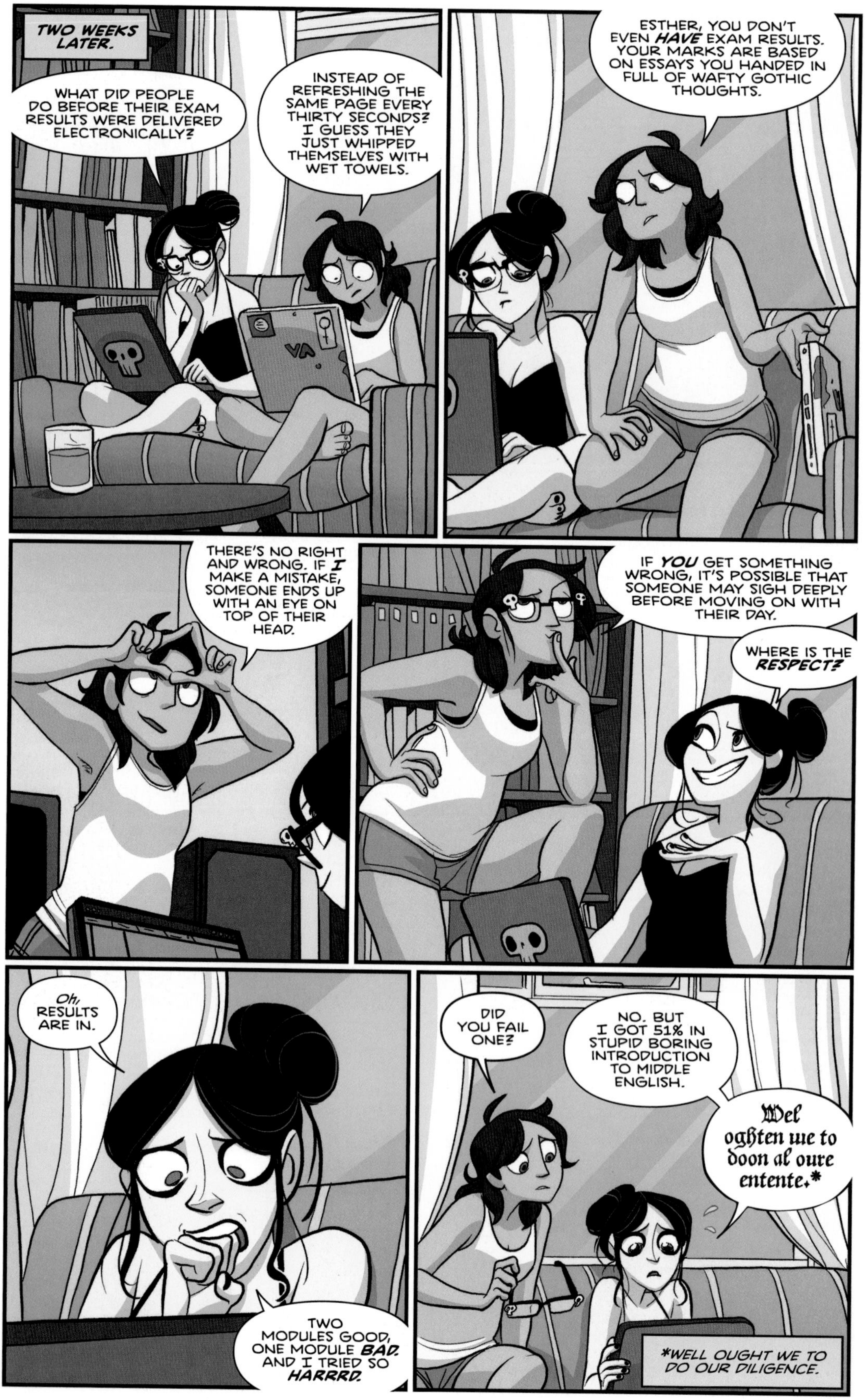
TWO WEEKS LATER.
WHAT DID PEOPLE DO BEFORE THEIR EXAM RESULTS WERE DELIVERED ELECTRONICALLY?
INSTEAD OF REFRESHING THE SAME PAGE EVERY THIRTY SECONDS? I GUESS THEY JUST WHIPPED THEMSELVES WITH WET TOWELS.
ESTHER, YOU DON'T EVEN HAVE EXAM RESULTS. YOUR MARKS ARE BASED ON ESSAYS YOU HANDED IN FULL OF WAFTY GOTHIC THOUGHTS.
THERE'S NO RIGHT AND WRONG. IF I MAKE A MISTAKE, SOMEONE ENDS UP WITH AN EYE ON TOP OF THEIR HEAD.
IF YOU GET SOMETHING WRONG, IT'S POSSIBLE THAT SOMEONE MAY SIGH DEEPLY BEFORE MOVING ON WITH THEIR DAY.
WHERE IS THE RESPECT?
Oh, RESULTS ARE IN.
TWO MODULES GOOD, ONE MODULE BAD. AND I TRIED SO HARRRD.
DID YOU FAIL ONE?
NO. BUT I GOT 51% IN STUPID BORING INTRODUCTION TO MIDDLE ENGLISH.
Wel oghten we to doon al oure entente.*
*WELL OUGHT WE TO DO OUR DILIGENCE.

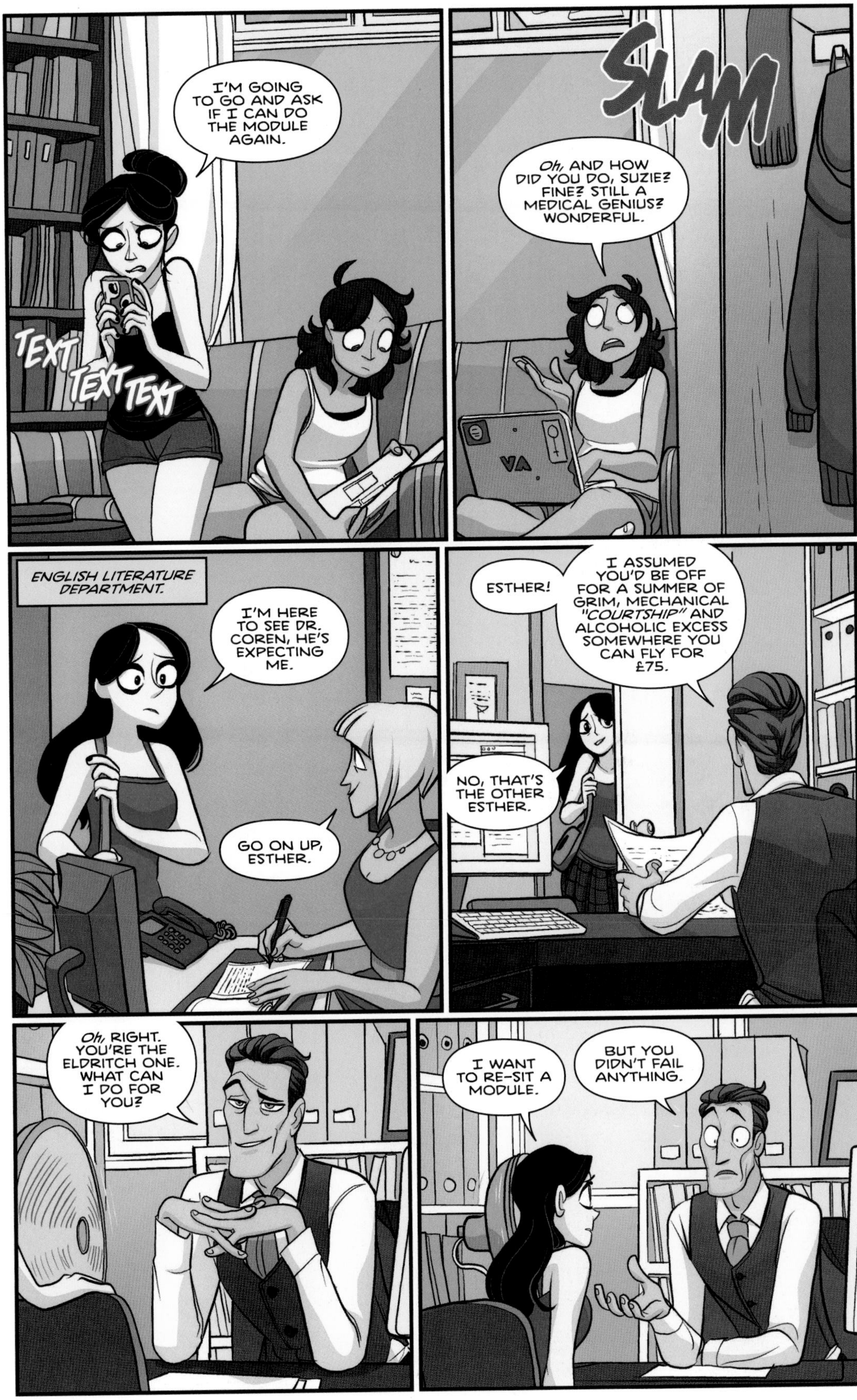
I'M GOING TO GO AND ASK IF I CAN DO THE MODULE AGAIN.
TEXT TEXT TEXT
SLAM
Oh, AND HOW DID YOU DO, SUZIE? FINE? STILL A MEDICAL GENIUS? WONDERFUL.
VA
ENGLISH LITERATURE DEPARTMENT.
I'M HERE TO SEE DR. COREN, HE'S EXPECTING ME.
GO ON UP, ESTHER.
ESTHER!
I ASSUMED YOU'D BE OFF FOR A SUMMER OF GRIM, MECHANICAL "COURTSHIP" AND ALCOHOLIC EXCESS SOMEWHERE YOU CAN FLY FOR £75.
NO, THAT'S THE OTHER ESTHER.
Oh, RIGHT. YOU'RE THE ELDRITCH ONE. WHAT CAN I DO FOR YOU?
I WANT TO RE-SIT A MODULE.
BUT YOU DIDN'T FAIL ANYTHING.

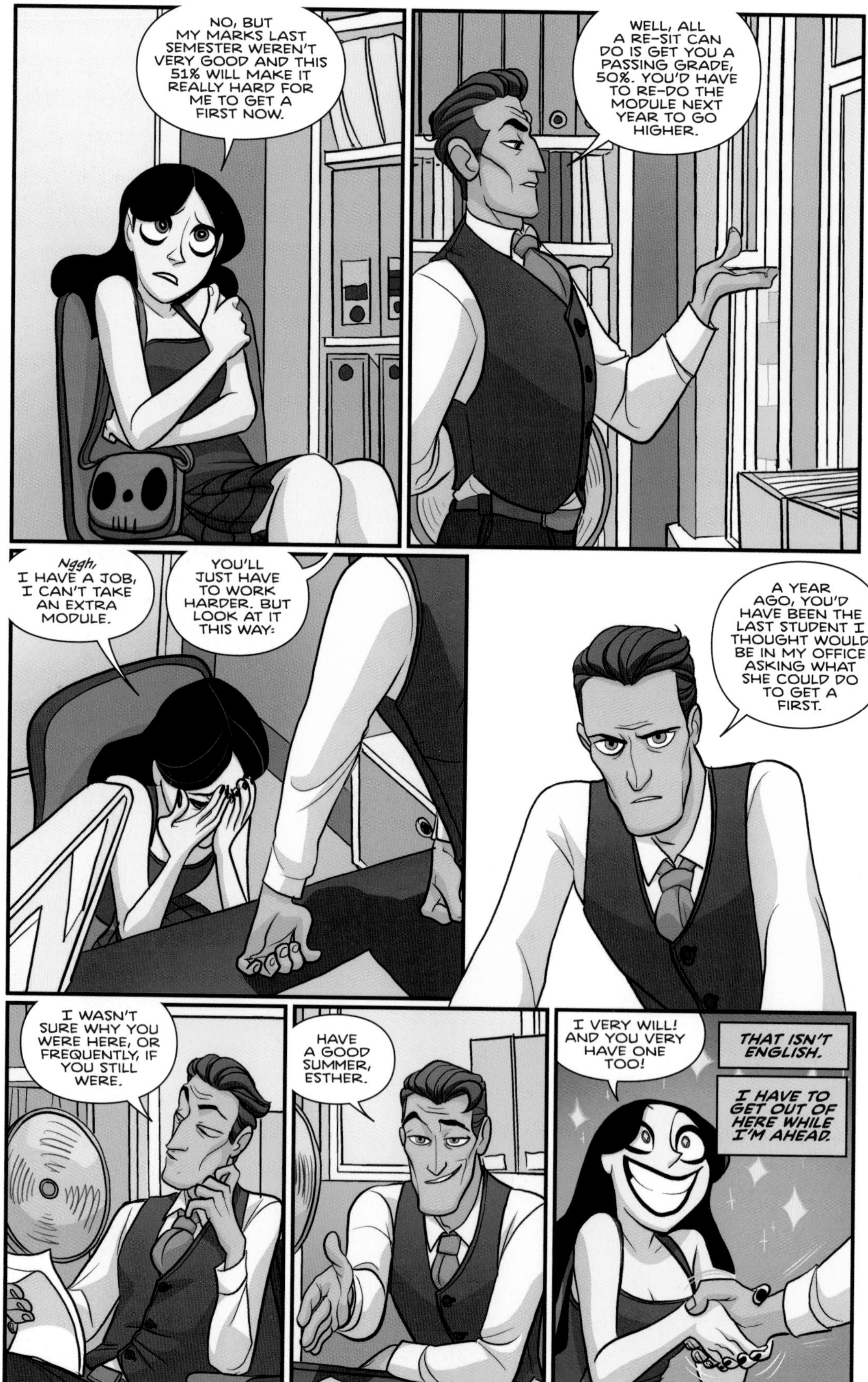
NO, BUT MY MARKS LAST SEMESTER WEREN'T VERY GOOD AND THIS 51% WILL MAKE IT REALLY HARD FOR ME TO GET A FIRST NOW.
WELL, ALL A RE-SIT CAN DO IS GET YOU A PASSING GRADE, 50%. YOU'D HAVE TO RE-DO THE MODULE NEXT YEAR TO GO HIGHER.
Nggh, I HAVE A JOB, I CAN'T TAKE AN EXTRA MODULE.
YOU'LL JUST HAVE TO WORK HARDER. BUT LOOK AT IT THIS WAY:
A YEAR AGO, YOU'D HAVE BEEN THE LAST STUDENT I THOUGHT WOULD BE IN MY OFFICE ASKING WHAT SHE COULD DO TO GET A FIRST.
I WASN'T SURE WHY YOU WERE HERE, OR FREQUENTLY, IF YOU STILL WERE.
HAVE A GOOD SUMMER, ESTHER.
I VERY WILL! AND YOU VERY HAVE ONE TOO!
THAT ISN'T ENGLISH.
I HAVE TO GET OUT OF HERE WHILE I'M AHEAD.

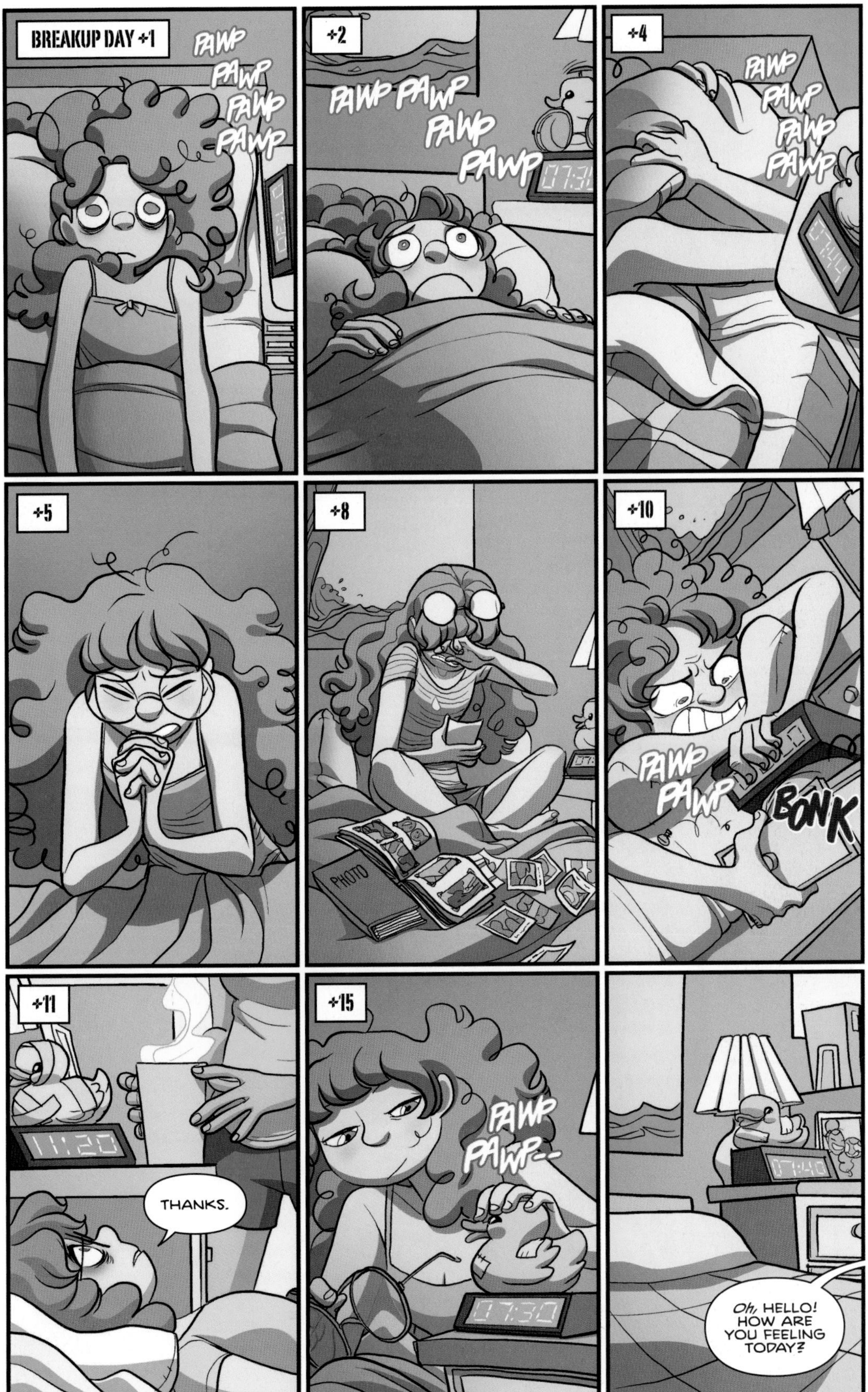
BREAKUP DAY +1
PAWP
PAWP
PAWP
PAWP
+2
PAWP PAWP
PAWP
PAWP
+4
PAWP
PAWP
PAWP
PAWP
+5
+8
PHOTO
+10
PAWP
PAWP
BONK
+11
11:20
THANKS.
+15
PAWP
PAWP-
07:30
07:40
Oh, HELLO! HOW ARE YOU FEELING TODAY?

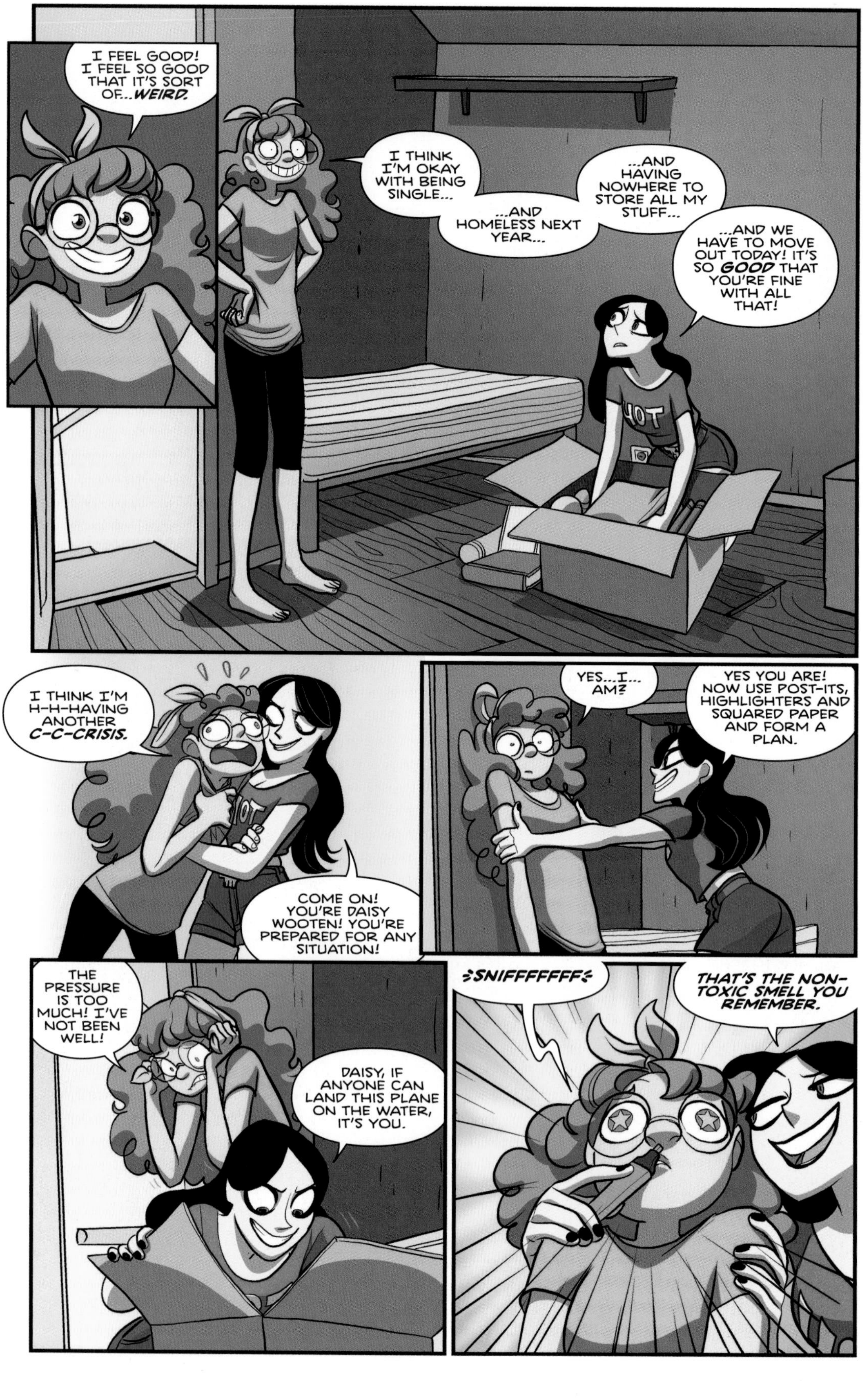
I FEEL GOOD! I FEEL SO GOOD THAT IT'S SORT OF...*WEIRD.*
I THINK I'M OKAY WITH BEING SINGLE...
...AND HOMELESS NEXT YEAR...
...AND HAVING NOWHERE TO STORE ALL MY STUFF...
...AND WE HAVE TO MOVE OUT TODAY! IT'S SO *GOOD* THAT YOU'RE FINE WITH ALL THAT!
HOT
I THINK I'M H-H-HAVING ANOTHER *C-C-CRISIS.*
COME ON! YOU'RE DAISY WOOTEN! YOU'RE PREPARED FOR ANY SITUATION!
YES...I... AM?
YES YOU ARE! NOW USE POST-ITS, HIGHLIGHTERS AND SQUARED PAPER AND FORM A PLAN.
THE PRESSURE IS TOO MUCH! I'VE NOT BEEN WELL!
DAISY, IF ANYONE CAN LAND THIS PLANE ON THE WATER, IT'S YOU.
SNIFFFFFFF
THAT'S THE NON-TOXIC SMELL YOU REMEMBER.

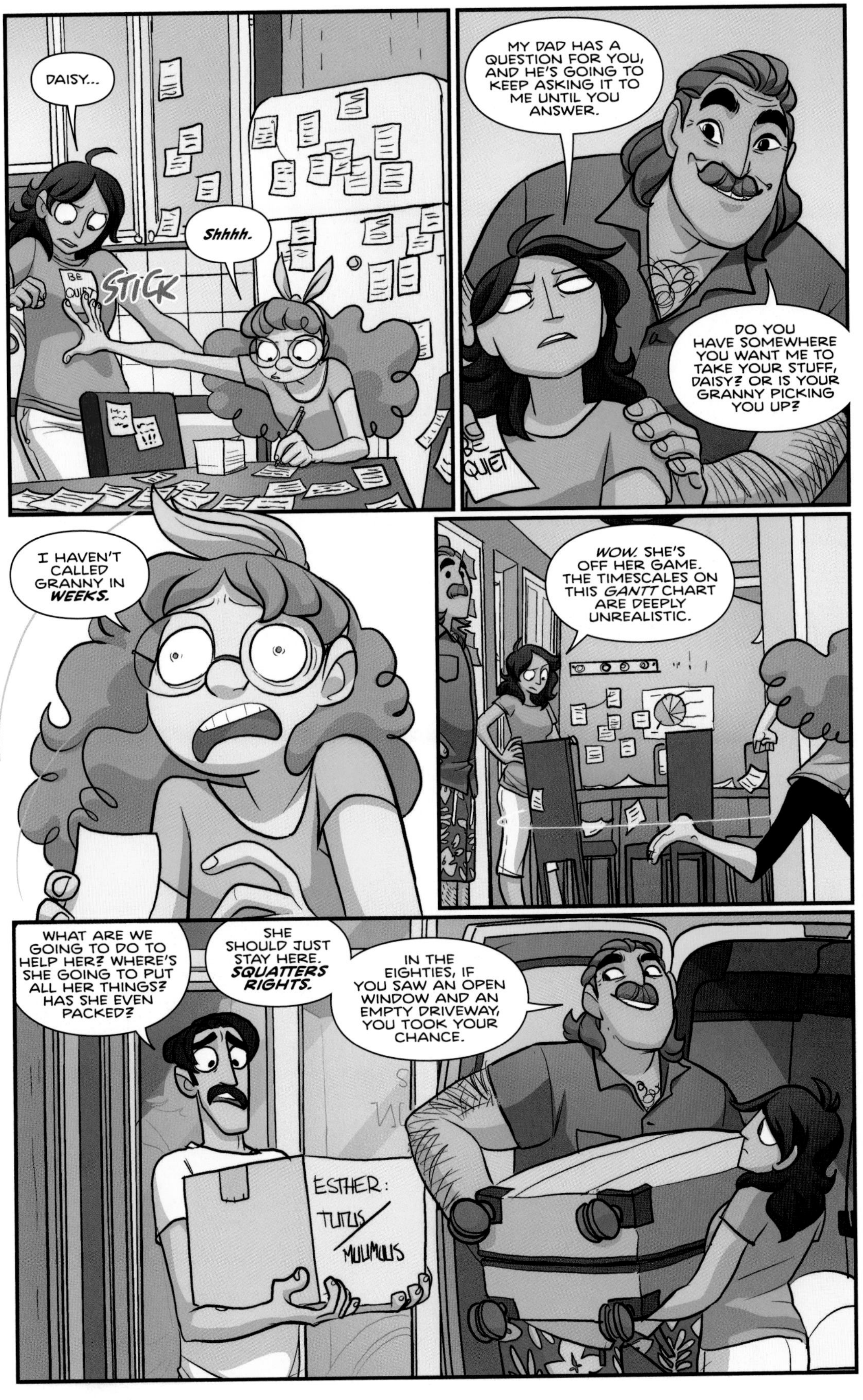

DAISY...
Shhhh.
BE QUIET
STICK
MY DAD HAS A QUESTION FOR YOU, AND HE'S GOING TO KEEP ASKING IT TO ME UNTIL YOU ANSWER.
DO YOU HAVE SOMEWHERE YOU WANT ME TO TAKE YOUR STUFF, DAISY? OR IS YOUR GRANNY PICKING YOU UP?
BE QUIET
I HAVEN'T CALLED GRANNY IN **WEEKS.**
WOW. SHE'S OFF HER GAME. THE TIMESCALES ON THIS *GANTT* CHART ARE DEEPLY UNREALISTIC.
WHAT ARE WE GOING TO DO TO HELP HER? WHERE'S SHE GOING TO PUT ALL HER THINGS? HAS SHE EVEN PACKED?
SHE SHOULD JUST STAY HERE. ***SQUATTERS RIGHTS.***
IN THE EIGHTIES, IF YOU SAW AN OPEN WINDOW AND AN EMPTY DRIVEWAY, YOU TOOK YOUR CHANCE.
ESTHER:
TUTUS
MUUMUUS

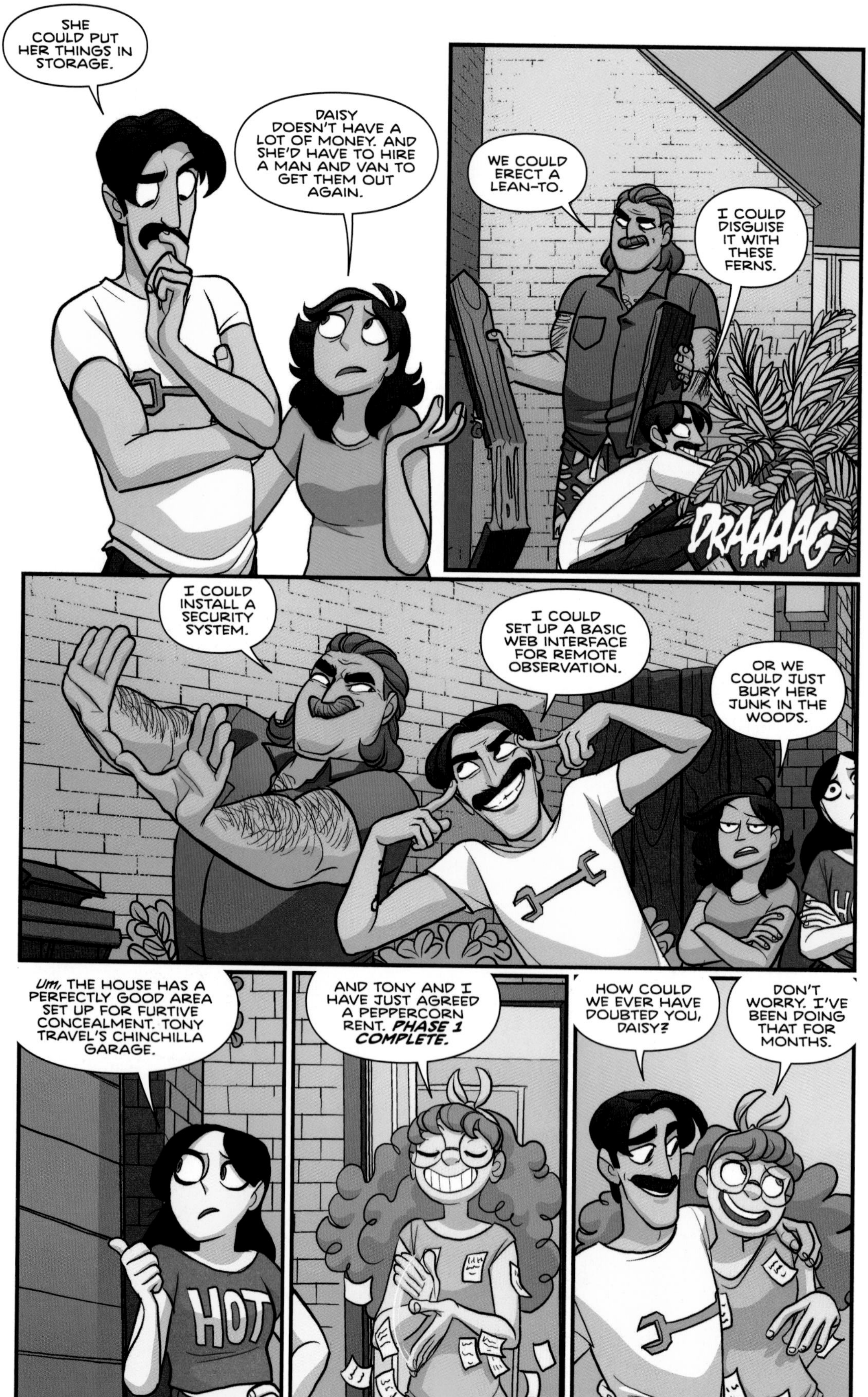
SHE COULD PUT HER THINGS IN STORAGE.
DAISY DOESN'T HAVE A LOT OF MONEY. AND SHE'D HAVE TO HIRE A MAN AND VAN TO GET THEM OUT AGAIN.
WE COULD ERECT A LEAN-TO.
I COULD DISGUISE IT WITH THESE FERNS.
DRAAAAG
I COULD INSTALL A SECURITY SYSTEM.
I COULD SET UP A BASIC WEB INTERFACE FOR REMOTE OBSERVATION.
OR WE COULD JUST BURY HER JUNK IN THE WOODS.
Um, THE HOUSE HAS A PERFECTLY GOOD AREA SET UP FOR FURTIVE CONCEALMENT. TONY TRAVEL'S CHINCHILLA GARAGE.
AND TONY AND I HAVE JUST AGREED A PEPPERCORN RENT. ***PHASE 1 COMPLETE.***
HOW COULD WE EVER HAVE DOUBTED YOU, DAISY?
DON'T WORRY. I'VE BEEN DOING THAT FOR MONTHS.

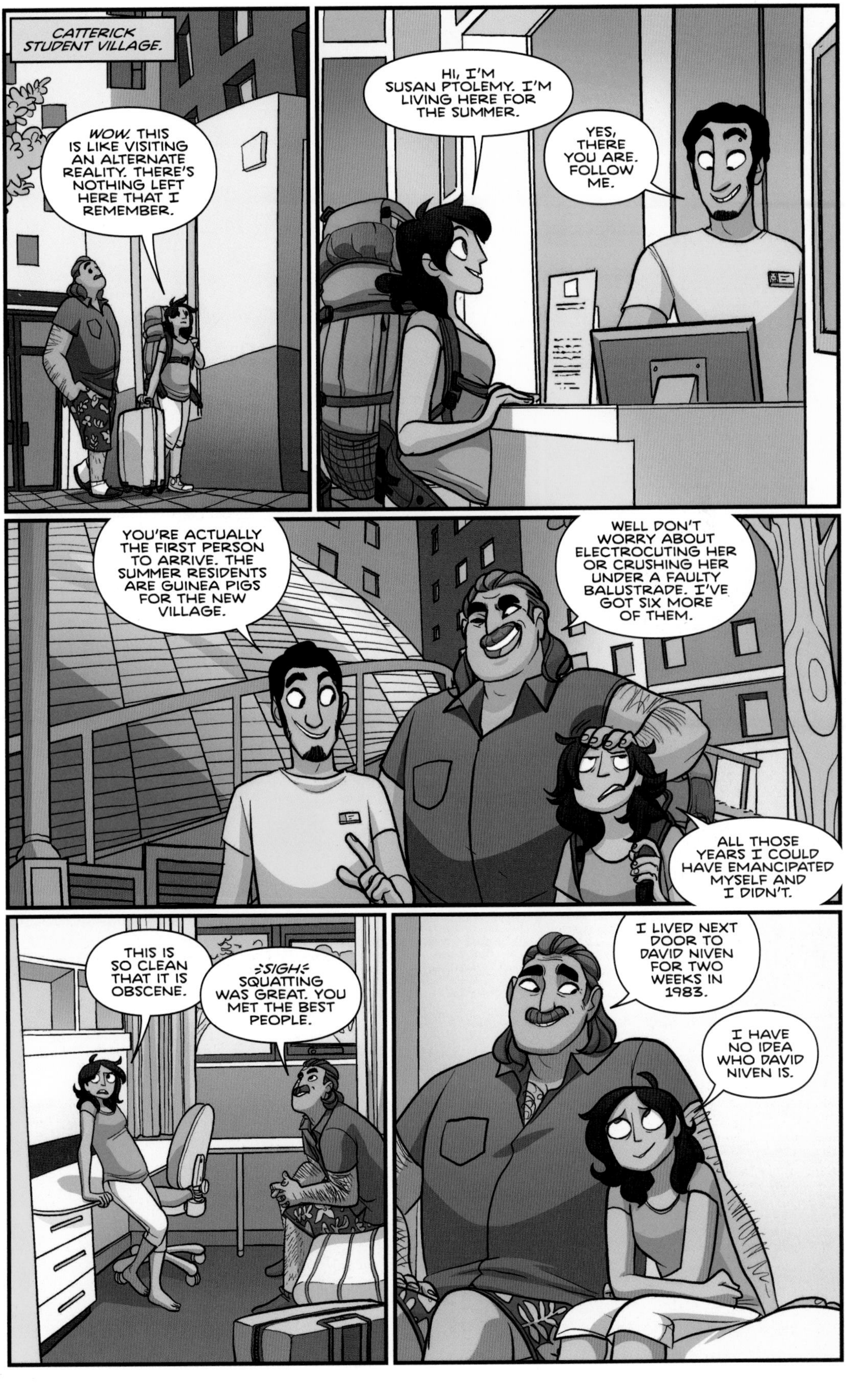
CATTERICK STUDENT VILLAGE.
WOW. THIS IS LIKE VISITING AN ALTERNATE REALITY. THERE'S NOTHING LEFT HERE THAT I REMEMBER.
HI, I'M SUSAN PTOLEMY. I'M LIVING HERE FOR THE SUMMER.
YES, THERE YOU ARE. FOLLOW ME.
YOU'RE ACTUALLY THE FIRST PERSON TO ARRIVE. THE SUMMER RESIDENTS ARE GUINEA PIGS FOR THE NEW VILLAGE.
WELL DON'T WORRY ABOUT ELECTROCUTING HER OR CRUSHING HER UNDER A FAULTY BALUSTRADE. I'VE GOT SIX MORE OF THEM.
ALL THOSE YEARS I COULD HAVE EMANCIPATED MYSELF AND I DIDN'T.
THIS IS SO CLEAN THAT IT IS OBSCENE.
SIGH
SQUATTING WAS GREAT. YOU MET THE BEST PEOPLE.
I LIVED NEXT DOOR TO DAVID NIVEN FOR TWO WEEKS IN 1983.
I HAVE NO IDEA WHO DAVID NIVEN IS.

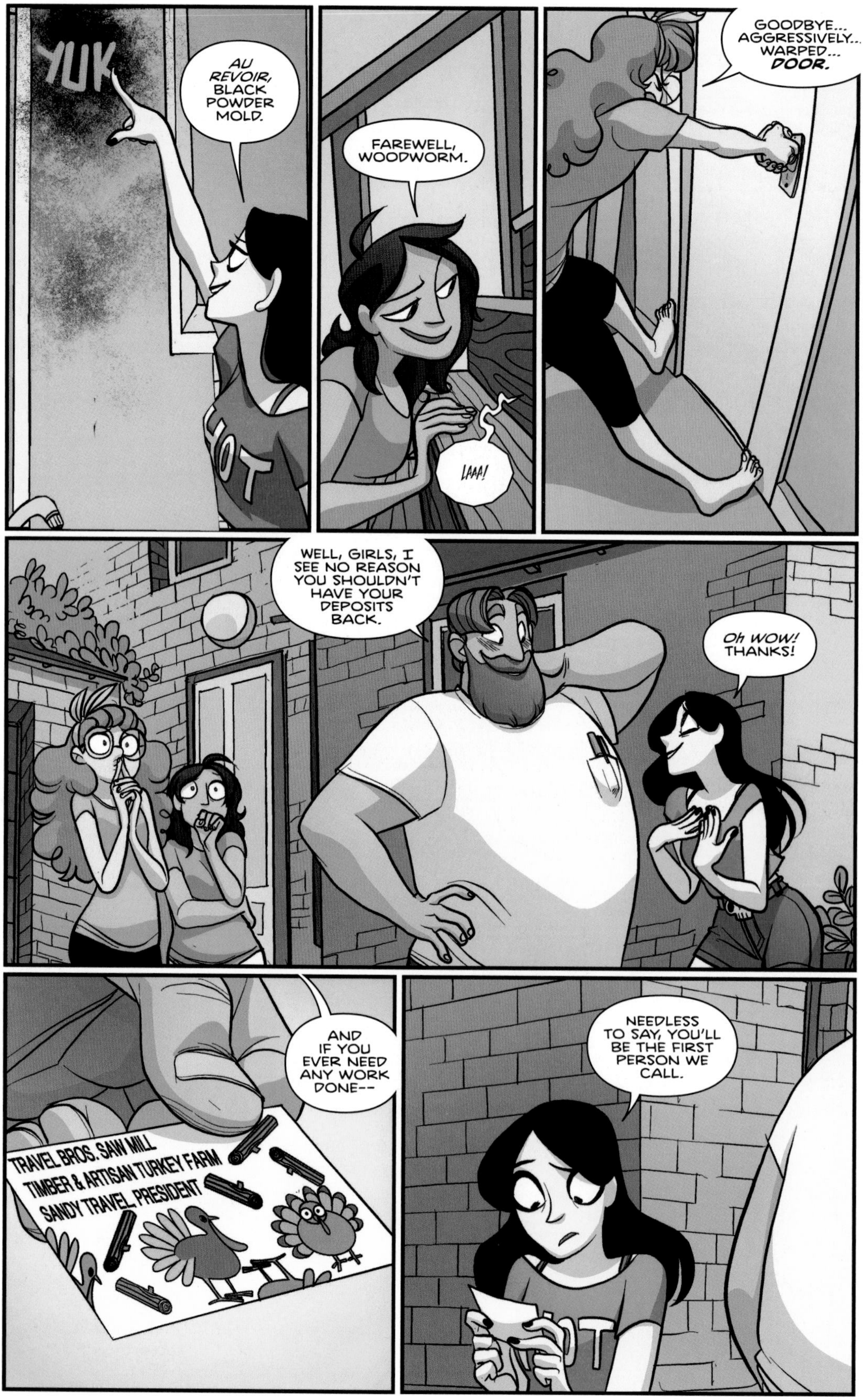
YUK
AU REVOIR, BLACK POWDER MOLD.
FAREWELL, WOODWORM.
LAAA!
GOODBYE... AGGRESSIVELY... WARPED... DOOR.
WELL, GIRLS, I SEE NO REASON YOU SHOULDN'T HAVE YOUR DEPOSITS BACK.
Oh WOW! THANKS!
AND IF YOU EVER NEED ANY WORK DONE--
TRAVEL BROS. SAW MILL
TIMBER & ARTISAN TURKEY FARM
SANDY TRAVEL, PRESIDENT
NEEDLESS TO SAY, YOU'LL BE THE FIRST PERSON WE CALL.

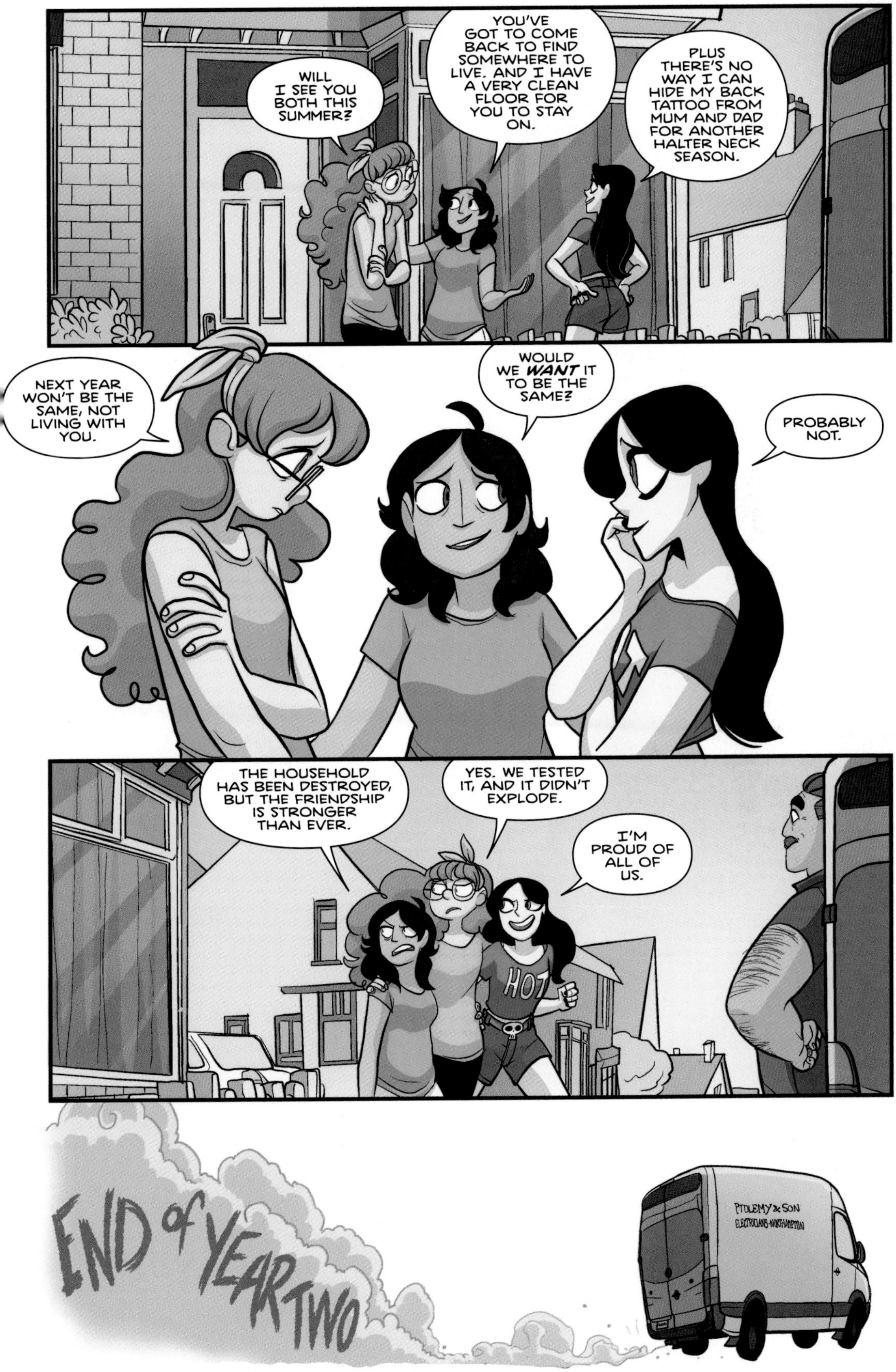
WILL I SEE YOU BOTH THIS SUMMER?
YOU'VE GOT TO COME BACK TO FIND SOMEWHERE TO LIVE. AND I HAVE A VERY CLEAN FLOOR FOR YOU TO STAY ON.
PLUS THERE'S NO WAY I CAN HIDE MY BACK TATTOO FROM MUM AND DAD FOR ANOTHER HALTER NECK SEASON.
NEXT YEAR WON'T BE THE SAME, NOT LIVING WITH YOU.
WOULD WE WANT IT TO BE THE SAME?
PROBABLY NOT.
THE HOUSEHOLD HAS BEEN DESTROYED, BUT THE FRIENDSHIP IS STRONGER THAN EVER.
YES. WE TESTED IT, AND IT DIDN'T EXPLODE.
I'M PROUD OF ALL OF US.
HOT
END of YEAR TWO
PTOLEMY & SON
ELECTRICIANS · NORTHAMPTON

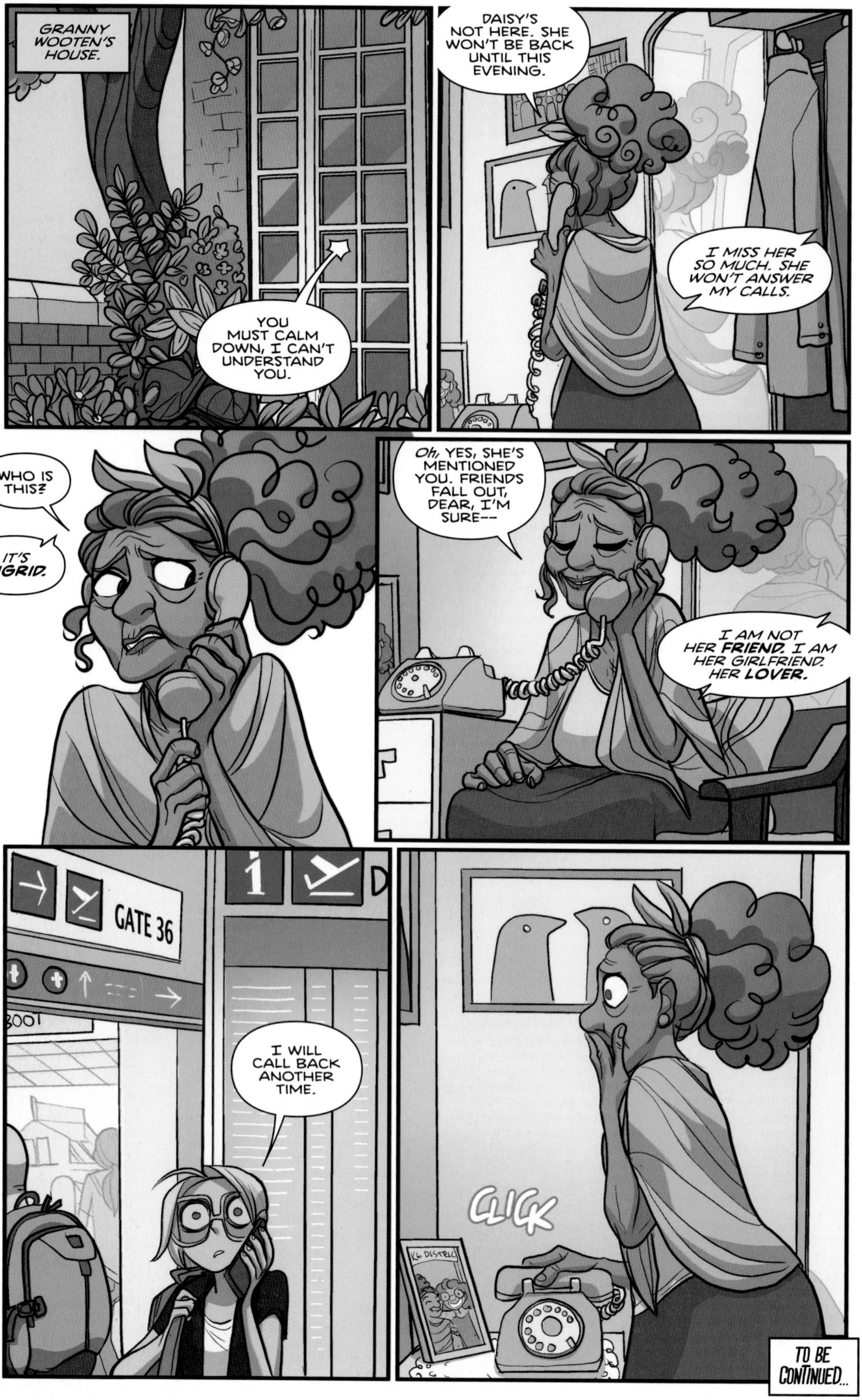
GRANNY WOOTEN'S HOUSE.
YOU MUST CALM DOWN, I CAN'T UNDERSTAND YOU.
DAISY'S NOT HERE. SHE WON'T BE BACK UNTIL THIS EVENING.
I MISS HER SO MUCH. SHE WON'T ANSWER MY CALLS.
WHO IS THIS?
IT'S INGRID.
Oh, YES, SHE'S MENTIONED YOU. FRIENDS FALL OUT, DEAR, I'M SURE--
I AM NOT HER FRIEND. I AM HER GIRLFRIEND. HER LOVER.
GATE 36
I WILL CALL BACK ANOTHER TIME.
CLICK
TO BE CONTINUED...

COVER GALLERY

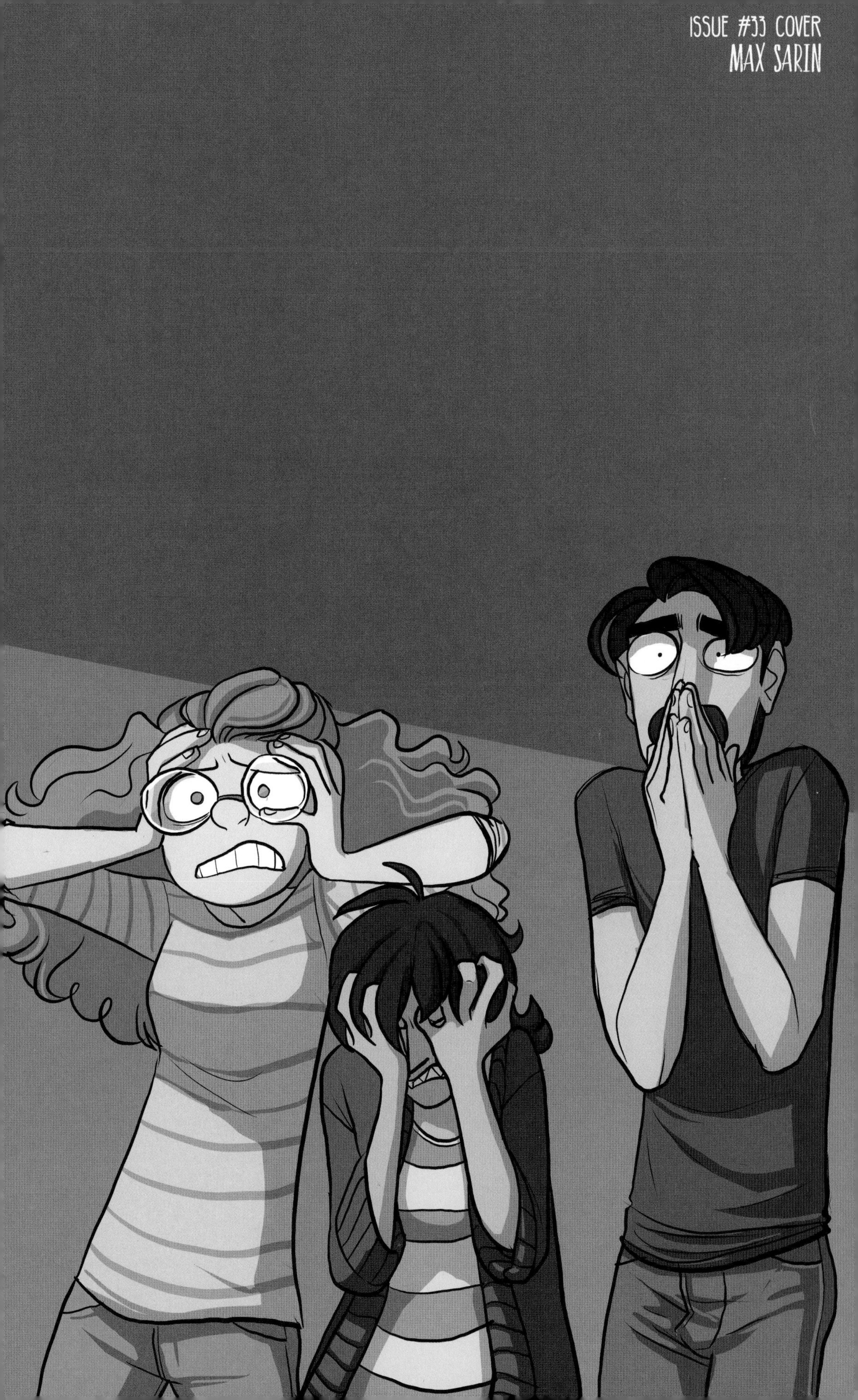

ISSUE #33 COVER
MAX SARIN

ISSUE #34 COVER
MAX SARIN

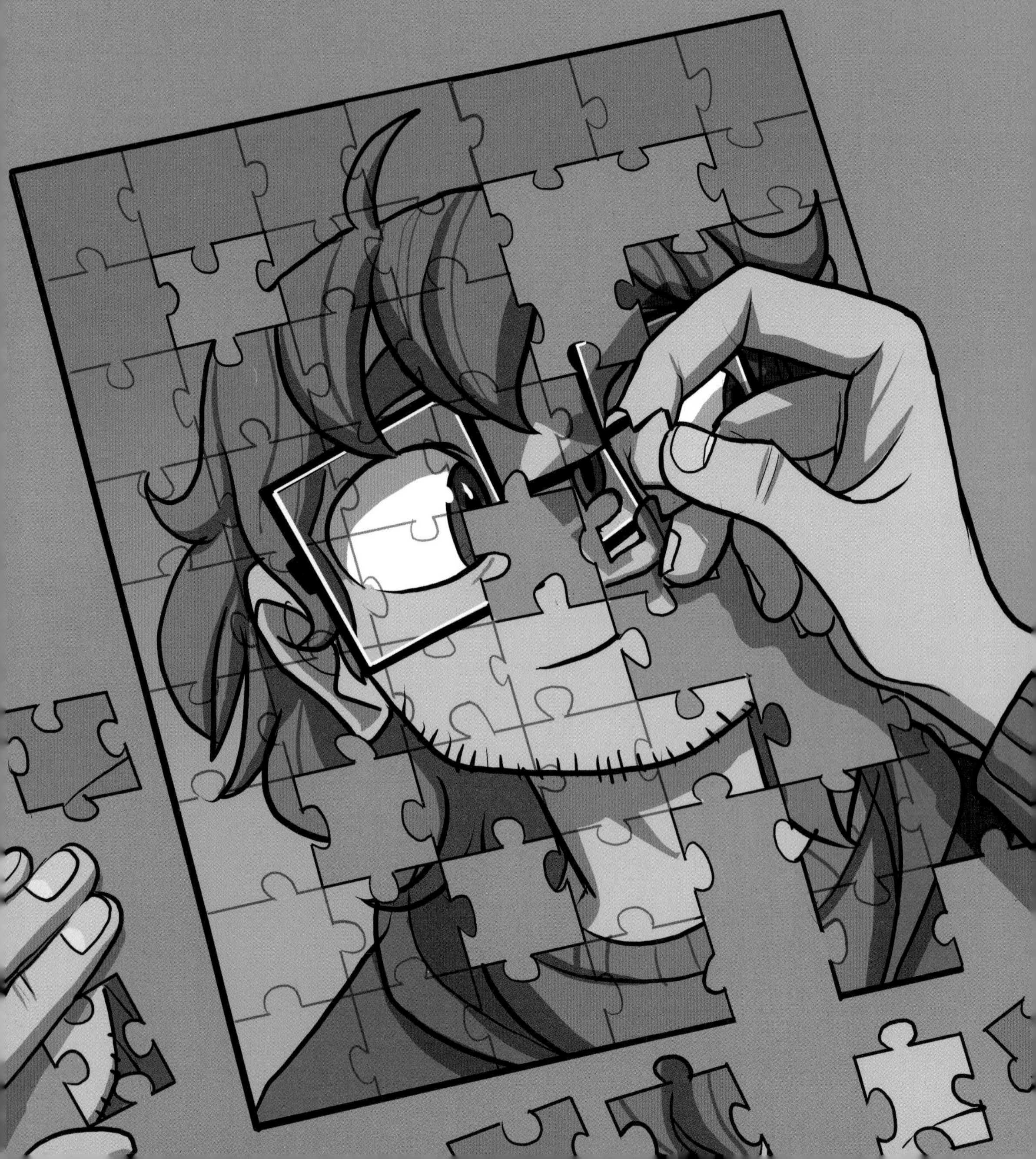

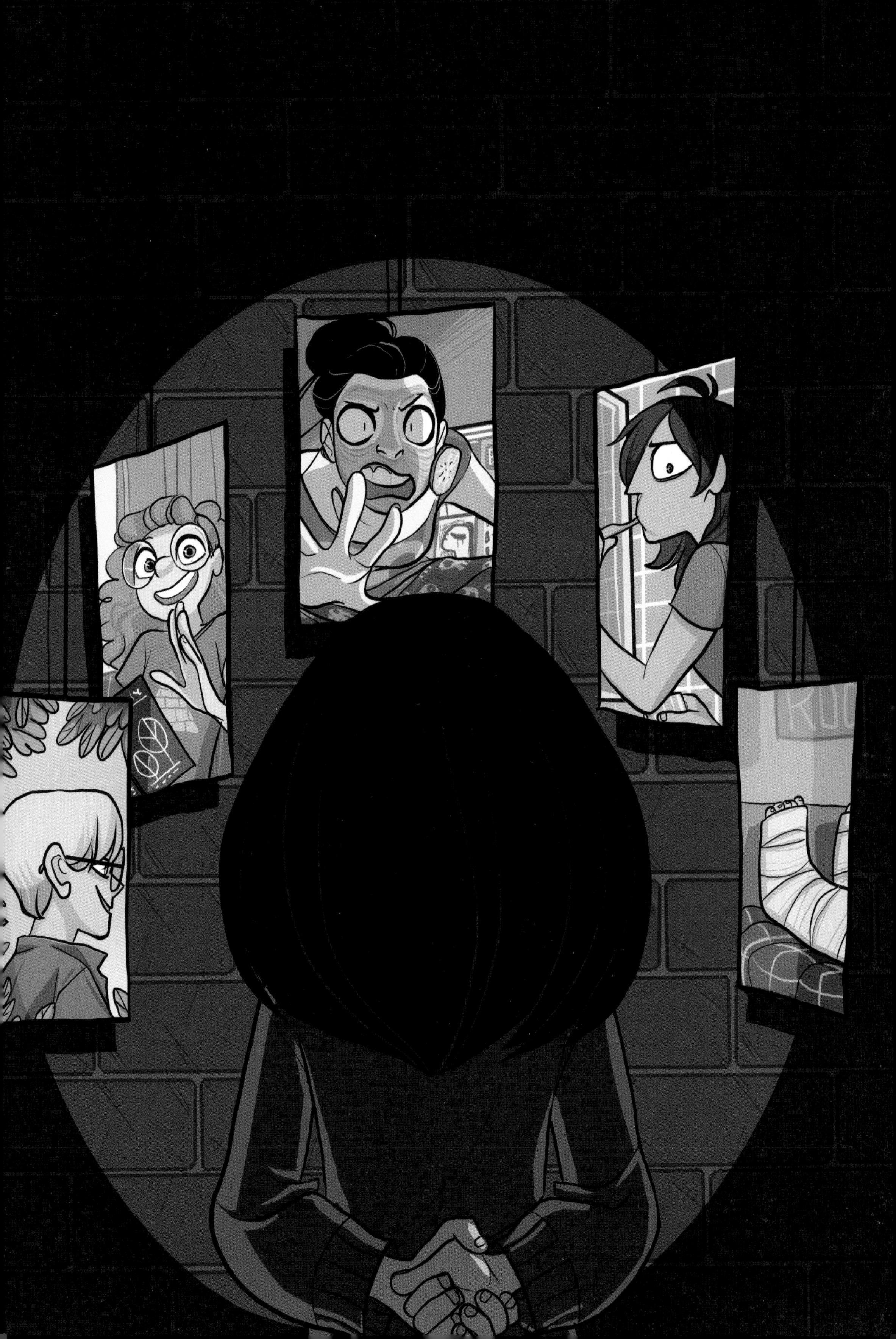

ISSUE #35 COVER
MAX SARIN

ISSUE #36 COVER
MAX SARIN

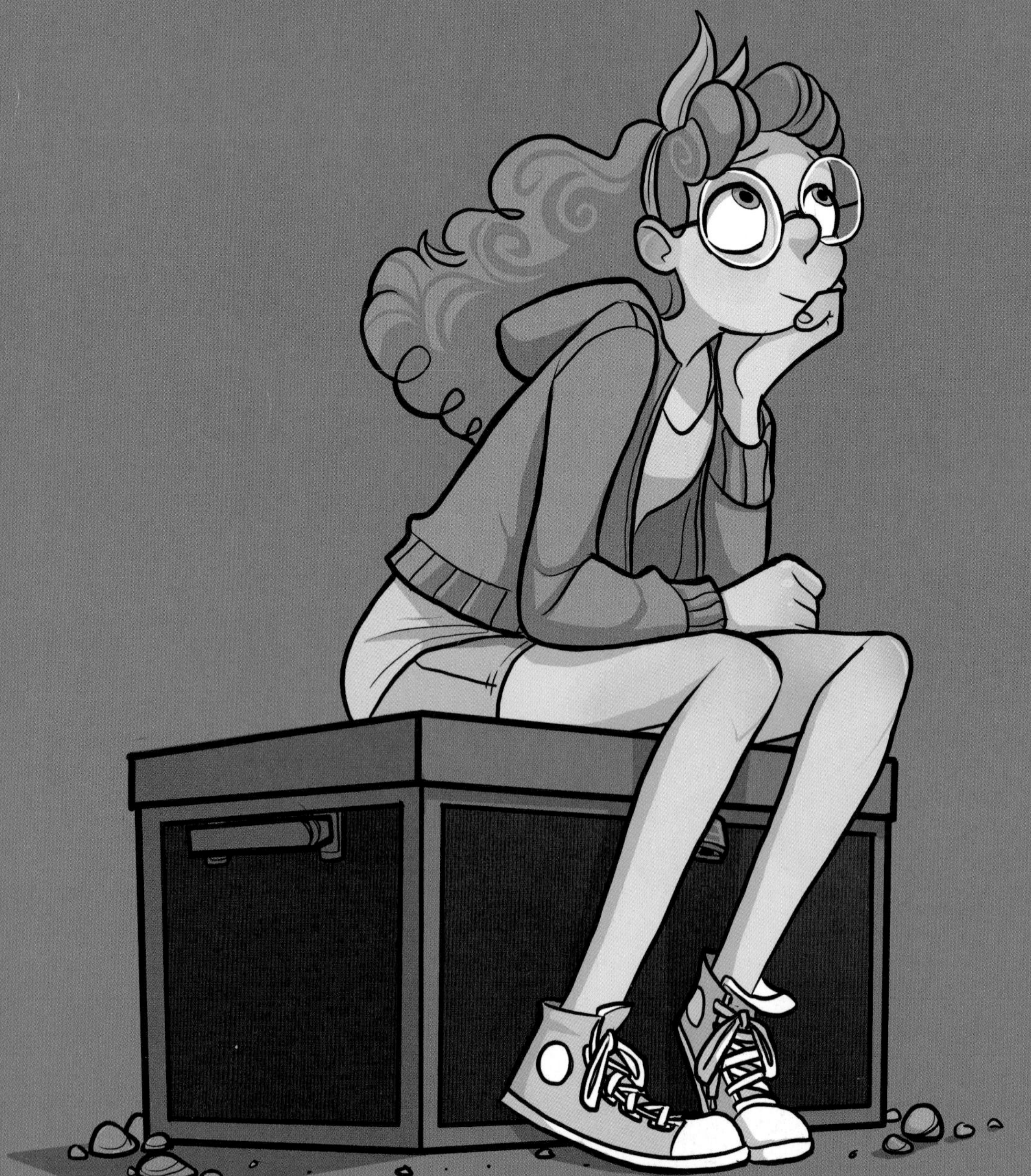

SKETCH GALLERY

SKETCHES BY JOHN ALLISON

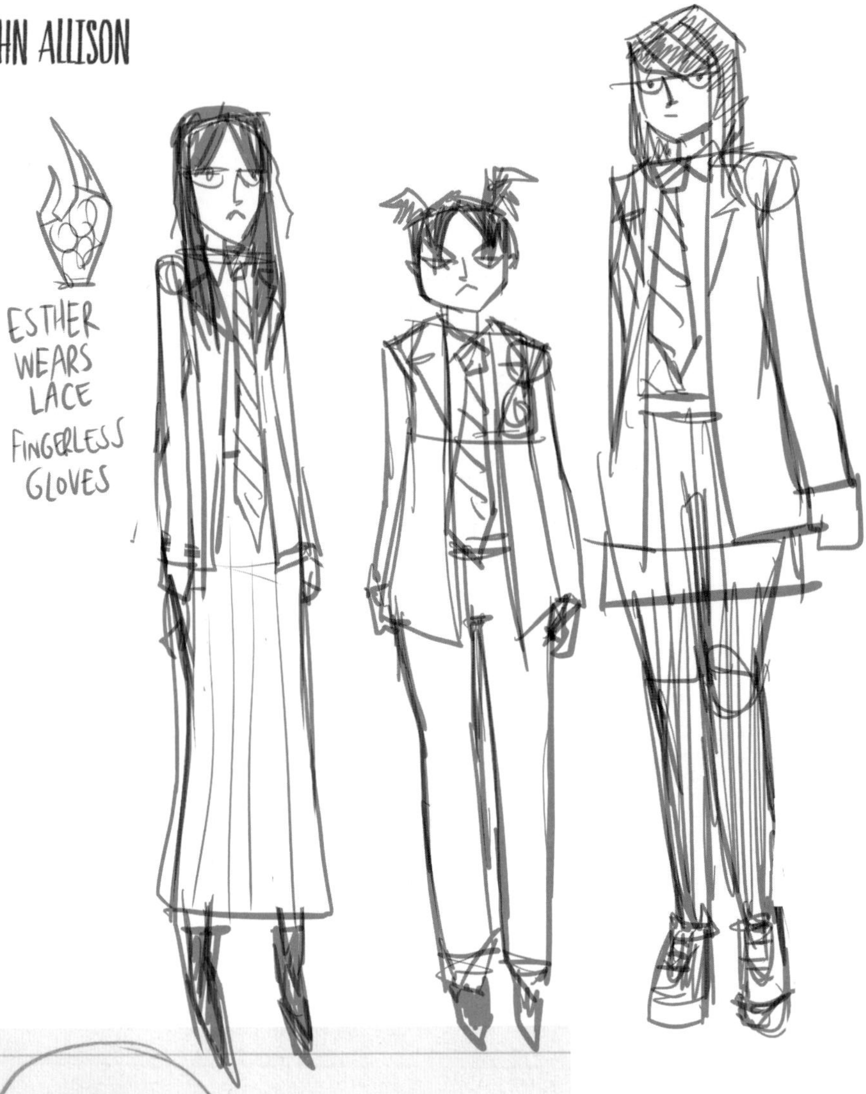
ESTHER WEARS LACE FINGERLESS GLOVES

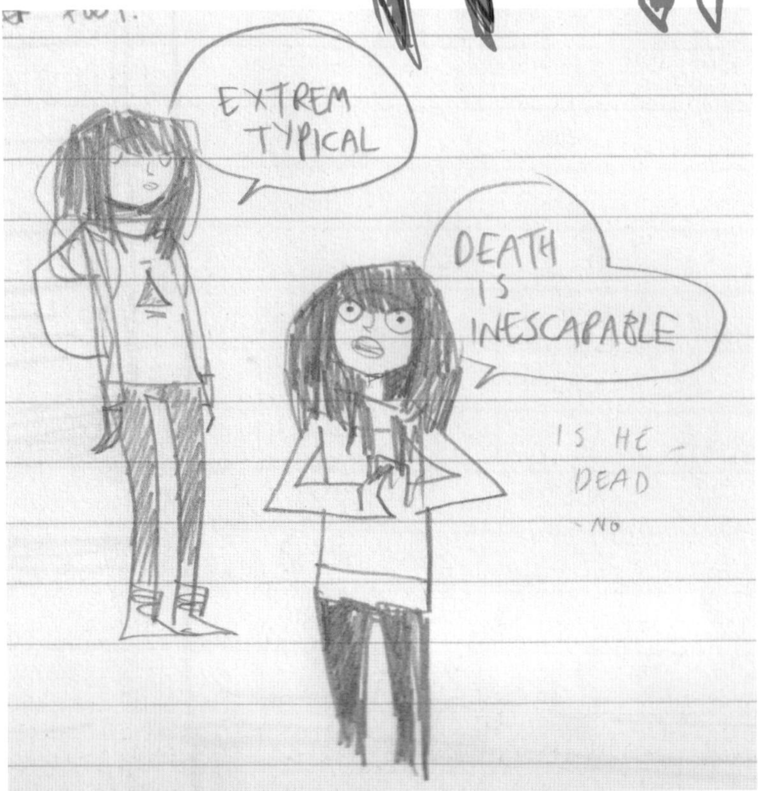
EXTREM TYPICAL
DEATH IS INESCAPABLE
IS HE DEAD
- NO

SKETCHES BY JOHN ALLISON

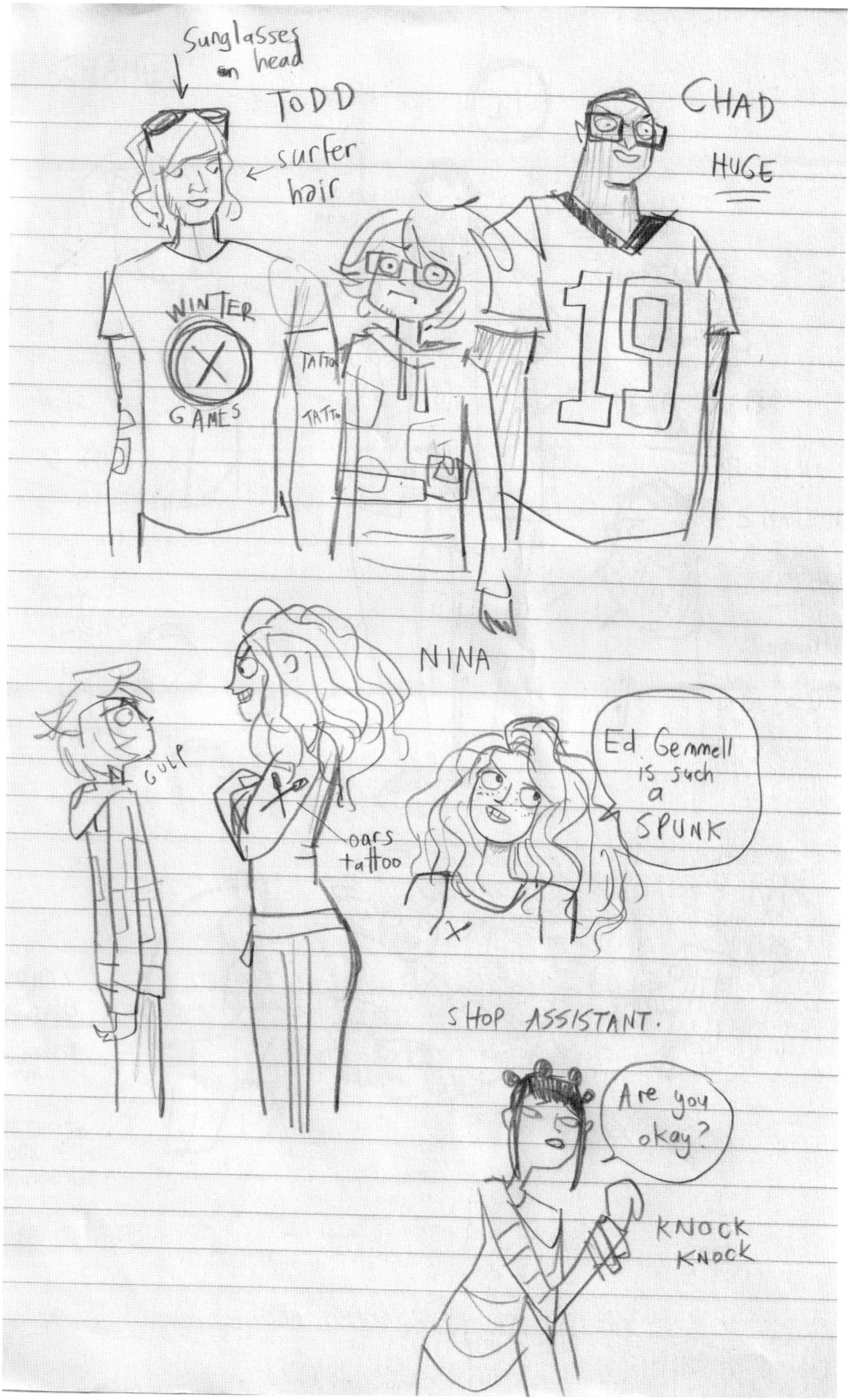
Sunglasses on head
TODD
surfer hair
WINTER
GAMES
TATTOO
TATTOO
CHAD
HUGE
19
NINA
GULP
oars tattoo
Ed Gemmell is such a SPUNK
SHOP ASSISTANT.
Are you okay?
KNOCK KNOCK

SKETCHES BY MAX SARIN

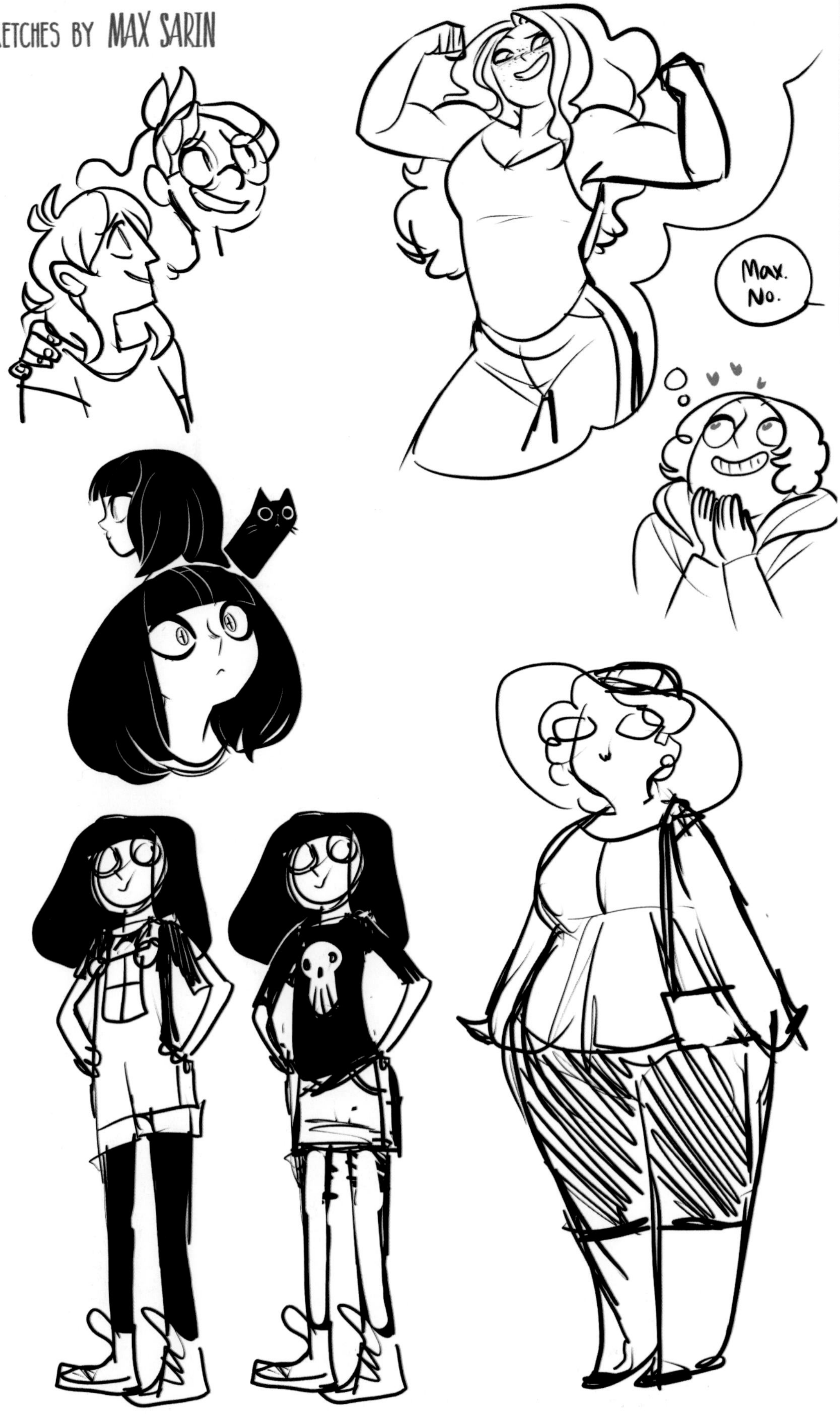
Max.
No.

SKETCHES BY MAX SARIN

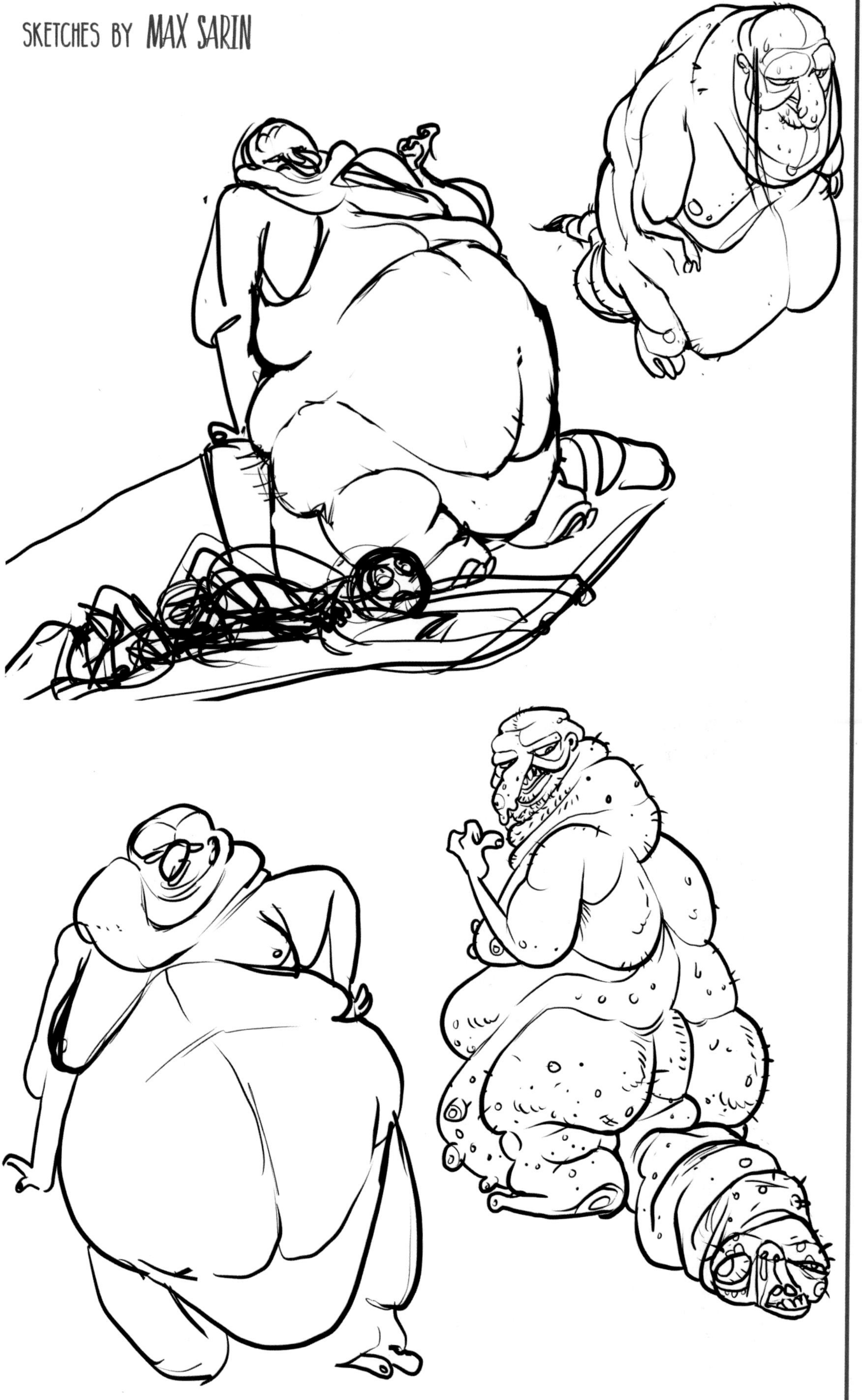

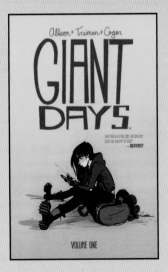